Listener in the SNOW

This book is for Carol

and

for my readers.

Acknowledgments

I am grateful for a wonderful cadre of readers who have suggested improvements, corrected my bountiful missteps, questioned my intentions, and most importantly, read and reported faithfully their experiences with the text.

Chief amongst these are Mary Walfoort who organized and led my readers' soirees; Stuart Lord, an indefatigable reader with a merry wit who labored incessantly on my behalf; James Richter whose insight encouraged me and whose precise reading saved me many a woe; Amy Eden Jollymore whose help with the global issues of storytelling shaped the novel; and my chief supporter and love, Carol Squicci, who read installments hot off the processor and was responsible for the first rounds of revision and for urging me on. Without these five the book could not have been completed.

I need also thank Dennis Hamlett, Fred Diviney, Gina Vaughn, Marylene Cloitre, Bonnie Wold, and Dave Marrons, who read the work, some of them twice. Their commentary has been helpful.

I acknowledge my debt to Wallace Stevens whose interest in metaphysical naturalism spawned *The Snow Man,* my epigram, from which I take the titles and inspiration for each chapter and for the book itself. Stevens said, "The world about us would be desolate except for the world within us," something that moves much of the action of this story.

I am indebted both to Jack London whose writing about the natural world expressed his appreciation of its power over humans and its ability to transform them, and to Hans Christian Andersen whose story *The Snow Queen* scared me as a young reader but showed me the allegorical relationships that bind us to nature.

I give my thanks to the Algonquin peoples and their traditions, in particular to the many Mi'kmaq and Ojibwe tribes who orally passed down the stories I adapted to Nebe's, Banook's and Granny Bassett's telling, and to Tatty's visions. These stories had been written down as early as the 19th Century.

I thank Ulf Furu of Kokkola who monitored my Finnish; Anne Fox, my copy editor; Professor Emeritus, Marvin Rintala, Davyd Morris, Michael and Jenny Bates, and Jim Farrell, my proofreaders; and Davis Hammet Proulx who years ago told of a windigo chase, a tale that eventually grew into this book.

Tim Jollymore
July 2015

Listener in the SNOW

Tim Jollymore

FINNS WAY
B O O K S

Printed in the United States of America. For information, address Finns Way Books™, 360 Grand Avenue, Suite 204, Oakland, California, 94610; or contact www.finnswaybooks.com

For information on Finns Way Reading Group Guides, please contact Finns Way Books™ by electronic mail at readinggroupguides@finnswaybooks.com

The lyrics on page 41 are from R. P. Sebastien in Mi'kmaq and French from the *Chant national de Micmacs* printed in 1910.

Wallace Stevens' acknowledged comment appears in "The Relation between Poetry and Painting" in "The Necessary Angel: Essays on Reality and Imagination," p. 169. Alfred A. Knopf, Inc.™ 1951.

ISBN 978-0-9914763-0-5

Listener in the SNOW

The Snow Man

One must have a mind of winter
To regard the frost and the boughs
Of the pine-trees crusted with snow;

And have been cold a long time
To behold the junipers shagged with ice,
The spruces rough in the distant glitter

Of the January sun; and not to think
Of any misery in the sound of the wind,
In the sound of a few leaves,

Which is the sound of the land
Full of the same wind
That is blowing in the same bare place

For the listener, who listens in the snow,
And, nothing himself, beholds
Nothing that is not there and the nothing that is.

Wallace Stevens, 1922

Part I

Moving North

It experienced a vague but menacing apprehension that subdued it and made it slink along at the man's heels.

Jack London, *To Build a Fire*

At Thief Lake confidence is low. After all, a man had drowned out there, and that made the lake people nervous. To harden their resolve took two weeks of subzero temperatures, until, finally, they dared set their fish houses out on the ice.

Now, along my brisk walk from the southern shore, I see whole communities of shacks scattered along crooked trails. Each little house is tacked together solidly enough to stand for no longer than the remaining two months of ice fishing season.

I stop near the longest array of these cabins. I've walked half way across the lake, tracing the edge of an underwater shelf that, only forty yards out, follows the arc of the western shore. I have to rest.

Where I'm headed two small clusters of fishing houses crouch in the middle of the lake. They are three quarters of a mile out above productive deep holes where the big walleye are caught.

My lips are already chapped, but I spit anyway. I'm not sure it's safe to go out there.

That clump of shacks and each darkhouse in it are connected to the others through a network of paths packed hard by snowshoes, insulated boots, and snowmobile tracks. The paths are low and dirty in comparison with the snow covering the frozen lake. They have been traveled. It should be all right.

I trek out to the trail that branches off toward the furthest group of fishing houses standing over what they tell me is the best fishing hole on the lake. I walk, at first testing the solidity of the ice with each step. Here and there I slip and skid, but the ice is solid. My thick clothing compounds the struggle and my unsteadiness. I plod like I am walking up a steep hill. My breath clouds the still morning air.

At the end of a particularly zigzagged path, I pull the glove off my right hand and knock on the low door of a shack. Someone inside lifts the burlap curtain from the window. A stranger's face presses the pane. I wave. In a minute the door opens, and a man made huge by the fish house doorway greets me. He's dressed in underwear and socks. He shades his eyes with a hand and steps aside. He beckons me to enter.

"Martin?" I ask.

"In the flesh." He catches my sleeve and pulls me in. "Get in here," Martin says. He guides me over the threshold.

I shuffle my way into the pitch-dark interior of the cabin. Once my host closes the door, I am as good as blind. Taking a step, I feel my way with a boot.

"Just stand a minute right there until you can see. I don't want you falling into a hole." Martin says.

He stands close. He must be watching me. "So, you're Tatty," he says. His breath smells of coffee and maple syrup. "It's taken a while for you to come around."

"I've had the fever, Martin."

"Everyone calls me Tiny. I guess my brother-in-law should too."

"Okay." I nod. "Tiny." He pats my arm. "Granny fed me stew like there was no end, and I got my strength back at last.   I'm glad I could finally come out."

My eyes adjust a little to the gloom. Tiny's bulk looms before me. "You have the time?"

"I got nothing but time," Tiny says. "Fish don't make appointments. You've got to wait on them."

Inside the fish house is hot. When Tiny moves off, I look around the single room. In one corner, the barrel stove stands on angle-iron legs; shelves run behind and butt into the far wall. Fitted on the adjacent long wall are two-by-six frame bunks. The room is stuffy.

A sleeping bag drapes over one side of the upper bunk. Two pillows anchor one end of the bag. The odor of sleep permeates the shack and drives up my nostrils. I sneeze.

Across from the beds, a small table and two chairs stand under the window between the stove and door. Burlap bags carpet the floor, but in the center of the room, neatly bordered by hemmed bags, two square holes in the ice, each a foot wide, shimmer. Tiny was right, I could have fallen into either of them.

Tiny points to the shining holes. "Them's my TVs," he says. "And the programs are pretty good."

He has rigged a short fishing pole at each hole, their handles staked into the ice. The translucent fishing lines fall to the water, seem to crimp at an angle, and disappear in blue darkness further down. A small bell dangles from each pole tip.

Into the dark cabin, the lake beams up through the holes. Now more certain of my sight, I move closer to look down the nearest hole. I follow the line as it bends below the water's surface to plunge beneath the thick slab of ice. I have to check myself. I don't want to imagine what could be down there under the ice.

Instead, I look around the cabin deliberately. "Comfortable."

Tiny follows my gaze. "It gets me out of the house. I

bring in a few dozen fish a week," he says. "Put your duds up on the bunk. Have a chair."

Tiny moves to the shelves where the Coleman stove sits. "Coffee?"

"Yes, please." I rub my hands and hold them out to the barrel stove.

Tiny pours the coffee. "Milk?"

He reaches behind a tarp hanging across the corner below the shelves and brings up a bottle. "It never freezes inside, but you can keep stuff cold." He lifts the tarp. Behind it a store of food sits on the clean-scraped ice floor.

I sit at the table. Sunlight filters through the weave of the burlap curtain. Through its ill-fitting door, the barrel stove pushes a glow into the room.

Tiny fiddles with the fishing lines. The bells tinkle as he adjusts the poles. He takes his seat. He stirs his coffee. "I'm making toast. Want some?" he asks.

"No, the coffee is fine, thanks."

Tiny sips. He waits for me to speak. Maybe he's decided not to ask about Mary or the babies. Anyway, he must have seen them while I was down with the fever.

I'm uncertain, flu-hollowed. I search my brother-in-law's face. "I don't know what you think about this."

Tiny looks at me, then at the bread toasting on the wire gizmo he's rigged atop the Coleman stove. He says nothing.

"I guess I have some questions about what happened at Tillie's."

Tiny reaches to turn the bread over. "I wasn't there. Don't know if I can give you any answers."

I look to the burlap curtain and release a long breath. "I just feel that I should tell someone. I mean, tell my part of the story. My version, I suppose. To someone, someone at the lake."

"So you chose me because we hadn't met yet?" Tiny rises and steps across a hole to retrieve a plate from the shelf. He picks the toast off the gizmo. He sits to butter the slices. "I suppose, because I wasn't here for any of it." Tiny catches my eye in a friendly way. He stabs the knife at the fishing poles. "Well, as long as them bells don't ring, I'm listening."

Even though this is what I've come for, I can't seem to start.

I look to the window. Outside the morning brightens. It is still early. I imagine the shacks on the long, arced street across the lake sending up plumes of smoke into the crisp, clear day. I picture right below us, beneath the two-foot thick ice, monster walleye curling by Tiny's dangling lines to inspect his bait. Then I shake off my visions of sky and water. I return to the cabin. I'm ready.

I blow across the coffee cup and sip. I'm not going to meet Tiny's gaze. I look again to the window and begin.

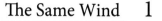

I COULDN'T SLEEP. The plane ride was smooth enough, and the novels I brought for the four-day trip were sufficiently dense. But every minute while the fifteen-hundred-mile distance between us shortened, thoughts of Mary poked at me and kept me awake. We'd been drifting apart for months, and I was coming north to see if I could patch things up. Maybe "drifting apart" isn't the right term.

From the time she had heard about the twins to be born into the family, Mary had grown more and more distant. She took on more and more of those Native trappings we'd let fall from us over our fifteen years of marriage. She even went to a nearby Seminole powwow before she flew to Minnesota a month ahead of me.

It was a strain to talk about her trip.

"I know it's been a while," she said, "but I'd like to see some of the old faces."

"Sure, if that's what you want," I replied, trying to keep it peaceful. "I just don't have the time to spend up there."

Mary twisted her lip. "I didn't ask you to come."

I felt hurt but tried not to show it. She pushed me away, hard. Rather than be distanced further, I stepped back to give Mary the room she seemed to want.

"It's all right. I just figured you'd want me there."

She softened. "Maybe after the delivery. For the

naming ceremony."

But the events in the north had another effect on her, one that threatened me.

Mary talked more and more about the possibility of having children, something we had long before dismissed.

I countered her dreamy ideas. "Aren't we a bit old to be thinking of this?"

She set her jaw. "Women near forty are having children these days."

I shook my head. "Maybe, but not first children."

Mary let it drop, but she had little to say to me for days afterward.

For all those problems and a whole series of disagreements, I couldn't sleep on the flight. Possibilities and worries scurried in circles around my mind.

I wondered if traveling north intensified my fears. My experience as a boy going to Canada for my father's funeral had left its mark. It had turned not just my body cold but froze my spirit with horror. That winter trip to Nova Scotia disturbed my sleep for years with dreams of yawning graves, Indian women flying through dark skies, and stories told in gibberish. For months, I awoke in cold shudders at three in the morning.

This trip to Minnesota already was blowing me off my course, threatening to loosen my grip on the comfortable life I had spent years building. I wanted nothing of Native spookiness, oddball stories, or backwoods, roughshod behavior. Nor anything to do with children. Just thinking of snowstorms, Indian ways, or kids chilled me. In my window seat an hour south of St. Paul and miles above a northern hurly-burly, I sat shivering beneath the thin airline blanket.

I landed ahead of the storm, but my connection

north wasn't going to happen. Duluth International, the airport to the north, was already battened down against weather barreling south out of Manitoba at fifty miles an hour. No one was flying through Duluth, and no one in Duluth was going anywhere else.

Despite the distance that had grown between us, I knew my coming was god-awful important to Mary. "Yes," she said. "You should at least make the christening of the twins." If attendance had been optional, I would have snuggled up in a downtown Minneapolis hotel to wait for the storm to pass, for the skies to clear.

That would have been the reasonable thing to do, but I knew too well that Mary would get as wild as a demon if I slighted her. I had seen it—shattered dinner plates, forks and knives flying through the kitchen with enough force for blades and tines to penetrate the sheetrock and embed themselves at odd angles to the wall, looking like a Dansk porcupine. I had seen the sacks of flour and sugar bursting over a carton of broken eggs she'd slammed across the floor. It would be better to brave the winter highways that night and drive north—despite the meteorologists' warnings—than to face the thunderheads of Mary's wrath. The knot in my stomach told me that much.

The quavering deep in my chest, too, told me that my motives were not selfless. I cursed my craving for Mary's approval. I shamed my avoidance of her stern unpleasantness, but I knew what a real storm was. I wasn't about to let a blizzard or Nature herself overcome my decision to avoid a scene with Mary.

Behind it all, though, was desire. I wanted to lie naked with Mary and to make love a long time. I hoped to bridge the distance of the previous three months. If I spoke honestly, it had been even longer than that.

Although Mary could conjure up a howler on my head much worse than what I would have to drive through, neither proved as haunting to me as reentering the wintry Algonquin world I had years before culled from my life.

"I can make it if I have four-wheel drive," I told the car rental agent at Minneapolis-Saint Paul International.

He recommended a Jeep hardtop that could plow through snow, steady and straight. While he donned his parka and boots to retrieve the vehicle, I went to the lobby phone to notify Mary of the change.

I dialed the number Mary had given me but could only leave a message with a woman who answered the phone. "I hope no one has gone to Duluth to fetch me," I said. "I'll be driving,"

"Good," she simply said. "Keep in touch."

The rental agent met me at the curb. He pointed out the knobby tire treads that would grip anything and the perfect body of the Jeep. He briefed me on the simple array of controls. The feeling of utility in the firm seat and spare cab encouraged me. I rumbled away from the curb and followed the signs north. I basked in the wisdom of my choice.

For the first hour and a half, I made my way easily—but then the storm that had shut down Duluth International swept across the highway.

"The nor'easter," as the radio called it, hit like a Northern Pacific freight train—a gigantic, invisible locomotive whipping a line of boxcars through an invisible whistle-stop, scattering automobiles as if they were snowflakes. Before I knew it, the first gust blew me and other cars across both lanes toward the shoulder.

I struggled to keep the Jeep from leaving the road. Winter pierced my body and flooded my mind. All I could think of—though I couldn't remember it right— was a line from a poem: *you have to have been cold a long time / to see the cedar trees shagged with ice.*

Frost seeped through the rental car's insulated panels and fogged windows. The frigid air crept through my thick jeans and the leather jacket pulled over two cotton layers and a wool sweater, even through the long johns Mary insisted I bring. Cold pierced the big boots and thick socks she bought before she flew north ahead of me. Riddled by shivers and driving into the teeth of a blizzard, I felt I understood that poem for the first time. I was to learn winter in a physical sense, would come to know it in my bones. I wasn't blue-cold, not numb—at least not yet—but at the core where my liver struggled to keep blood warm, I could feel the danger, the steely clutch, the confusion of the swirling, snow-filled air, and the ghostly darts of screaming wind gusts.

Back in Florida, Mary had told me the Indians called these same winds winter-windigoes.

"They're frozen spirit-people," she'd said. "Some claim they are cannibals that gnaw on ice-solid limbs." Then she'd grinned.

I'd snapped the newspaper in front of my face and snorted, "Save it for someone who cares, Mary."

She persisted like a pugnacious imp. "Windigoes move on air, hunker down."

I'd folded the paper. "Woo, woo."

She'd come off her chair, squatting and dancing around low to the floor. "They're solitary, ready to slice your jacket sleeves." She'd laughed wickedly.

I tried to wax poetic. "I suppose they are just waiting to run a lance of chill up my spine and to threaten freezing the very life from my flesh."

Mary'd feigned astonishment, "You believe! I can tell it in your look." She'd risen merrily on her haunches and stared into my face with widened eyes.

I'd shut my eyes and gave her an emphatic, "No! I don't."

Mary had stood. "You'll find out."

In the Florida sun, her talk had sounded like mumbo-jumbo to my practical ear. Mary had just been having fun, yet she knew suggestion held power over me. Because of that sway, I had been relieved to finish my literary studies. The strength of stories in novels and tales the Anishinabe people told, once I opened to it, could send me spiraling off my path like so much hurricane debris. I'd pooh-poohed the windigo in front of Mary then, but now, in the frozen wildness of a snowstorm, her stories were not so easy to dismiss. Here they didn't seem funny at all. I wouldn't let it happen, but Mary's windigo rushed to spirit me off.

Defying my insistence to keep my mental feet on the ground, out of the corner of my eye, I caught sight through the windshield of what looked like misery itself in the snow—a wavering, almost transparent figure, like an ice-white flame. It whirled just beyond the crossed beams of my headlights, churning ghostly arms wildly, swimming against a raging current. The hypnotic movements this edge-of-the-blizzard phantom performed solidified Mary's spirit story in my mind. I saw it plainly. I gasped sharply, pulled the steering wheel firmly to avoid that illusory, twirling figure ahead. The Jeep bumped and groaned against the wall of frigid air that pounded its square little body, then it grabbed the pavement. I broke a sudden sweat.

Jerked from wavering visions to solid alertness, I clutched the wheel tightly and glued every bit of attention to the road that disappeared foot by foot into an onslaught of swirling snow and descent of preternatural darkness. Some poor souls out there had been blown right off the platform of that midnight whistle-stop into the snowbanks. Did I have a ghost to thank for saving me? Only a few of us had regained the pavement. Once righted after the first mighty blow, the survivors laced along the road, a string of red lights just visible enough to follow. Our taillights formed a dim crimson arrow shooting ahead into an abyss of churning white and black. I hoped that whoever was in the lead knew where the road ran. I prayed that he would not drive too fast.

I had no experience driving in a snowstorm. Blinded by horizontal rain, I had churned through the margins of hurricanes. I had ducked flying debris, but anything I knew about the north, about cold and snow, I had learned from books read in the warm embrace of Florida. Northern winter? I had wanted to experience none of it.

Maybe I shouldn't be out here, I thought.

The radio had called this the storm of the century. The announcers preached caution. Listen to the old-timers' wisdom, my mind nagged. Don't be a fool.

"Hooey!" I bellowed. I squelched the radio. I shook off negative thoughts. If I were courting disaster, I didn't want to be reminded. Bravado and ignorance would blanket the warnings of the frigid air. Still, it came to me that a man alone here could freeze and quickly die no matter what he thought or didn't think. Couldn't you suffer the same fate as that man trekking the Yukon? I asked myself. He hadn't listened to the old-timers. You could be found next spring decomposed, perhaps half-eaten. I clamped my hands firmly on the wheel. Hooey.

Pressing on, though, the failure of my Jeep's heater to keep up with the driven, icy onslaught of howling wind, rattled my courage, cooled my thighs and my hope of reaching the cabin on time. I lacked Mary's stalwart constitution. I visualized the family, Mary's Chippewa, stoically sitting through six months of frozen darkness like night herons hunching through short winter days. Doubt plagued me. I could have turned back, but I had just begun fighting the storm. Even after a four-hour flight and the anxieties that changed plans produced, I was still fresh. I had only two or three hours remaining to reach Thief Lake, tucked just a few miles below the Canadian border. I should have been looking forward to the christening of my wife's twin cousins, but it was a warm fire inside a snug cabin that pulled me onward.

The storm settled into a steady, grinding blow. I followed without mishap the loose-knit caravan of taillights scudding through knee-high drifts. All seemed under control.

This is not too bad, I thought. This isn't as treacherous as the Yukon.

I emptied my mind of doubt. I kept a keen, observant focus on the road and allowed my thoughts to drift to the friendly welcome that lay ahead. I shied away from fearful images of freezing bodies elongating in the snow. I avoided thoughts of disembodied, miserable gnomes crouched in snow-covered, cedar copses. I wrestled down all phantom visits of ghostly worry. I rumbled along the highway, easily keeping pace with the crimson line of lights which began slowing as the density of the snow in the air and on the road increased. I let my thoughts turn to what I hoped would be my wife's warm embraces and a cheery celebration of new life in Mary's family.

For all the years we had known each other, most of them spent as man and wife, this was the first time I would meet any of Mary's kin. I hid my reticence to get involved but had little enthusiasm to meet (now, Tiny, don't laugh) what I thought would be a bunch of reservation Indians who had never traveled further south than Duluth. From what Mary told me about the family, there was little to like.

"My parents are long gone. If they had an influence on us, it was a bad one," Mary said once. "As usual, we were staying with Granny, the responsible one in the family. The parents took off one Saturday night. They just never came back. Some said they froze to death in Canada."

Though Mary spoke fondly of Granny, the woman sounded much like my own grandmother, Banook, who I remembered as a funny little Indian woman full of stories and advice. The resemblance didn't make me want to meet Granny.

"Well, she cares. That's for sure," Mary said.

She told me about the family members, and maybe she wasn't exactly fair. Mary was one who often embellished or shaded the truth. "My brother had trouble keeping his moccasins on," she said. "He was always a buck in rut."

(A crooked grin spreads across Tiny's face. "She got that right, but, even if she's your wife, that girl is no one to talk."

"That's fair," I say, "but she portrays you as the prolific branch of the family." I continue my story.)

Mary said, "He sired his first son at sixteen and added two more by other women within a couple of years. George made him a grandpa at thirty."

Since we had no children, it all sounded like criticism. "At least my nephew kept his spewing in the family," Mary said. She laughed about it all.

Her soft spot was for George's wife, Beanie, and her own so-called cousin, Windsong. "Those girls have real courage. Raising kids at the lake is not something I would do."

When I learned this was Beanie's third and that Windsong was expecting twins, it appeared unrestrained and impractical. There were too many kids around for my taste. That part made me nervous even before I got here.

Once she decided to travel, Mary grew enthusiastic about going north. "I missed both of George's boys, what, five and eight years ago. I don't want to miss the birth of twins." Windsong, Mary hinted, was the product of a thirty-year-old local medicine man and a very young woman. She had been born near the same time Mary left Thief Lake. "Granny raised her, too. I think it was easier this time."

Windsong was carrying two. None of those earlier births had drawn Mary back home. I thought it was the triple addition, Beanie's latest and Windsong's twins, that roused a yearning strong enough to overcome her inertia and her own strong resistance to the north in winter. Mary insisted that Windsong would have girls, identical twins. This prediction was ironclad. She knew it. The change of heart toward family that the far-off pregnancy engendered took me by surprise. Actually, I was shocked by all of it. Mary didn't delve into divination or fortune telling of any sort and had long since sworn off having her own children. So Mary as a seer and as a nervously expectant godmother led her away from my idea of a comfortable world. I did not like it at all.

She broke the news at one of our quiet dinners together. "I got a call from Minnesota."

"Really? What's that about?" I asked, not letting the strangeness register.

Mary told me the call had come a couple of days earlier.

I was sifting through the day's mail. "No one died, I hope."

"No. But I might have to go up there."

That possibility and her tone drew me from my sorting. "It's freezing up there," I said. She read it as an objection, which it was.

Mary held her lower lip between her teeth. She seemed to be debating, then, said, "Granny needs me. She didn't say so, but it sounded like it."

I wasn't even aware that Mary had reconnected enough to know anything going on up here. I didn't know that she shared her whereabouts with family. "Did you start writing to your grandmother?" I asked. "Is she sick?"

"No. The girl, the woman she raised, Windsong, is having a baby. Actually, twins."

"So?"

"So it'll be a big deal. It'll be a lot of work. And Granny won't have anyone to help. Beanie is pregnant, too."

My sweet married-couple world suddenly was becoming populated by strangers. "Who's Beanie?"

Once up north, Mary told me she would set up residence at Granny's cabin.

I groused about it. "A whole month ahead of the due date? That seems uncalled for. What about me?"

Mary lost patience. "Three babies are coming at the same time," she yelled, "and you don't seem to get it!"

She was right. I didn't understand, but Mary knew I wouldn't risk a knock-down, drag-out battle. "All right, all right! What do you want me to do?"

In her plan, I would arrive to help celebrate the births at the naming ceremonies, where she would introduce me, her husband of fifteen years.

"I don't want to be paraded before a whole bunch of people."

"It won't be a huge number."

"How about just the family?" I asked. "Just your grandmother, brother, and a few others?"

Mary was boiling. I could tell she was holding down anger. "Look. This means something to me," she said. "I'll include the family and a few friends. It's a couple of hours out of your busy little life."

Things had been bad enough long enough that I didn't want more discord. I agreed.

Over the next few weeks, I eyed Mary carefully. I couldn't tell which draw was the strongest for her—the reunion with Granny, me meeting the family, or the naming festival for the newborns—but I was pretty sure it was the birth of the two girls. Soon, though, I entered the busy pre-hurricane season of my storm shutter business and paid less attention to what Mary was telling me after the plan was set. I did notice the long, hushed calls to her cousin Windsong.

"Can't you call her when I'm working?"

"No!" she insisted. "Windsong can only make it to the phone over at Martin's house in the evenings, and it's earlier there."

She made those calls late when I would rather she come to bed with me. Since her excitement centered on what was happening just south of the Canadian border near the frozen Rainey River rather than in her own palm-shaded Florida home, I turned my face to the wall when she finally did slip in beside me.

Still, Mary's growing excitement gave me all the more reason to join her in time for her big event. I had to do something to keep our marriage intact, something to keep her grounded in the south. I knew less about Ojibwe ceremony than the little I knew about my own Mi'kmaq heritage, but I understood that the birth of twins was strong medicine. Over the twenty years I had known her, I had not seen Mary enjoy such contentment and anticipation. She acted as if she were carrying a child herself. She stirred my jealousy, but I kept my words in check. Fortunately, Mary did not chat on about the event, incessantly knit little things, or hum sweet nursery songs. No, Mary lived more deeply than that maudlin housewifery.

This excitement inhabited her more like the imperceptible movement of the dark amber backwater flow of a channel, rich with the fullness of life beneath a quiescent surface. Her former tenderness rose; she caressed me with a musing gentility. She touched the poet in me.

Each movement she made now stirred from far within, suckled by roots reaching deep into a fertile bottomland of memory and meaning. She was a muskeg island, floating, still on long waters, moving on an unseen current. She was as enchanted as daybreak full with the splendor of promise. She grew both more alluring and more distant.

Then one time after love-making, Mary jarred me out of my lyrical dreams with impromptu ideas about going north.

She betrayed her thoughts to the ceiling. "It's going to be all right," she said.

"What is?" I thought she would say, "Between us."

"Oh, things at home." She sounded far away.

I wanted to bring her back. "Here?"

"No. Well, with us, yes. But I was thinking of Granny and Windsong."

Her preoccupation with others deflated me. "I'm sure it will be fine," I said, turning away.

She lay still. She was traveling north. I could feel it.

After a lingering sigh, she said, "It's been so long."

I turned to her again and drew her to me for comfort. "You'll be all right. I'll come get you." She said nothing more and was soon asleep.

Mary fell under a mantric spell that called her northward, smoothed impediments of wintry travels, and dispelled the tension with which she had always regarded a return. I feared that leaving with no mention of her coming back spelled truncation of our marriage. So because the emotion she kept private daunted me and separated me from her, I agreed without observable reluctance to make the trip after her.

My second in command, Al, would run the shutter business through this busiest time of year, when we were still repairing last winter's damage and were installing shutters before the start of the next storm season. Leaving then was a sacrifice, but I could bring Mary back only if I went after her.

This had happened before. There had been strong premonitions like Mary's just before my birth. Mother had told me about some kind of stirrings that ordered my father to vacate Nova Scotia when she was pregnant. He had listened to the voices, and they turned out to be, for me at least, the best forebodings he followed in an otherwise short, drunken, and chaotic life. Though, after his interment in Canada, he left behind little but the flat-nosed evidence of his Native blood on my face, a pile of unpaid bills on the kitchen table, and the flimsy house we lived in—one cut above shack-with-lean-to—Mother and I had something to come back to, southern warmth.

A return south after his funeral nearly didn't happen. Only eight years old, I forced the issue with tears when I discovered Mother's hope of staying in Nova Scotia. Through strength of will fueled by fear, I prevailed on Mother to return to the only home I had known. I won back then and would now use all tactics to bring Mary back, too.

Years before, transplanted in the south, I basked in the odd fortune of my father's alcohol-driven wandering that had brought us to Tallahassee. As if in compensation for what I came to see as my unlucky Indian heritage, he left me to grow up in the warmth of Mother's love and the Florida sun. So, if returning south with Mary meant meeting her on her home turf, that's what I would do.

I was against moving around and—after burying my father and, ten years later, returning Mother to Nova Scotia—was done with the north. I prospered in Florida.

Right after graduation I abandoned the imagination-driven languor of a career in literature. There was little hope for a job in teaching, anyway. So I adopted the practical pursuit of business, joining two college friends in an ill-fated strip-mall development scheme. When the venture failed, I dispatched the ironies of an Indian—even an undercover one—operating in the land development business in favor of a new job, selling and installing storm shutters. That business rooted me all the more deeply in hurricane-prone Florida.

After life with my father, disaster preparedness felt right. And though both my parents had been migrants, I never planned to move. I built a life with Mary in unhaunted sunshine and practical mundane activity. Successful as I was though, I still needed her with me.

So on I drove through that Minnesota blizzard. I hoped the mysteries that had drawn my father to Florida would prove stronger than those that had drawn Mary away. Her new familial magnetism had turned her north again, with me in time-delayed tow. From what I had experienced years before in Nova Scotia and from what I had seen so far in Minnesota, the frozen north was not a place I wanted to stay. We could not thrive there. I could not survive. Would everything, as Mary hoped, be all right?

Mary had told me about the cold. She made fun of me when I shivered at forty-five degrees, saying, "You don't know what cold is!" True, at that time, I hadn't been out of Florida but twice, and the coldest Florida weather I had experienced—covered in blankets, dressed in an old World War II parka—was something still above freezing. I met Mary soon after she arrived at Pensacola from the north. She swore from the first that she would never return to what she called that god-awful refrigerator. Though I didn't know her to ever wear a sweater or a jacket, she claimed to be tired of freezing in the dark and wouldn't be dragged back kicking or screaming, alive or dead.

She was nineteen then.

"Then why did you stay so long?" I'd asked.

"We always said, 'It builds character,' " she told me. "It sure does. The state is full of them. Too stiff to quit, too dumb to know better."

Cold, the kind I knew and the kind I could not yet know, did not worry her. The place and people rather than the cold and dark was what she wanted to escape. And I've found out it was a whole lot more than that. Deep in her roots that trailed the bottoms of the northern channels' heavy acidic murk, acerbic welts stung her. Mary's wounds had grown old but began to pulse again like hurts inflicted yesterday.

Mary had seldom looked back. We married in a tiny civil ceremony, attended by a couple of hired witnesses— friends of the Justice of the Peace—and my college roommate, who bore the rings. She did not invite family. In fact, I didn't think that she let anyone up north know. I hadn't written anyone myself. We were unconcerned with family, hers or mine.

Who found her? I thought it was through our loose association with the American Indian Movement. How else could word be brought north? I suppose she might have called or written at some point. If she did, she didn't tell me. I guess I didn't ask. It doesn't matter now. Whenever she made mention of the family, I listened but didn't say much. I thought it best to let the ghosts of her past rest.

In that icy Jeep, my meditation on Mary drowned in a wave of snow-filled wind, washing me, the car, and the guiding red string of taillights down a curl of whirling white.

The car and I were falling. I clutched the steering wheel when a huge, gloaming fist burst past from behind me. The fist punched the face of the storm and with that glancing blow plowed my Jeep to the edge of the earth. The giant clenched hand roared along and exploded through the white wall of the blizzard. I hadn't driven in weather like this before. So it must have been instinct or deep winter ancestry that told me to let off the gas. The fist, its arm and shoulder catapulted by, intensifying the wind-whipped, whiting world. I forgot to breathe then gasped and gulped frigid air. The cab's glacial atmosphere entering my lungs snapped me back to attention.

It was a truck that had stormed past, a tractor-trailer rig barreling along as if this were a clear, balmy, summer's day. Through the fury of driven snow, I stared after its amber running lights and at its red tail lights speeding ahead. "You have to follow them." Over the roar of the flying truck, I couldn't tell if I had actually spoken. I redoubled my speed. I chased what seemed to be my only hope of following and staying on the now invisible road. I found to my horror that I had fallen into reverie, lost my string-of-lights escort, and had been crawling along at twenty-five miles an hour.

"You've got one hope, Tatty," I said aloud, squinting after the semi. "Keep up with him."

I had learned to follow big rigs under much different conditions and circumstances but on an occasion filled with as much palpable danger. On a summer trip through the Mississippi night, I had followed first one semi, then another through wisps of dense ground fog along wooded lowlands populated with night-roving deer. I had nudged into the windy suck of the trailer's wake, close enough to benefit from the warning the eighteen humming wheels gave the wandering deer and far enough back so the trucker could see my car and be mindful of me. All I had to do was watch for the rig's sudden braking.

Now, in the gale-driven snow lashed by the stinging turbulence of the wind, I followed the same course. I stayed back to avoid some of the blinding whirl of snow kicked up by the truck. I kept my braking distance as wide as I dared, should something happen. In tandem with the truck, I cruised on.

Against my will and best intentions, I inevitably let my guard down. I imagined that we strove onward against the storm, we two, a giant, moving fortress and a trundling wheeled-hut chained together by hope. The imagery I invented warded off fatigue. This practice insulated me from the frosty fear that I was alone on a deserted and beleaguered road in a strange wilderness.

I settled in, sheltering behind the semi. I had grown tense gripping the wheel for an hour. The effort left my shoulders aching, my hands sore, and my neck stiff. In half the drive I had traveled a respectable eighty miles but after the storm hit only forty miles more. Fighting the blizzard felt like wrestling a famished, albino alligator whose snapping jaws constantly threatened to tear me up if I let go. The leeward shelter of the truck had weakened the gator. Now I could loosen my hold. For the first time in hours, I let the wheel go one hand at a time, cranking the air with the freed arm, working the stiffness out, then, lifting the other limb to bring life back to it. I grasped the wheel again and focused solely on the semi's taillights.

We cruised the night, pierced the storm in single file, melding into one machine tethered by my phantasmagoria of imagination and frozen flakes twisting in the Jeep's dual beams of bluish light. I rubbed my eyes to dispel visions. Nevertheless, at some moments the phantom shape of Mary's windigo formed. A waif danced across the trailer's door panels, jumped onto the Jeep's hood, and finally dissolved in the vortex of wind-blown snow.

It reappeared looking hungry and sad. I shut my eyes as long as I dared and still beheld the vision behind my lids. I looked again. At times it hunched, riding the driven snow itself. Sometimes, it perched on the hood and cocked its head as if to listen to what I was thinking. The gnome turned its big sad eyes on me. "You must have a mind of winter to be at home out here," it said. It nodded.

"Enough!" I shouted.

I twisted the wheel to dislodge the sprite from the hood. In my effort to shake off the figure that camped there, I sent the Jeep into a skid first one way then the next.

"No!" I screamed.

I straightened the wheel, steadying myself and the car. It isn't real, I said to myself. Forget it.

I might have become a believer in windigoes or, like another time in my life, in poetry, but even if I refused to believe as I did before, I hoped whatever phantom force existed in the storm would be benevolent. I fixed my gaze on the truck's door panels moving thirty feet before me. They hypnotized me. The truck I stared at drew me on like the howling winter-windigo that Mary had warned would sing a siren's song in the north.

The storm raged on, sounding at times like angry voices in hissing feuds, like the beating of gargantuan wings between guttural explosions of warring giants' yells. I listened to the cacophony the wind incited. More disturbing were voices from quiet corners tucked behind the edges of the wind's outbursts. There were shouts in the blasts, but whispers lisped, too, in the lulls of wind. Discomforting messages lurked within both, thoughts like "Freezing isn't so bad" or "Sleep, you are tired." Between the bass blasts and sibilant melody in the hush, I heard my father's voice. It sounded first like a Mi'kmaq chant intoned when he was three sheets to the wind:

> *Ne-noi-te-te-me-netj ge-li-gen*
> *Tan ga-ga-mig set-an e-oei.*

After a particularly strong gust, I heard different words following the same tune:

> *Ouvrons nos yeux a sa lumiere.*
> *Ouvrons notre Coeur a sa Loi.*

The harmonic memory played the stiff chords of my neck, tugging me toward that primordial spinal base of the autonomic brain that felt like a tuning fork resonating with the wildness of the nor'easter. I knew it was dangerous, but that did not seem to matter. The vibration, whether real or imagined, soothed the ache of my shoulders. It warmed my chest and limbs. I floated with the harmony that the oscillating weather, the rumbling road, and my quavering neck chords intoned.

Silent screeching of bursting red blew my reverie apart, vaporized my dream, and drained my veins in a bloody paroxysm of burning snow. I snapped to my senses.

The truck had braked. Fortunately, still tethered, though the leash had grown slack and the distance between us shortened, we had started grinding slowly up a grade.

The storm had immersed me in exactly the psychic state I wanted to avoid. I'd followed the truck up a highway exit in a dream. The incline had naturally retarded my advance toward the steel bumper of the rig. In my trance I'd slowed enough to afford a full stop. The Jeep skidded and slid to rest just three feet behind my partner-in-storm. I breathed in. I blew air at the windshield. My trucker-guide lurched out of his stop. I followed his hard right turn, fishtailing with the uncertain traction.

I was both awestruck and irritated—like a man surprised when coming home to a birthday party. I found myself in a parking lot awash in neon glow of a brightly lighted travelers' stop. Bundled-up pedestrians waded toward a restaurant amid cars stopped at all angles, some half-buried in drifted snow.

Destiny, providence, or, against my best intentions, that will o' the wisp dancing above the highway, had led me here. The implication was clear: whatever luring hand beckoned me to follow—in a dream, practically comatose at times—seemed, right then, glowing and fortunate, rather than, as I had feared, dark and malign.

A green, amber, and red neon sign mounted over a steeply pitched café roof announced: Bobbie's.

The first time I traveled north was by train. Just before my ninth birthday, Mother and I brought the embalmed corpse of my father to his hometown, to his people in Nova Scotia. That trip left deep wounds. We were sad. Mother wept. I pretended to cry with her. My father rode four cars back in his casket. I was scared, but at that time I acted brave. It was Mother, I thought, who needed comfort.

I had known only a small number of emotional expressions—anger, want, and depression seemed innate—others, like bravery, tenderness, and generosity, I had read about in books. I wore bravery especially as a protective coat without knowing that it also isolated me. Bravery was armor holding in a firmament of furies I could not name but that bloomed darkly in me whenever I thought of my father. The kitchen of my childhood had flashed with marital battles. Even from the solitary darkness of death, my father slandered me with churlish accusations.

For years on end he filled our yellow kitchen with vicious verbal stabs at Mother. He shouted his disappointment in me and in his own dismal fate.

I heard him accuse Mother. "All you care about is that goddamn kid!"

Mother spoke quietly. "Shush, Peter, you'll wake him."

"Wake him? That jiggaboo needs a good waking. You baby him too much."

"He's only five. He's your son, Peter."

I heard his chair scrape back against the linoleum floor. "I wonder sometimes."

"Not that again, Peter. He is as Mi'kmaq as they come. He looks like you and Banook, too."

"Leave her out of this. That kid has to be tough to make it as an Indian. Stop coddling him all the time."

The voices echoed off the yellow walls and bounced, still hot and stinging, down the hall to my bedroom. There I writhed in fury and plotted the murder of my father. Those arguments ended with doors slamming, and my father leaving, sometimes after hitting Mother.

I could still hear her sobbing, "Peter, you hurt me!"

"That's not all you'll get!" he roared.

"No. No. I'm all right. Don't leave now."

"Get out of my way. You can't stop me."

I heard him stomp out the door. It slammed on Mother's weeping. Later, I would hear her at the sink, washing dishes in between outbursts of tears and heaving sighs.

"Shit," she said. "Oh shit!"

Fear and anger paralyzed me. I couldn't bring myself to talk about it, not even to Mother. Though I wanted him dead at these times, I did nothing.

Then he did die.

If I cried, it was only because Mother was pained. I felt relief and guilt at the same time.

On the train, it was easier to be brave than to feel the misery my father's death would rain on my life. Even years later, when I met Mary, I was convinced that the event had helped rid my life of a tyrant rather than hamper Mother's and my progress. When Mother was gone, too—ten years after my father, returning to Truro, where her sister still lived and where Mother died, slowly, painfully, quietly—the cold spirit of my father still slapped me, reached out of the darkness to arrest my breath, to bring me up short exactly as he had done when alive.

As I crossed through our living room, his disembodied voice would spring out of the whiskey-laced air in the lightless room where he nursed his bottle, "Where do you think you're going?"

I was silent but thought, You been lying on the couch waiting for me, haven't you?

I halted, stiff and afraid. "Nowhere," I said, "just to the kitchen."

Derision filled his voice. "Don't snivel," he said. "What? To eat the food I put in the fridge?"

"No. Well, yes. I thought I could have an orange."

He mocked me. " 'I thought I could have an orange.' Well, you can't. I'll tell you what you can do. You can turn right around and get on back to your room."

Later, just as on those nights, he stood, whether alive or dead, a constant sentinel over my life, ready to yank the chain his drinking and rage locked to my collared neck. I could not slip by him. Even thirty years later, my dread of his spirit lived on.

For a long time I refused to see and admit that my father was the quintessential drunk. Then, on a sodden winter evening, he showed me plainly enough. Coming in the back door on shuffling, uneasy legs, he muttered too loudly as he negotiated his path through the kitchen. Mother and I were playing pick-up-sticks on the living room floor.

"Well, isn't this cozy?" he said, swaying over us, "The domestic duo."

He swept an unsteady foot over the pile of sticks, scattering them.

"You're drunk, Peter."

"The hell you say."

"You're just plain mean. Mean and drunk."

"Who says?"

Mother looked at me. "Look at your father, Tatty. He's drunk, isn't he?"

I hung my head. I couldn't look at either of them.

"Yeah, Tatty," he said, "I'm not drunk, now am I? Tell her." When I shook my head, meaning yes and no, he bellowed. "Tell her now!"

I could manage only mumbled words. I wanted to strike out at him, to end the night. But the words turned to cotton in my throat. I gagged on my thoughts.

"See?" my father said, "he knows what's what."

He leered at Mother. "Well, I think I'll join you two. Let's have a game."

My father went for the chair. I watched in horror and disbelief as he sat nearly three feet left of it and tumbled to the floor.

"See, see," Mother said, laughing, "you missed by a mile. You're blind drunk."

He floundered on the floor, raging against the truth.

"You pushed me!" he bawled.

Mother stopped laughing. "From over here? No."

"Wha' the hell you know, woman? Ne'er work a day in yer life. You an' momma's boy there can go to goddamn hell." He kicked out at us but was too drunk to hit his mark.

I couldn't say it then, but from that night to his death and beyond, I knew it was true. My father was a boozer. A common drunk. And a cruel one, too.

It was a funeral train. We two rode coach and paid more, Mother said, for my father than for the both of us. Our mood was solemn. Mother grieved more deeply than I could understand. I couldn't shake fears of my dead father, so I hid behind false bravery. Always, though, father's body following us four cars back haunted me. His presence muted my excitement of traveling on rails.

I had never ridden a train before—have not since our return trip six days later. Despite my wonderment, I did not feel right about exploring the long line of coaches. When I ventured forth, usually at Mother's urging, I never went back toward the cargo compartments. I returned quickly. Other passengers eyed me sympathetically, I thought, as that boy whose father died. I told Mother I didn't want to leave her alone, but really, I hated being stared at. Once when I returned from the observation car, I saw Mother hurriedly wipe tears away. That saddened me. I felt responsible. So the three-day trip northward was not one to enjoy. Like a mind of winter, the somber mood and the cold, fearful beginning of a different life chilled my bravery and my dignity, especially on the edges of sleep.

I felt the presence of my father. I wouldn't tell Mother of my fear that he could come through the coach door at any time. Maybe it was just worry, but even months later, I still expected to hear him clearing his throat as he opened the back door at home.

Mine was a morbid fantasy, but my father also cast a pall over Mother's spirit. She tried for my sake to be cheerful, but she brought him back with each sigh. Her reddened eyes were constant reminders that he was with us. Maybe his corpse was some strange comfort to Mother who twice I knew about visited the cargo car that carried him along with us. I had viewed it at the funeral in Tallahassee, and I was unnerved that the body trailed behind our coach class car like a blind hound on the scent.

I pictured him inside the casket still wearing the white carnation the undertaker had placed in his lapel. I wondered if someone had removed the gold wedding band that had looked to me so shiny and lone on his rough hand. I worried—as some of the boys at school had told me—that his fingernails were lengthening, that his hair and whiskers were growing long. I felt he was not yet done living. Would my nightmare end at his burial in Tattamagouche?

I woke, sweating and moaning, with nightmares of my father making his way down the aisle, eyes rolled back, zombie-like, stiff-legged, heavily bearded, clicking inch-long fingernails on the leather backs and hand grips of the seats. Mother tried to soothe me with whispers of comfort and kisses on my damp forehead. Especially toward night—even in the excitement of that first snowy evening moving north from New York City toward Montreal, my first ever view of real snow—I grew morbid and afraid. I obsessed silently, unwilling to burden Mother about the black casket to the rear that cast its shadow over me. Try as I might to hide my fear, Mother knew. She told me stories to divert my attention from these dark, unspoken musings.

She worked to focus my thoughts away from my father. She spoke of her side of the family, of the "Finlanders."

"You don't remember Grandma, do you?" she said.

"Your mother? I do, too," I countered. "You have pictures. I've seen them."

"You know that when she was your age, she lived on an island between Finland and Sweden. She spoke Finnish at home and Swedish at school."

"Did she speak English, too?"

"After she moved to Canada, yes. And some French, too."

Though I knew Grandma only from bent-corner photos saved in the keepsake box Mother had shown me four or five times, her truly brave soul impressed me. I was cheered to be descended from her. In one photo she knelt alongside a patch of vegetables, one hand caressing a squash gourd, the other modestly anchoring her apron and flowered skirt around her knees. Another showed her aged, terribly wrinkled, stout and jowly, standing before an entry door, purse in hand, the opening of her long coat showing a boat-neck dress and the same string of pearls I had seen Mother wear. Grandmother Strang looked reserved and stately in both photos.

She had crossed a frigid ocean at sixteen. She came alone and unschooled in the ways of the new country. Mother's stories of her lent me courage and fed the feeling that I had come from sturdy stock. That helped.

I found it easy to admire my grandmother, enshrined as she was in filigreed metal frames. Mother portrayed the languages Grandma spoke as mystical knowledge. I could hear her words dance in jolly cadences from behind her photographic gaze. Peasant though she was, she spoke more languages than anyone I knew.

The talk of languages reminded me of my Canadian-born father, who spoke three tongues, though when sober he kept quiet all but English. I had heard him speak Mi'kmaq only when drunk. He spoke French very badly, he admitted.

He had forbidden Mother to speak Finnish in his house. "I don't want to hear any of that old-country gibberish here."

My father seemed intent on squeezing my grandmother's and Mother's influences from my character. It did not work. His strategy only enflamed my curiosity about the Finns, that strange breed that seemed even more clannish and odd than my father's Mi'kmaq people. Now that he was gone, I felt a new freedom to explore my Finnish side.

Somehow though, guilt rose to greet that thought. I suppose because I was to meet my father's Indian mother once we arrived in Nova Scotia. I should be curious to know about her, but I resented her being alive while Grandma Strang was gone. I felt pulled first in one direction, then in the other.

"Didn't Dad speak French in Canada?"

"Not much. His family was English-speaking, but he talked mostly Mi'kmaq with his mother and cousins."

"And what did you talk with your mother?"

"Mostly Finnish, but after the school recommended it, English."

She put her hand on the side of my head, hugged me, and combed her fingers through my cowlick. "Your grandmother was something, *Pikkupoika*," she said, using a private Finnish name she had given me. She told me the story as if I had never heard it before.

"Grandma's name was Ellen. She left a small island

in the west, just across the sea from Sweden. She called it '*Gombligotiliboo*.' "

I played the part of an innocent listener. "What sea was that?" I asked.

"The Baltic Sea, I think," Mother said. She coaxed my hair into place. "She was just fifteen, one month shy of her sixteenth birthday."

"That seems old. Not real old, but older than me," I said.

"She was following two cousins who had bought farms near Fort William in Ontario. She told me about getting there." Mother adopted Grandma's voice to take over the telling:

" 'I worked. A maid in a rich house in Montreal. I needed twenty-five dollars to take the train to Aune's. They gave me a tiny room on the third floor of the house. At night I practiced French with Claudette. She was the cook's helper. She called herself a sous-chef. Claudette was good to me. She lent me books to look at and read. Children's books.' "

Mother's imitation of Grandma's voice amused me. I didn't think about my father in his coffin. I pictured myself in her place, sitting up late, poring over Claudette's storybooks. Her dedication bolstered me. In Grandma's voice, Mother told me that hard work was native to all Finns.

Mother took up her mother's lilting accent. " 'I was made to be a farm wife, not a maid. But it took six months of cleaning house to save enough to join my cousins in Ontario. When I got there, I worked in the kitchen and in the poultry yard. We raised turkeys, ducks, and chickens. I fed the big tom turkeys, but sometimes they chased me. I'd hike up my skirts and run. Aune would see that and laugh.

"'I gathered eggs in my apron pockets. I prepared the fryers for dinner. In the yard, I would lay the squawking chicken's neck across the big wooden block and chop its head right off.'" Mother said this in a curt, sharp voice, slicing suddenly, quickly through the air with an open hand. "'And that chicken? It ran circles around the yard. It left its head right in my hand. Of course, it couldn't make a sound.'"

I visualized our yard back home filled with headless chickens and turkeys running in all directions, colliding with each other, bumping into the house, tripping over the sandbox, and, finally, falling over, feet kicking the air. The gruesomeness of the scene did not chill me. I laughed with Grandma and Mother at those headless chickens.

It was good to hear Mother laugh. She continued, "*Voinko kertoa suomeksi*? Should I tell it in Finnish?"

I shook my head and laughed at the funny, foreign sounds.

Mother resumed in her own voice. "Grandma had to pull all the feathers out and clean the birds for cooking. She baked them in a wood-burning oven. She had to chop the wood, too."

It all seemed like adventure to me. I pictured myself living a pioneer farm life. The work Mother said was grueling—sixteen-hour days of hard farm labor—seemed charming and fun to me. Grandma's fortitude, stamina, and practicality were useful. Her story starched my flagging bravery.

Mother's intention was to divert me, but it was clear that she got helpful lessons and qualities from Grandma's life to use in her own. I imagined Grandma being exactly like Mother, a diminutive, fair haired, wry-witted, hard-working, and practical person who took life in stride. She described Grandma's grit as *sisu*, a Finnish word that she translated as "we made it through the winter," a quality that made the Finns tough survivors. On that train ride, sitting attentively at Mother's side, I took *sisu* as my own, a useful word and a handy tool.

The train carried us northward into cold darkness checkered by snow, but I felt that I could make it through the winter of my father's death with the warmth of Mother's stories and stoutness of their truths.

"Within a year of her arrival, Grandma married. She moved to a neighboring farm to become the wife of Andrew Torppa. I was born that year." Mother described her own childhood mornings with a longing that made me want to relive them.

"I heard Grandma in the kitchen, stoking the big cast-iron stove. She rattled grates, tossed wood into the firebox. Sometimes I would wake to the crack of her splitting cordwood outside the kitchen. She clattered and clanged the pots and pans as she began to cook breakfast. The smell of coffee rose to my loft over the parlor to tell me the stove was hot. Then I jumped out of the warm covers and skipped down the ladder.

" '*Hyvää huomenta, Äiti*,' " I said. " 'Good morning, Mother.' I warmed my clothes across a chair back while I waited. I lifted my nightshirt to heat my backside at the stove. When my clothes were toasty, I dressed as quickly as I could, right there in the kitchen.

"Her yeasty wheat bread bulged as if ready to float off the shelf like a balloon following the stovepipe to the ceiling. It grew over the sides of the metal pan. It rose in the heat of the range. Mother took the loaf to the floured table, punched the growing mass down with her fists clenched at her thick wrists, and kneaded it again and again.

" '*Yksi, kaksi, kolme* . . . ,' she counted. The sweet smell of flour puffed out with each stroke. She nestled the dough in the pan again and put it on the range-shelf to rise once more."

Mother said, "You have to have a wood stove to bake decent bread, crusty, dense, and chewy."

"We don't have a wood stove, but I like your bread," I told her. It was true.

"Oh, it's nothing like hers. She made peasant bread, brown, speckled inside, dense, with a hard crust that kept the flavor locked in. I make white bread. It's easy."

We had always prized Mother's bread. I pictured my father cutting a loaf in our kitchen. Now, my father's sudden absence prodded me to wonder about Mother's dad.

Before I knew to stop myself—I only felt it was mistake after it was out—I wondered aloud about Mother's father of whom she'd said little. "And what happened to Grandmother's husband?"

Mother was thoughtful, more tactful than I, and took her hand to the side of my head with a caress, smiling faintly. "This will never happen to you," she said, lifting my chin to look into my eyes, "but in those days on a farm, a woman had to have a man. So when my father died in the sanitarium, Grandma remarried later that same year. I was four."

Her voice carried so much disappointment that I lowered my gaze. "I'm sorry."

"Don't worry. I don't need to remarry like my mother did. You and I can manage without your father, just the two of us."

I looked into her face, "And we can still live in our little house?"

Mother turned to the window.

I had not, until that moment, thought about our future. At nine years old the present had been enough to keep me occupied. Would the future be simpler than life had been so far? Though she didn't reply, Mother's look betrayed doubts. Despite my uncertainty, I asked no more. I laid my head against her side.

"Tomorrow we'll be in Halifax," she said and looped her arm around me to arrange our blanket over us. I was asleep immediately.

Tiny suddenly lifts a finger. He rivets his attention on the fishing line closest to him. I stop talking.

Tiny barely whispers, "He's nosing the bait." The line stirs so slightly that the tiny clapper does not roll inside its bell. Hardly breathing, we wait for the fish to strike. Nothing happens.

Finally, Tiny moves. "Give me your cup," he says and reaches toward the barrel stove where he keeps the pot warm. He fills my cup and points to the milk bottle and toast left on the table. "Have some toast to soak this up."

"Thanks," I say.

Tiny pours his own untouched coffee back into the pot. He's a big man. He sits away from the table. His face is larger and rounder than mine, his nose a bit more hawkish, and his hair six shades darker, nearly black, but our Algonquin kinship from an eon back preserves a resemblance that could have easily served to mistake us for cousins.

Tiny folds his hands on the table and pushes his full-moon face toward mine. "Strange. I didn't know my father. You knew yours. We both had bad luck." Tiny lifts a corner of his mouth in a canted grin. "Granny raised me. We're close like you and your mom. I didn't know my mother, but you didn't know your grandmother."

I have to smile. "Indian luck?"

"Rotten, but we keep going anyway."

Tiny laughs big and jerks backward in his chair, palms raised like he is pushing a load of irony at me across the table. I tip my chair back on two legs. It isn't that funny, but I wrap myself in both arms. We chuckle a bit together.

I sip my brew between chortles. "Coffee's good."

Tiny gets up to refill his cup. "Okay, I'm curious. What was going on at Bobbie's during the storm?"

I let my smile fade. I look again at that burlap curtain. The filtered sun runs woven patterns over the table. Tiny thins behind the glare off the checkered oilcloth of burlap-sifted sunshine.

I recede into my story about the café.

Inside, Bobbie's was everything the desolate blizzard-wracked road was not: alive with warmth given off by the cinnamon buns standing on racks at the cash register, friendly with roiling talk of some sixty souls, and punctuated by the clatter of plates the busboys stacked in tubs to rush through the swinging kitchen doors.

The aroma of coffee overcame a peculiar scent of snow-sodden wool and wet cotton-lined nylon emanating from the coat rack at the door. Below, rubber overshoes surrounded the rack base. Newcomers like me stamped and shuffled in the vestibule and unzipped their boots, kicking them off, building another circle round the rack. Some kept their coats on, and all moved toward the pastry counter, where buns, donuts, and Danish sweetened the air.

"How are ya?" the waitress said. She smiled, pressed lips together, raised her brows, and waited for me to order.

I was still on the highway, a deer frozen in the headlights.

She gave me a second to process the greeting. "Quite a storm we've got tonight. . ."

"Yes," I finally blurted out. I was having more than a little trouble talking.

"Would you like one of our famous cinnamon

buns, Sweetheart? A coffee? Would you like to sit at the counter?"

"Yes."

"Which one? All?"

"Yes." It had become my blizzard-born mantra.

"Right this way." She pointed and deftly grabbed the coffee pot with her right hand and a plated cinnamon bun with her left. "Regular, I guess."

"Yes."

She sat me between two coffee drinkers who seemed to be wondering what to do with sticky hands they held above the remains of glazed buns. The hostess set my cinnamon roll down, turned my coffee mug over, and poured while asking, "Room for cream?"

"Yes."

"All right, Honey. Sugar and cream are on the counter. Anything else?"

I was finally able to vary my monosyllabic response, "No." Adding, "Thank you." I was beginning to think I could talk again.

She topped off the coffees right and left of me. "You'se need wet naps?" she said, depositing two small foil wrappers before each of my companions. Then she was gone.

The man on my left held a foil packet to the light, "Looks like a condom." He opened the foil to take out the moist napkin. He worked at cleaning his hands.

The man on my right looked at me. "Quite a storm we've got out there tonight."

I responded immediately. "Yes, it is."

He hunched closer to make conversation. "Where you coming from?"

"Saint Paul, tonight."

"I wouldn't go down there for nothin'. Came south from the Falls to get his uncle." He nodded in the direction of the man on my left. "It was pretty bad up there."

I must have looked puzzled. He added, "International Falls, ya know?"

"Well, looks like we're just crossing paths," I said, turning into a veritable chatterbox, "I'm headed up to Thief Lake."

He screwed up his mouth and twisted his neck, touching an ear to his parka hood, "You might make it."

"It's that bad?"

"Power's mostly out everywhere. They're plowing with all they got, from what I saw. Might get through. But all the way to the lake?" He shifted his pursed lips up aside his nose, "That's going to be interesting."

"I think it's right near the main road."

"More'n five miles off. I know some people there. Whose place?"

I was eager for more information. "Martin Bassett's," I said.

"Tiny?"

The nickname threw me off. "I'm not sure."

"Hey, Cooley." He hunched over the counter to get a clear view of the man on my left, who was working on his second wet nap. "He's going up to Tiny's cabin. Ain't that something?"

These two were together and had left a stool between themselves not for conversation-making with strangers but to accommodate their ample girths. The man on my left turned nothing but his head. He gave me a broken-toothed grin. "Goin' see all them babies be born?" He seemed like a mind reader. "You missed the first one. Beanie's already had hers."

The man on my right spoke softly to the countertop, "Yeah, Windy might be another matter."

Their familiarity startled me. The storm had blown me magically between probably the only two people in Bobbie's, or for miles around, who knew the people and the place where I was headed. I must have been staring with my mouth open. Had I gone miles further than I had thought? I wondered how far my hypnotic driving had carried me. It seemed as if I had arrived. On the left, Cooley turned back to his coffee. "Good luck."

As if a flash of headlamps lighted his mind, the man to my right said, "Hey! I bet you're Mary Bassett's man, aren't you?"

"Well . . ."—I felt tentative and cautious—". . . she's Mary Langille now." I felt like bolting to the car. Eerie feelings crept along and had followed me indoors. "Strange," I said. "Small world, huh? You know them?"

"Know, knew, both. I grew up with all three a' them." He hadn't yet used the wet nap, so he rubbed his puffy, rough-looking hand on his napkin and somewhat apologetically extended a handshake, "Hooper Daniels. Call me Danny. I'm practically family."

Here I was, miles to go and already meeting "family." I responded automatically, "Langille. Tatty Langille."

"That's Cooley Jokinen."

"Isn't that a Finnish name?" I asked.

"Acts like one too," Danny said.

I nodded to Cooley. "I'm half, myself."

"We won't hold that against you," Danny said. He grabbed a clean napkin and looked toward our waitress. "Lois, borrow me that pen."

Lois, showing practiced efficiency, grabbed the coffee pot as she came with the ballpoint. She made a final note on her pad, slapped the bill and her pen in front of Danny and topped off all three coffees.

"Watch these two. Especially when they give directions." She turned away.

"Hey, lady, watch the tips," Cooley warned, but Lois was gone.

"Look here," Danny was already sketching on the napkin. "You leave the main road at Hongisto's Implement. They're all covered with the snow, but look for them tractors. There's a big sign, too. Go right."

I examined his map. He had drawn a crude tractor at a "Y" of two lines.

"You go down that road five or six miles. It curves around a lot, but they're usually plowing like crazy down there. You can follow the grader if he's around. You'll pass a two-story building on your right, Tillie's."

Now he sketched a two-story façade. It looked something like an old-time, western saloon.

"Go a little ways past, I can't say how far. Turn left at the gas station. Tiny lives up that road." He shoved the napkin at me.

Cooley lunged at the rough map, pawing it toward him. "The hell. You go right at the '66."

Danny screwed up his face again, "Okay, okay, right at the station. Cooley knows everything. He's right-handed, too."

Cooley scribbled something on the napkin and drew an arrow. "Turn three-tenths of a mile past Tillie's. And don't stop in there, either."

"Where?" I had to ask.

"Tillie's," they said together.

"Salt 'n' pepper," Danny blurted out. He seemed to be playing a game with Cooley.

"Stuff it, Danny," Cooley said.

I looked at the map, turning it around to find the right orientation. Cooley grabbed it again, added a huge "N" over the arrow. He shoved it back at me. Both of them got up.

"We got to get Uncle Joki."

Danny pounded my shoulder. "Nice meeting you, Tatty. How'd you get that name?"

"From his parents, fool," Cooley said.

"It's short for Tattamagouche. It's my dad's hometown," I said.

They spoke together. "Good luck."

"Salt 'n' pepper," Danny said. "We're always sayin' the same thing."

"Shove it, Danny," Cooley said. He was tired of the game.

He stood over me. He wavered in his boots, seemed to be thinking deeply. "Listen, we're going to pick up my Uncle Joki ten miles south a' here. We'll be half an hour behind you on the trip back. We'll keep an eye open, just in case you have trouble. What you driving?"

"A little dark-green Jeep. Hardtop."

"Okay then."

"Thanks, but I probably won't need the help."

Cooley looked at Danny and then at me, "You might if you stop in at Tillie's. Don't mess with them people."

They shuffled to the cash register in their unzipped boots. I saw Danny slip the pen under the folded bills he laid on the counter, then put his hand in his coat pocket.

"Hey. Leave that pen," Lois said over her shoulder. "Change?"

"Naw," they both said.

"Salt 'n' pepper."

"Shut up."

Even though they had their puffy coats on, the two turned to the coat rack. Danny reached up and unhooked two wool hats, the kind with earflaps that tie under the chin.

Just the kind of bumpkins I expected to meet up north, I thought. Kept their jackets and boots but hung their hats.

I looked down at my half-eaten bun and decided to leave it.

Back at the coat rack Cooley seemed to be working on Danny. He did the talking and once or twice tipped his head in my direction. Danny looked down, probably trying to think, then shook his head. Cooley shrugged.

They donned their hats, zipped their jackets, and both looked back at me like two stuffed, oversized puppets. Danny touched his plaid cap brim in salute. Then he smiled.

Christ, I thought.

Cooley wavered a second or two at the door, bit his lip with what seemed indecision, finally shook his head, and then pushed Danny out by the shoulder.

Lois was back. "More coffee?"

"No. But how far is Thief Lake from here?"

"Didn't you ask Danny and them? I'd say sixty miles on the main road."

"Thanks, Lois." I got up to leave.

"Good luck."

"Thanks. That's what everyone is saying. Got a phone?"

Lois motioned to the back, "Round the corner by the men's room."

This time my call did not go through. Dead silence,

not a single click or ring sounded. But something must have connected somewhere, because my two quarters dropped to the cash bin as soon as I cradled the receiver. I was on my way. Mary would have to take that on faith.

The storm hit me full in the face as soon as I came out of Bobbie's door. The parking lot was even more a melee of cars and trucks all catawampus, their lights crisscrossing the whirling firmament at all angles. Several men with shovels and pails of sand worked to loosen a low-slung sedan that had bottomed-out in a drift. I heard one of the men say to the open window of the Chevy, "You should just pull it over and park. There's rooms at the motel still."

It sounded inviting, but with only sixty miles to go, I did not feel like giving up. The coffee break had helped. The sticky half cinnamon bun lay warm in my stomach. The Jeep had been a good idea, high up and built for snow. I could make it.

Down the other side of the overpass I entered the highway that had been plowed to a one-lane width while I warmed myself in the restaurant. The going was good, slow but fine, and it afforded me time to readjust without having to fight both the storm and the road at once.

The road did call for attention. What the plow had cleared was piled high along the shoulder, but the snow, now fluffier, falling fast, but with less swirling in wind, was quickly covering the scraped pavement, and it drifted against the bank on the shoulder.

The combination of drifts, clear-scraped pavement, and patchy packed snow beneath new-fallen fluff made traction spotty, sometimes slippery, other times suddenly gripping. More than once I hit a high drift and felt a tug as snow grabbed the tires, pulling the car toward the shoulder. I had to gently correct. Once I overdid it and skidded sideways for a moment. The tires sure hold kept me from being dragged into the banks.

Winter driving lessons were not what I came north for, but they were being offered, demanded, and came free—as long as I was able to stay on the road. Though I was happy for my quickness to learn, storm-driving tired me.

Father might have been proud of me, I thought. Though I needed to focus on driving, I found myself ruminating on his legacy.

"Might have been . . . . Be serious," I said aloud. There had never been a time that he expressed anything but lack of interest, annoyance, or disgust regarding my doings or accomplishments. I had more reason than Mary did for not wanting children. Mine was a simple desire to avoid my father's mistakes. Nature has its way, but some people have no business bringing children into the world. My father was one of those. I'm likely another. The difference between us was that he bumbled along making chaos and mayhem, while I followed plans to keep order and peace in my life, at almost any cost. Had I fathered children, I would have destroyed myself and my children as well as peace and order.

No, he would not have been proud, I said to myself.

I thought of the fifteen years Mary and I had been married, during which the question of children was always answered with a resounding, definite, and dual, "No!"

Mary's decision may have had everything to do with her wayward parents. "Grandmother raised me," she said. She seldom mentioned her ghost parents. I was not sure how well she knew them.

Mary's reasons were in line with the feminist ideals and a fierce desire to break the ties of tribal culture that had early on kept her in the backwoods. If she did not want to raise a child as an Indian off the reservation, the best way to avoid it was not to have one. We made a good pair that way.

Our marriage was fine, despite some troubles we had been having lately—well, more than just lately. I was looking forward to being with her again even in the embrace of family. Mary had been gone three weeks—had traveled in good weather—to be present at the birth and to act as the midwife for both women. Beanie was having her third. Mary felt she didn't need much help, but Windsong was young, alone, and no doubt scared. Granny was hearty but old. They needed Mary there.

Mary called me the night Beanie went into labor. Just yesterday? It was a report but acted as my travel call as well. Windsong's labor also seemed imminent. Though I was expecting the call and hid my reticence, that didn't soften its sudden intrusion.

Years before, traveling north to my father's funeral had kept me cold a long time. Even now at forty, that trip chilled me, and this Minnesota storm brought Banook, my Native grandmother, into my thoughts with her obtuse, enigmatic world of the Mi'kmaq. I felt little different than the child I had been then: terrorized by disembodied denizens, harbingers of death.

I couldn't help but touch those scars now on the narrow, newly plowed road bounded by high banks of snow that invoked the chimera of those November train tracks from Atlanta to Truro, Nova Scotia. The closer I came to Thief Lake, the more I felt wobbly and unhinged, like a fool lured again into a hostile world.

THE TRAIN RIDE NORTH to my father's funeral terrified me, but Mother's stories carried me peacefully through that night. When I awoke, we were in the train station at Halifax. We struggled to bring our small cache of luggage to another train, a shorter one, and boarded with help from the porter.

"I'm here!" A woman with long blonde hair tied back with a bright scarf threw her arms out, revealing an ultramarine shift beneath her heavy, unbuttoned coat. She danced down the aisle, her arms waving excitement above her pill-box hat that was accented by a pheasant's tail feather. Her sheer nylons shimmered in the sunshine that seemed to stream in just to light her path.

"Elsie," Mother said.

The woman wrapped Mother in her arms, coat, and scarf all at once. "My lovely Elizabeth! You look wonderful."

"No, I don't, you liar," Mother said. "Look at my eyes!" She bent her head back to gaze into the woman's face. "Oh, I love you, Elsie."

The woman peeked down at me from over Mother's shoulder, winking, then pushed back from Mother and said, "And this is Tatty? You've sure out-grown those pictures." The woman knelt to me, rushing me into her arms in an invisible cloud of lilac and summery warmth. "I'm your Aunt Elsie. Your mamma's sister!"

"I didn't think you would come, so I didn't tell Tatty," Mother said. Looking at me, she added, "It's all right, Tatty."

Elsie grabbed my valise and Mother's large suitcase, took my hand, and led us down the aisle. "Come. We'll all sit together. I have the best seats in the house." She giggled and threw smiles back at Mother. "Plenty of room. I had the conductor move the seat around so we can face each other. Look, Tatty, we can raise the table so you can draw pictures and read your books!"

Aunt Elsie took over. She bubbled, merrily fussed, and brooked no frowns. "Let me see that face," she said raising my chin in her soft palm. "Hmm, let's try this." She forked her fingers each side of my mouth and drew my lips into an upward tilt. "Look. He can smile." She tickled me under the chin, quickly kissed me again, and playfully pushed me back into the seat across from her. "Sit!" she commanded. Then barked, "Rrruff!" I had to smile. Then she was up, grabbing the last bags from Mother, and like a porter, stowed them in the racks above my head. She gave Mother the same treatment as she had me—kissed her profusely, turned up her mouth into a smile, and set her down next to me.

"You haven't eaten," she informed us. From a basket on the seat next to her she brought forth muffins and a thermos. "We're going to have an Elsie-fête. A homemade muffin breakfast with good, hot coffee. You do drink coffee, don't you Tatty? Of course you do!"

I did not. I looked to Mother, but she was gazing at Elsie, smiling broadly. Did she have tears in her eyes? I nodded. It was impossible to daunt or disappoint Aunt Elsie.

Mother tried to slip in a word but to no avail.

"Good," Aunt Elsie said. She looked at Mother. "It's mostly milk, Lizzy. Lighten up, sis. You, too, Tatty." Then in a lusty, bold voice she announced, "This," holding a finger to the air, "is a celebration!"

Elsie whirled drapes of sheer energy and warmth around us. We ate, laughed hard, and listened to stories of Elsie's life in Truro. She tattled on the odd customers who visited her busy millinery shop. "One old man totters in at least once a week to steal a button or a thimble, whatever he can pocket. We call him Mr. Kiper. A lady dressed to the nines is another regular. She haggles over the price of thread. I always refuse to discount. At least for her." Elsie laughed and took Mother's face into her hands.

Mother basked in the glow of her sister's love and generosity. They had not seen each other since my parents' wedding in Tattamagouche. They talked incessantly, so much so that none of us realized our train sat still in the station.

Mother suddenly hushed, staring out the window and stopped chatting. I saw, and my stomach leapt up. The porter who had helped us onto the train and a baggage handler wheeled my father's coffin along the platform on the way to the rear of the train. A pall fell over Mother's face.

Aunt Elsie would not have it. Even to this solemn event she brought light and gaiety. "Oh, there goes the master of ceremonies now," she said. She took my face in her hands, put on a serious look for a split second, and said, "I am sorry, Tatty." Then she smiled broadly, kissed me, then Mother, and immediately resumed her jolly chatter that held us enthralled. She erased everything else, including the motion of the train leaving the station. Morose thoughts, sadness, and fear fled before her banter.

Mother and my aunt looked very much alike but were temperamentally foreign to one another. Though I clung with devotion to Mother, Elsie fascinated me. Mother now appeared smaller, more hesitant, a bit reserved—like Grandma in those pictures—perhaps not as stately, and definitely less sure. Elsie was bold, almost brash, assured, and effusive in her talk and with her laughter.

They were half-sisters. Elsie, nearly five years younger, was favored by her father, the dire stepfather of Mother's childhood. Despite their differences, their bond and love had survived, stretching over the years-long separation. Ten years later, when Mother asked me to drive her to the Halifax ferry to return to Nova Scotia for good, it was to Elsie's care she commended herself.

Mother's return to Nova Scotia, to her sister, completed a circle in her life. The two had left the farm in 1940. Mother had just turned twenty; Elsie was sixteen. They joined the war effort in the Halifax shipyards. The work paid cash money and liberated them from isolated farm life and its thankless labor. The sisters roomed together, worked side by side. Then Elsie married. For six years more before Mother met my father, the two lived next door to each other. Elsie led the way, even in marriage.

The three-hour train ride from Halifax to Truro seemed to pass quickly. The sisters engrossed themselves in talk, reminiscence, and teasing. I napped, looked on, and read for the first time since leaving home. As I read Hans Christian Andersen, Mother absent mindedly fondled my hair. I could finally relax my vigil over her and against the coffin in the rear of the train. Mother seemed well-cared for. My father, having been dispatched by Elsie's frivolity, was more distant on this second train.

As this peace softened my tense muscles, I slept again.

In dreams I heard two women talking. Their voices seemed blown along on wind. I could not make out the words at first. In the dream, I crept closer, trying to hear the muffled conversation. Though they kept their voices low, their meaning grew clearer. Someone had died.

"No, I'm not sorry," one said.

"Have you told him yet?" asked the other.

"I haven't found the right time. I'm not sure about it myself."

"Should I have a chat with him?"

"No, I'm his mother."

I recognized the voice. I came out of the dream, but with eyes still closed, I listened for more. The words tumbled like blown leaves one over another. It was something about working.

Then Aunt Elsie came through steadily saying, "The shop won't support two, but at least you would have a place to stay."

Mother replied, but I couldn't hear. I felt her rise from the seat. Then she was gone.

I squirmed and stretched. When I opened my eyes, Aunt Elsie was looking at me.

"Well, well. You sawed some wood, there, Tatty."

She leaned across and kissed my forehead.

"We'll be coming into Truro in a few minutes. It won't be long now. Lizzy is in the biffy. She'll be right back. Another muffin?"

We arrived at Truro. Tattamagouche, the town of my father's birth and his burial place, was close by.

Funerals are punishing to young boys. I had already suffered through a ceremony in Tallahassee. I had behaved bravely then and all along the train ride, but I did not look forward to added funeral torture.

With her bold eye for the trials of others, Aunt Elsie took care arranging things for me. For my part, I saw that Mother was in good, cheery company, which relieved me of the need to support her. Mother told me I was excused from the church service but would attend the interment. Fair weather had prevailed the previous month, and the ground was soft enough for digging. I would return, for the sake of relatives in Nova Scotia, to the graveside farewell and wake.

During the funeral service I was to spend time with my father's mother, Banook. We met her outside the rear entry of the church. Mother and Elsie stooped to hug her in turn. She wouldn't attend the service.

"I will go to one more funeral," the little woman announced. She turned to me and said, "My own."

"I said goodbye to your father," she said, "when he left the Mi'kmaq way of life."

Mother lowered herself to me, balancing on her high heels, and held my hand. She caressed my neck as my tiny grandmother spoke.

"He was my eldest son," Banook said. She let her words fall to the ground. She stood, small but solid.

I felt uneasy. Despite the relief brought by avoiding the service, this was another plan I had not heard about. First, Elsie joined us unannounced. Then Mother and she had been whispering about telling me something. Now I was being passed off to my grandmother. Though there were advantages to me, I felt wary.

Mother, teetering on heels, held me firmly by the shoulders and looked straight into my eyes. "Tatty, you will be all right with Banook. She will care for you. I promise."

I was more comfortable with women than with men, even than with boys, with playmates—the death of my father confirmed that. So, despite troubled feelings, I followed when Banook simply took my hand and said, "Come." It seemed as natural as being at home with Mother.

Even after my early childhood years, I preferred to stay at home, stirring batters and soups in the kitchen with Mother, reading with her or on my own—the Andersen's fairytales I had brought along were favorites—or quietly watching Mother's calm and careful manner of sewing, sweeping, doing laundry, or making beds. I watched her, adoring the way she brushed her hand over the sheets to smooth them before covering them with blankets. Doing most everything, she would pause and stand back, her hands catching her hips, to gaze carefully, critically at her work, usually nodding as if to say, "Job well done," before moving on to the next task. It was when I, myself, became her task that I felt most complete.

Just weeks before entering second grade, I fell ill. Mother told me I was on the verge of rheumatic fever. Her voice grew serious, but she tried to hide her concern. That two-week recuperation, though dull at times, was full of warmth and love. Between her visits to my bedroom, I lay quietly, letting the fever work its way out of my system, and listened to Mother bustling throughout the house.

I memorized the routine she kept—one she followed when I would be at school or playing outside. Her deliberate, purposeful steps sounding through the house on the bare floors and over the carpeted living room telegraphed her location, her activity, and where she was headed. I could tell by her steps when Mother was making soups (short steps between counter and range), or when she was bringing a bowl of broth on a tray garnished with toast or crackers (a measured step in the kitchen, slowing cautiously over the rugged areas, stopping to pivot at the hall entry, then quickening and nearing, getting louder as she came down the hall to my room).

At her approach to my room, I propped myself up on pillows. She set the tray across my lap and swept my legs aside to sit and talk with me while I ate. Even in adulthood—long after her death—I can still feel the smooth palm of her hand, a hand as reliable as any thermometer, reaching across my forehead, checking the progress of the fever. "You're as cool as a cucumber," she said with satisfaction, patting my chest. "You'll be starting school next week, hale and hearty."

It was not just Mother I preferred. As quickly as I would with Mary many years later, I fell in love on the train with Elsie. Her boisterous goodwill and immediate attentions won me over. She eased my efforts to be a brave funeral-boy. Even as she engaged Mother, passengers, porters, or conductors, she included me: "Did you hear that, Tatty? The conductor tells me we have an hour to go." To be bathed in her radiance was a soft and lovely thing.

Banook, though she did not enthrall me with gentleness and soft words, captured me and allowed me to set aside my misgiving about being shunted off. As odd as I found her, I could trust her. Afterall, she was a woman.

My grandmother and I were nearly the same height,

I slightly taller. I had grown three inches the preceding year, passing the four-foot mark, and looked down at her from my full fifty-one inches. Though she seemed stern, her diminutive stature and the soft, rounded lines of her cheeks, eyes, and upper chin lent her a hopeful look. Her eyes were wide set, and the space between them seemed to flow prominently, high and wide, onto a foreshortened forehead, a brief plateau below a starkly defined hairline. She wore her hair long under an embroidered hoodlike cap that trailed broad, decorated flaps down each side of her head. Banook formed a pointed contrast with Aunt Elsie, but they shared a firm, strongly determined manner.

"We will walk downtown. I have someone there to see," she said. We walked on the side of the road past the clapboard church. Above the simple white-painted structure, a bell tower poked up over the central entry between long gothic windows. Either side of the belfry, a pointed-arch window was recessed in the façade. The doors housed in the base of the tower were wide open, and there, Mother and Elsie greeted mourners entering the church.

"Come," Banook said. We turned toward the little business district three blocks away.

Along the road, we met two people. Dressed in dark clothing, they were headed to the church. "I have said farewell to Peter," she told them. "This is his son, Tatty." She said it matter-of-factly, inclining her head slightly in my direction. The man and woman nodded condolences to us and moved on toward the church. "Old neighbors," she explained. Her practical way of meeting people, her plain words telling of the death of my father, her child, assured me, gave comfort, and offered promise. Her small brown hand squeezed mine as a confidence between us.

We crossed the road at a string of squat one-story shops—one looked like a butcher shop. We moved to the sidewalk. Banook said nothing but continued to hold my hand. In the next block the buildings looked much like the church would have looked without its bell tower, each two-story, some with wooden stairways climbing alongside. One carried an awning sign, I.O.O.F.

"What is "eye—oof?" I asked.

Banook looked up at the sign. She kept her pace. "A white man's club," she said.

At the end of the second block of two-story frame buildings—a grocery, a bank, and a beauty parlor—we turned off the street, down a gradual short hill. We stopped before a very small, bare-wood house. It looked perfectly suited to someone my grandmother's size. "Nebe lives here. She is a storyteller."

Banook led me around the side of the house. Far down in the back yard we approached a woman even smaller than Banook seated on a wooden apple crate. From a pile higher than her head, she was feeding wood chips, a few at a time, into a smoldering fire below a square, metal-sided chimney. She used a stick to stir another larger fire that burned in a pit beside her crate. Though her back was turned to us, she announced, "Banook brings a new friend." She dropped a few chips below the chimney and turned, still seated on the box.

"This is my grandson. Peter's boy," Banook said.

Nebe looked very much like Banook, the same round features, the same hopeful expression, and the same slight bulge of her lower forehead.

She looked up at me. "It is the way of the Mi'kmaq world. We come into it with nothing. We leave in the same way," she said and rose to her feet.

"Stand to meet the boy," Banook said.

"I am standing, Banook."

Both women laughed. They hugged each other.

Nebe sat again, tending her fires. "There are two crates by the back door. Get them, Tatty." She spoke my name.

Nebe explained she was smoking fish in her metal chimney. She had caught them that night. The river flowed past her land to the sound that widened to a sea not a half-mile from her house. "Nebe fishes at night, the Indian way," Banook told me. "Only whites fish under the sun."

"Fish traps are the best way," Nebe said.

Several oddly shaped wooden boxes were piled near the chimney. "Want to see?" Nebe asked.

"We have no time," Banook said. "We came for a story, little one," Her voice teased.

Nebe fed the chimney. She put two more pieces of cordwood on the pit fire. It sprang up to the new fuel. She turned to me. "Who did you come with?"

"Just Grandma. Banook."

"No, before that? On the train?"

"Mother. Then my aunt. My father. He's . . ."

"So two women and a dead man. Hmmm. I know no story of two women and a spirit. But there is a story of two sisters, one younger than the other, one curious and wild, the other sorrowful and tame." Nebe fed the smoker. "This is an old story. It happened not long after Glooscap was stung by lightning and found the Mi'kmaq world."

She did not need to coax me, but Banook said, "Listen to Nebe. Listen to her story."

Nebe stirred the fire. She spoke into the flames. "The sisters lived in a time when travel between the land-world and the sky-world was still common. It is the sky-world that the French-Indians later called *autremonde,* the other world. Travel brings new things, allows them to happen." She turned from the fire and looked at me now. "Always watch carefully at the beginning of a journey."

Nebe passed her hand over the pit fire, as if catching a handful of smoke, then, as if sowing seed, made three passes each side, with her hand loosening the smoke in three directions. Her hands fluttered to her lap where they waited as we did for the story to begin. Nebe crouched on her stool, as if in pain.

" 'I ache, sister,' the young sister said. 'I have man-ache.'

" 'You always ache. Be still in yourself,' the older said twisting reeds to fashion a fish trap." Nebe angled her face toward Banook. A smile hovered at the one edge of her mouth and the opposite eyebrow rose.

" 'It is a terrible pain. It tells me I must look for a man.'

" 'There are no men here, they have gone for the long hunt.'

" 'We will climb *le ciel* and search *autremonde* for tall men.'

" 'Not for me, little one,' the elder replied." Nebe again raised her head and smiled at her friend. " 'But I will go with you to the hill.'

"The sisters, hand in hand, climbed the hills, the path to *autremonde*, hiking always upward, past forest and cloud, around hillcrest and crag.

"Little One pointed to the distance beyond a cloud top, 'Look, sister, the end of my pain.' Not far off stood two tall men talking and looking down toward them. The young sister leapt forward and ran fast to meet them.

" 'Dignity, little one. Patience, young sister,' the elder called after her.

" 'Patience before virtue, sister,' the younger called over her shoulder. She ran faster. The older followed steadily, slowly.

"So it happened. The sisters took up living in skyland in *autremonde*, sharing the blankets of the sky-men, tending the fires as I do now, preparing the food, smoking the fish, again, as I do.

" 'Little wives,' the tall men said to the land-women, 'we go to join the hunt. Will you obey us when we are gone?'

"The younger sister spoke first, 'In every thing you have taught us, yes.'

" 'I will do my best,' the older sister said.

" 'Then two things: make sure the fires do not die out, and of this flat stone before the entry to our house, leave it lie as it does. Do not raise it up or look beneath it.'

" 'In every thing you have taught us, yes,' said the young one."

Nebe tossed more chips below the smoker and poked the pit fire with her stick. "And do you think the sisters did what they promised?" She looked at me with a pursed, crooked smile. A gleeful look lit her rounded features. "Banook knows that answer."

"Nebe knows better than Banook," my grandmother said. Her face impassive, still.

"The tall men had been gone only a short time. 'I ache, sister,' the younger woman said.

" 'Your man is just now gone. How can you ache?'

" 'No, sister, it is not a man pain this time. I ache to

know what is beneath the stone. Don't you wonder?'

" 'It does not concern me. Look if you must.'

" 'No, I have been taught well.'

"The sisters worked in the morning tending the fires. They worked in the afternoon repairing fish traps and washing clothes. The sun was growing golden-red on their skin when the young sister said, 'I ache, sister. I must look. Come.'

"So together they lifted the great stone that lay before the doorway to their house. And below it? What did they find?"

Nebe opened her hands to me in question. Her elbows rested one to a knee, her legs splayed to the fire. "What did they find?"

"I don't know. What?" I hung on her words.

Nebe looked to the ground as if she had lost something. She stared intently.

" 'Look, sister,' said the young one looking through a hole hidden beneath the stone, 'It is Mi'kmaq land, and there is the house of our parents below.'

"The sisters crowded at the hole. 'There are the hunters returning,' said the older sister.

" 'Where? I do not see them.'

" 'On your side, look.'

"And sitting on her knees looking down between them, the young sister stretched over to see and tumbled into the hole. Her big sister grabbed for her feet, but Little One had already fallen, and the older sister clutched only air. Then she lost balance and, too, fell head over heels through the hole in the sky."

I broke spellbound silence, "Will they die?"

Grandmother answered quietly, "Listen to Nebe tell the story."

"The sisters fell away from *autremonde*, away from the hole in the sky, into the land-world they had left. Little sister was falling first, below. Then, above, her big sister tumbled over in the air. As they fell, the older sister saw the younger twist and tumble in a swirling mist, a manitou, a spirit wind. Little sister was blown like a dry leaf far off, growing smaller, a tiny petal on a mighty wind, until the big sister could no longer see her against the mist of the hills.

"The older sister reached out and caught the top of a pine tree that bent with her weight. She straddled the trunk with her legs and climbed down to the ground. She returned to her people, alone."

Nebe stirred both fires.

"And what happened to the younger sister?" I asked.

"The manitou took her away. That is what the story tells."

I felt empty. "Nothing else?"

Nebe looked to Banook, then, shook her head. "No. Nothing else."

I persisted. "But what is the end of the story?"

"Mi'kmaq stories are like life," Nebe said. "They end. You accept."

I hid my disappointment. If Mi'kmaq stories ended this way, I wasn't sure I wanted more of them.

Banook rose. "We must go now, little sister."

"When the fish are done, I will bring you some."

Nebe again turned to the fires. We left as unceremoniously as we had arrived. Grandmother and I walked back along another street toward the church and its cemetery across the road.

"What is a manitou?" I asked.

"No one knows. Some say a great wind. Some people

call it 'windigo,' saying it eats people. Others swear it is a light that lures Indians to death at sea. My grandmother saw one as a shining moose walking over lake water."

"I still don't know," I said.

She walked on. "When you see one, you will know."

This brief encounter with my Mi'kmaq relatives rekindled my queasy worry. I tried again to understand.

"Are you two sisters, Banook? You and Nebe?" I asked her.

"In a way. Nebe and I are like two leaves of the same twig. Her name is Leaf. That is what *nebe* means in our language, 'leaf.' "

She had my curiosity up again. "And what does your name mean, Banook?"

"*Banook* tells of the first lake you come to as you ascend a stream."

It meant nothing to me. Like the story, it just seemed foreign, strange. Still, I tried to grasp it all. I was far outside my ken. "Is the story about you and Nebe, as sisters?"

Grandma took my hand again. We stopped a block from the cemetery. She did not look at me, though she spoke not to the distance into which she looked but only to me, in a voice serious as Mother's pronouncement of rheumatic fever, "You are here now. Take but one or two things away with you. If the rest is important, it will follow." She squeezed my hand gently. We walked on.

"Where you live now, it is flat. But here, if you follow a stream up hill, you will come to a lake, a *banook*. That is the river's source, gives it its life. But also, when you approach the lake from below, you can see without being sensed—you see beaver, muskrat, deer and bear—all come to the lake, to the water for life. So, too, do you. We come to the water for life." She held my hand and rubbed it with the other. "We are here now."

Though I was certain of her affection, I was mystified by my grandmother's ways. I wanted to know, but even her explanations seemed like puzzles to me. I found Mi'kmaq ways confusing, impractical. I wanted to be back with Mother.

As if answering my call, Mother stepped down from the church walk. "Thank you, Banook," she said taking my hand.

"I will sit in the kitchen," Banook said. She climbed the stair without another word.

Mother knelt to me. "How was your little adventure?" she asked.

Now, within the circle of her arms, my tears erupted. She clasped me to her. My body shook, releasing feelings I could not name, whether sorrow, loneliness, fear, or relief.

"Oh, Tatty, it's all right. Everything will be fine."

I sobbed. "I don't want to live here. I don't want to be Mi'kmaq. I don't want strange stories," I said between choked breathing.

Mother was silent.

"You want to stay here. I can tell. I heard you and Elsie." I pulled away and looked into her eyes with as stern a stare as I could muster. "I don't."

Mother recoiled from the look as if struck. Still she said nothing.

"It is dark. Cold. Scary. I want to be in Florida. I want to be with you."

Mother stroked my hair. "Yes, Tatty. We will go back home. We won't be staying here."

We crossed the street to the cemetery and joined the small knot of people around my father's grave. The brisk wind off the confluence of the Waugh and St. Mary's rivers flapped the dun coattails and creased trousers that surrounded the grave. Mother turned up her collar, and Elsie drew her scarf over her head. I stood between them holding their hands.

The black coffin that had dogged my spirit from Florida to the southern shore of the Northumberland Strait now sat on a transom over a hole in the earth. It descended, like the two falling-sisters, into another world. The coffin and my father fell below, out of sight, and removed all but a winnowing memory of him from my mind. To me, his final going became more relief than sorrowful goodbye. My father's burial and all that surrounded it removed doubt and confusion from my life. I knew right then what I wanted.

It was not bravery, either feigned or true, that stopped my tears. There on the dormant wind-scorched grasses of the winter cemetery at the meeting of two rivers—so the meaning of *Takamegooch* was said to be—I decided, repeating the words firmly in my mind, to stay on the earth, work at the practical baking of life's bread, avoid the reading of fanciful tales—either Mi'kmaq or Andersen's Scandinavian stories. I would bury fearsome, haunting death in cold, northern ground, and flee to the warmth and vigor of the South, cheered by Finnish *sisu* and the caring of a steadfast mother.

The power of a dark sun that had torn me away from home was setting with my father's casket. I hoped never to see it again. I let go Elsie's hand and grasped Mother's tightly. So I broke with an inscrutable, northern and Native past I had only just encountered. Separate from the rest of the small knot of mourners, I turned toward the church kitchen, taking that one thing with me.

Tiny says, "You sure are a poet." He rises. "I always choked on those fifty-cent words."

From behind my own thin smile, I look inward. "I suppose that's a compliment."

The big man shrugs. "I'd take it that way."

He leaves the table and grabs his mitts from a peg. "Looks like you'll be staying for lunch. I'm going to thaw a trout in case those lunkers down there don't take my bait." As he pulls on the deerskin choppers, he stamps his stocking feet into the boots left standing by the door.

I am amazed. "Going out like that? In long johns?"

"We're having a heat wave." Tiny laughs and opens the door.

Sun bursts into the room. When he slams the door shut, I'm blind again. Waiting for sight to come, I listen to Tiny scruffling around out in the snowbank piled at the end of the house. I follow his movements as he stumps around the back of the shack. Then everything's quiet.

Cautiously, I lift a corner of the burlap curtain. The day shines, brilliant. The only detail I see is the dark fringe of fir and pine far across the lake. Everything else is a dazzling white.

Tiny is at the door again. I shut my eyes.

Coming in, Tiny chuckles. "Almost summer," he says. "You know, I've got a pee spot out back."

I shiver but say, "I can wait."

Tiny tosses the trout he retrieved from his snow bank into an enameled bowl. The fish clangs against the basin's steel sides. Keeping the choppers on his hands, Tiny ladles water from the hole in the icehouse floor over the fish. When the bowl is nearly full and the fish is soaking, he sets it on the shelf above the stove and pulls off the mitts. "Believe it or not, that water is much warmer than that trout. Should thaw in a hurry."

"I'm not that hungry."

"Well, you will be when that fish is frying. I'm going to cook it in beer batter."

Tiny carefully places two more chunks of pine into the stove and kicks off his boots. The wood is already crackling. "So how did you meet my sister?

Nothing That Is Not There   5

I MET MARY AT COLLEGE not long after I had returned
from a trip north. It was nearly ten years after my father
died, and this time I had brought Mother north.

On that second trip north up to Portland, Maine, I
escorted Mother onto the Halifax-bound ferry. I stowed
her Pontiac below and secured the trailer we had filled
with cartons and trunks of her belongings hauled up from
Florida. We met an older, more subdued Elsie on deck. I
brought them to their cabin. I held Mother in a hug that,
though I wanted to flee, I sustained long enough to say,
"I love you." I said goodbye to her, we both knew, forever.

Later that afternoon I boarded an airplane back to
Florida, this time to Pensacola, to college, to my future,
and, within two months, to meet Mary.

The return to Florida was poignant but abrupt. On the
trip back—my first experience flying—my excitement was
shrouded by that haunting sense of loss and abandonment
I had felt at my father's sudden death. Even though I had
not admitted that death was an integral part of this trip,
too, Mother's condition was serious, more serious than
she told. Perhaps she was sheltering me from suffering
through yet another parent's death fraught with horror,
dread and, this time, the painful wasting of cancer. I was,
she knew, better off at college, my studies undisturbed
by her medical needs to which Elsie and the Canadian
government could, anyway, better tend. Even though the

distance and her diminished presence would allow me to prosper, less fettered by responsibility and with greater concentration on my own tasks, I knew I was abandoning us both to suffering. Mine would be a solitary suffering as profound as that I imagined my father experienced (even beyond death) following Mother and me all the way north, separate and confined in his black casket. I was unsure I would be able ever again to connect fully with the external world. I wanted to live everyday life only through practical, mundane tasks, devoid of feelings. I went blind to the colors of my emotions, even though love for Mother had steadied me in the past.

I felt muted, latent terror. Though I knew better, it was no use. Terror bid me run, run from my fear, not to hide from it but to out-distance its advance. Looking over my shoulder to the north, I flew southward to a new life, a life without that protective soul who knew me best, who knew me—at least a younger me—completely. And though I neither knew nor felt it then, I realized later that I fled the ache Mother's leaving created. I did not know what I was looking for, but when I found her, I sought solace in the tender arms and searching heart of Mary Bassett, who, herself, was looking for adoration and love.

Despite my promise to live a practical, useful life modeled after my Finnish grandmother's, I had enrolled in literature courses and fancied myself a poet. The day I met Mary, I immortalized the event in these prosaic lines:

> *Coppery radiance of autumn light stretched beneath the sycamore branches lifting a pungency promising resurgent life, sprung of rich soil looking toward winter's rest.*

Wrens and orioles let chittering and throaty calls burst from the foliage of the wide-spread tree, the sound shimmering in a still, heavy air that coated the skin with a freshness that belied the impending fall.

Late summer bougainvillea littered the lawn with castoff rusty blossoms, and deep red moss rose and white impatiens huddled in the shade of a knee-high, quarried-rock wall that flowed around the periphery of the tree's spreading branches.

It was not simply the golden light, the enchanting bird-song, neither just the thoughtfully placed serpentine, limestone wall punctuated with floral blooms that could penetrate a poet's concentration of task and duty.

No. All sense of blind focus, of unseeing purpose fell instantly away at a stroke of prayer or luck, which all at once restored vision, direct and peripheral.

It was what he saw, this freshman poet, folded in dappling light at the very edge of the sycamore's shade, as in a canvas composition, that stopped him, arrested his heart and captured his inward eye.

She was the graceful center of the autumn day. The light glowed not on but from the ruddy skin of her forearms. One arm held on her folded knees an artist's tablet, the other caressing the page in ringlets of motion gentle as those flowing from a single fallen petal in a wind-kissed pool.

The fullness of the air was given birth from her tranquil breath. The soft, moist air sleeked her midnight-black hair straight over her dark, supple shoulders following the curve of her spine to her heels on which she sat.

The oriole and wren song wove a corona, practically visible, around her thoughtfully lifted face. She was Mary.

Though I read it a hundred times, committing it to memory, I never showed Mary that poetic idyll. It embarrassed me. Still, I won't forget how my lovely apparition paused, considered her next artistic stroke, nibbling her lip in reverie.

The day I met Mary, I strode the quad—this was six weeks into the fall semester at Pensacola JC—looking for a shady place to eat my lunch. I favored a sycamore grove away from the main path that usually mixed sun and shade. I sat in sun if it was not too hot, otherwise, shade.

A dark, slender, and graceful girl sketching on her artist's pad sat in my usual spot. She knelt, the striking focal point of a masterpiece. I could not have walked by.

The girl's willowy figure persuaded me to stop. She folded, bent over her drawing tablet on the lawn. Her long black hair curtained the page she worked on. I wonder if I recognized the artist as Native then, though I could not, even close up, see her face.

I circled up behind her. I paused. I stood, looking over her head trying to see what she drew. "Mind if I eat my lunch here?"

She brushed her hair back and fixed on me the darkest eyes I had yet seen. She was Native all right. Good, I thought. Her pupils and irises merged into unified, black orbs.

"Help yourself."

I sat to her left, her drawing hand, a little away from her.

She took a steady minute to size me up. Unabashed and direct, her gaze moved from my straight, brown hair, down this flat forehead, over these plain-set Mi'kmaq eyes, down the broad nose and over thin, Finnish lips and round, clean, bare chin. She nodded and returned to her work.

That was approval, I thought.

In a minute, she eyed my lunch bag. "What do you have in there?"

I had packed it that morning. "An egg-salad sandwich, an orange, and some cookies."

She looked at the drawing, then at the lunch, then at me again. She looked hungry. "Sharing today?"

A lunch-date with this stranger seemed right. My romantic senses jumped to attention at her cheeky invitation. She wanted to share what I had. I no longer felt that hungry. "Yes. Sure. It's a big sandwich."

A moment before she had appeared a vision. Now

in solid reality, she made the mess of splitting an egg-salad sandwich pure poetry. Mary watched as I prepared to tear the thing in half. I took it up, looked at it dumbly, and set it down again on the paper bag. She laughed and grabbed my wrist. "Wait." She opened her artist's bag and dug into a pocket, bringing forth a palatte knife. "Here. Be gentle."

Reeling from her touch, I stared, first at the knife, then at her. "Do you mean with the knife or with you?" My lame quip warmed my cheeks, but she took it well.

"Cut the sandwich with the knife. Be gentle with me."

I let my words follow my heart. "We'll be gentle with each other."

This was a case of enchantment.

We both missed classes. We both squeezed out drabs of egg salad onto our jeans. We crowed about it, laughed at each other. To me, sitting there under the musical sycamore was as captivating as being swept up in my aunt Elsie's magical loveliness, her soothing scarves and tantalizing perfume. It was as warm as evening conversations with Mother. I was not falling in love. I dove into love like the white pelican plunging into the Gulf. Ungainly. Sure. Quick. Entire.

We shared my three pecan sandies. I broke the odd one in half. Afterward, I looked at Mary, then to her drawings. I fingered her tablet. "Show me your work."

Though she was not shy—Mary was impious and bold—she pressed the portfolio to the ground. "I'm not sure you would like them." She lifted her chin with the disdain of a royal.

I leaned forward and placed my hand above her knee. "How will we know, if we don't look?" I asked.

I tickled her side, and when she jumped, slipped

the tablet out from under her hand. "Now," I adopted a professorial tone, "let's see here."

She moved close to me to see what I would look at.

I paged through slowly, pausing to admire. "Earth?" I wondered at her label of a drawing of a turtle.

"Yes. Turtle crawled up from the water, carrying the land on his back."

"Who says?"

"I say." She made a grab at the portfolio. I twisted away.

"Okay, okay." I flipped through other pages. She depicted beaver and horned deer. "Very detailed," I said, careful to sound complimentary and sincere. It wasn't hard. The drawings were good.

I came to a page of designs, figures marching across the paper over bands of brilliant colors. "What are these?"

"Seminole designs," she said. Pointing to several in succession, she named them—a series of interlocking diamonds in contrasting blues, "Mountain;" a double line of three-dimensional effect built like fountain pen tips opposing each other tip to shoulder, tip to shoulder across the page, "Storm;" finally, black figures dancing across an iridescent blue field, resembling a series of the Roman numeral two, "Turtle."

The turtle design gave me a chance to ask, "Are you Seminole, then?"

"No. Ojibwe. From Minnesota."

I teased. "Oh, that's what that accent is."

She gave back, mimicking my deep-South sounds, "Y'aaawl can shooor pick out an ak-cent!"

I laughed, then tried to sound Canadian. "My grandmother, Banook, is Mi'kmaq," I said.

"I thought you looked Native." She hurried to add, "I

like that."

"Are you full?"

"Who the hell knows that? But so they say. So my grandmother says . . .said."

I wondered if Banook, of whom I had not thought for a long time, was still living.

I asked softly, "Is she gone?"

"Oh, no. She's in Minnesota. I just have put a lot of space between us."

"Actually, I'm unsure if Banook, my grandmother, is alive or dead. I met her only once, more than ten years ago."

"Well," Mary said, "I'm not much on family myself." She pointed at a band of color on the page that looked like a series of black "f's" running on a field of orange red. "That's a man on horseback. Seminole."

"Why Seminole for you?"

"The mascot argument got me interested."

"What argument?" I wondered if my ignorance would matter, but I had to find out.

She told me about Florida State's struggle with the American Indian Movement over its mascot and team name.

"The movement forced their hand on 'Sammy Seminole,' " she said. "He was never played by a Native anyway."

I was lost. "I'm not really very political."

"I wasn't either until I heard Russell Means speak in Minnesota. Then when I got here, I started to feel the put-down."

I did not tell Mary then, though perhaps it was self-evident, that I didn't broadcast my Native heritage. The break I had made with my father, his family, and Nova

Scotia had seemed to me permanent. Since his funeral, I had never wanted to be identified as Indian. Now, I felt scared in the face of Mary's openness, her stridency. I didn't want my self-imposed exile to come between this woman and me, but Mary had already included me. She was the first person to whom I had admitted my heritage. My Pensacola JC application did not ask. I did not tell.

Mary looked into my eyes again. "You don't have to be political. But would you like to hear David Narcomey speak about it? He's coming from Oklahoma."

Any political speech would be all right if I were in Mary's company. "Sure. When?"

So even though our chance meeting blossomed, in a way, out of art, our first real date was a political affair. These two themes entwined themselves in our early love. Neither of us became members of the American Indian Movement. I never warmed to the political. And Mary, for reasons I did not understand until I got up to Minnesota, had as much aversion as I to signing her name to the AIM membership roster.

"I don't have to advertise to be involved," she said.

Our love and regard for each other didn't run on such narrow-gauge tracks, though. Our Native blood, my revived interest in Indian history and art, classical architecture, and academic leanings were minor accoutrements, compared to interest in each other. We were each without family, at least in Florida. We both had grown up in some sense parentless.

"Granny raised me. I remember my father, but my parents are really just shadow figures," she told me in a rare mention of her past.

"I'm used to being alone," I said. "I mean one-on-one. I grew up with my mother. I suppose you and your grandmother were a pair out there in the northern Minnesota woods."

She didn't say much more, just, "Yes, after my parents disappeared."

I thought she had cousins and, like me, playmates she had spent her days with, but Mary's preference for solitude and privacy, I figured, grew, like mine, out of the life of a small family rather than out of the isolation of living in the forests just south of the Canadian border. Anyway, she seldom mentioned family.

Times when her lonesome ways grew prominent were satisfying. She would sketch quietly for hours, while I read stories, essays, and novels required of literature majors. Her periodic excitement punctuated the quiet times with new interest and activities that enlivened our life together. She often rushed in, chatting about a performance of the Preservation Hall Jazz Band, a Seminole conference, or a new pizzeria she said we just had to go to. Those were good times, but Mary was not always fun. In fact, she sometimes horrified me. Her behavior reminded me of my father's dark outbursts. On occasion, Mary became an irresolute fury, dangerous to herself and to our love. I tried to show my care for her in these rages and to protect her from herself. Try as I might, where the fits came from, I couldn't discover. Though I could not tell what set her off, I had early on decided to let nothing that was not there in front of us cause us to split.

The first orgy of rage I witnessed came at two in the morning, four months after she had offered to share her apartment as a refuge from the haunting news of Mother's death. A sound of havoc woke me from a troubled sleep—I had been dreaming of Mother, in danger of falling, reaching out to me over the bulwark of the ferry. I stood on the wharf, frozen, gazing up at her departure. The dream and the activity on the dock at first prevented me from registering that the sounds I was hearing came from within our apartment. When I discovered Mary absent from bed, I bolted upright. Then I realized the shattering noises and weeping came from the kitchen at the other end of the place.

I padded wooden floors cautiously from our small bedroom through the dining room. I stopped short of the rectangle of light spilling from the kitchen. A dinner plate flew across the door opening, crashed into the adjacent wall and shattered, strewing its shards across the threshold between the rooms. Barefoot and wary of the jagged ironstone chips, I grasped the door casing and pivoted around the doorway to see and to announce my presence.

In the middle of the patterned faux-brick kitchen floor, directly under the bare-bulb overhead, Mary stood entirely naked, holding a dinner plate in each hand. She hung her head and wept. Her shoulders shook. She laughed, a sound strained through a mesh of tears, and raised an arm high. She swung a plate down savagely, letting loose, pitching it full force to the floor. The plate exploded at her feet. It was then I saw her legs and feet bled and had marked streaks across the linoleum. She raised the other arm.

"Mary, wait. Stop." At first I was unsure I had spoken.

Mary hesitated. She turned her head my way and through the disheveled veil of her hair, looked without recognition at me leaning around the doorjamb into the shaft of light.

I swung around the doorway. In three steps over pieces of broken plate I was there. I held one hand out for the last plate she had raised high. With the other hand, I lifted her hair over her forehead, swept it down her shoulders, touched her back, and drew her to me. "Oh, sweetheart . . . it's okay." Now, still holding the plate I had taken from her, I hugged her, feeling the heaving and tossing of her sobbing, labored breath.

Her wrenching wails made the minutes crawl. Eventually, her groans, sounding like heavy rope drawn hand over hand through tight grommets, quieted. I felt some of the plate fragments digging into my feet, but I held Mary, both lifting her weight away from the dangerously jagged floor and tipping her overflowing emotional pool to pour away from her own and on to my chest. Her wheezing, weakened spirits electrified my care. Strength sprang warm and supple from a reserve I had not felt before. I was of a single mind. I thought of nothing but the woman whose steadily heaving chest pressed tightly against mine.

In time, I shuffled her to a chair, fetched a blanket to quell her shaking, knelt and tended her feet, removing three bloody spears, before turning to care for my own. I swept the debris away from the doorway, lifted Mary in my arms, and brought her to the bath where I could clean and bandage her wounds.

This was no time to ask about her frenzy. I waited for Mary to reveal what lay behind it. She volunteered nothing. What destructive force, what buried anger had such a hold on her, she did not or could not tell. I thought of absent parents, isolated upbringing, and the stigma of the Native stamp that colored us both. It was frightening to not know why.

Since Mary's outbursts were few though fierce, I weathered them without having to figure them out. I could do little but comfort her and deal with what was there.

The care-taking posture I adopted in the aftermath of her plate-smashing episode was new for me. I worked tenderly, slowly, and methodically to clean, treat, and bandage Mary's bloody feet. I took less care with my own, wrapping each quickly and after guiding Mary haltingly back to bed. I neatly tucked the sheets and covers around her, smoothed her brow, patted her hands, and kissed her forehead. She was immediately asleep. I gazed over her in amazement. My ministrations had drained her fury. Her face grew smooth and placid, peace softened her mouth, and her long release of breath sounded a profound tranquility.

I left her in bed and returned to the kitchen to sweep the floor more thoroughly, clean up the blood, and remove other traces of the fit. Already, the kitchen scene seemed more a dream than an actual occurrence. It became something like my father's rants, which he did not remember the next day.

I could barely convince myself that, just an hour before, Mary had stood below that barren light bulb, as naked as she now slept, destroying the dishes she owned, plate by plate, glass by glass. Applying the practical promise I had made myself years before, I set the breakfast table with the bowls that were spared and slipped in beside Mary.

I could not sleep. The event played and replayed in my mind. I watched the destruction again and over again. My worry took a physical form. The cuts on my feet stung more urgently. I began to fear I had missed removing small bits of jagged china and glass. I imagined them working their way further and further into my feet. As

I lay in what had become my misery, magically—maybe diabolically—drawn into me as Mary wailed it forth, a forgotten story rose to my mind in shadowy form. I had pushed the story from my waking mind just as I had the Mi'kmaq tale Banook's friend told. Half awake, the story bloomed in my memory—fragments of glass that cut into a boy's eyes pierce his soul and chill his affection for a loving neighbor girl. His sight darkens. The shards cleave his erstwhile happy view of life. Then cold-hearted, the boy is captured and imprisoned in a castle of ice.

On the edge of sleep, I feared that Mary's outburst might infect me with discontent, that the cuts on my soles would fester inside to feed misgivings. As against previous nagging anxieties I had pushed to the back of my mind, I blinded myself to this dreamlike absurdity. I relegated fear to the darkness of night and the shapelessness of dreams. I buried the restlessness of my body and my consciousness, lay still beside Mary, rested, and fitfully slept.

Mary never spoke of the incident, but she tacitly acknowledged it. Within a few weeks, as positively energetic as ever before, she had resupplied us with crockery sporting a native turtle motif that an artist friend at school had thrown and fired for her. She had traded one of her paintings of her Minnesota lake for the dishes. Her canvas showed a stick-cabin in a white forest and a birch bark canoe on the shore of a cove. Each time I set the table or fed off those plates became a reminder of the untalked-of nightmare. Still, neither of us said a word about it.

Nor did we much talk about the dreamy part of our union, our love making. Having been something of a mother's boy, I never cared for the crass language, sexual aggressiveness, and crude joking of men—and my father was one of the crudest. I was initially grateful that Mary was strongly sexed and aggressive. Although, as she told me, she was minimally experienced, I felt I had to exaggerate the few exciting but far from complete encounters I had had in high school. Thankfully, Mary was a willing—and at times a wild—lover. As the first months of our encounter warmed through the winter break into spring, she freed me, ever so slowly, from my shame and inhibitions that worked to quiet my restrained but formidable drive. As humanly tender as we both could be, naked atop the sheets, wrapped only in each other and Mary's braided midnight hair, we, in Native fashion, became animal spirits in our dreamtime embraces.

Mary acted wolflike, straddling me, sitting on her haunches, the golden swell of her belly curving smoothly upwards beneath her breasts, which she lifted as if to a rising moon midst howls of the hunt, while holding me down, her vanquished prey. Her throat tensed and bellowed, alternating long inspirations with trailing, wolf-song rolling through her pursed lips that jutted above the perfectly thrust vee of her chin. In a line from howling lips, tremulous throat, twin pipes of wind and water, through tensed membrane and viscera to hidden caves, the message of her song gripped me, sliding around the pillar of my life. Mary, the she-wolf, arced now, hunching, her stomach hollowing to her own spine. She extended her arms, pushing shoulders high above her neck, her breasts now pendulums above her cratered gut. She looked at me, her culled calf, spreading a canine grin wide, lifting as if readying a final lunge to the throat. Instead, she rose, arching upward, pressing her vulva down against me to howl a universe full of unleashed joy.

My response was bearlike. Atop Mary, I was moved to embrace a desire that flowed up my chest and arms, a feeling muscular and hard, bringing me to roll up from below her ribs and press upon Mary's chest, to hold her there, feeling the swelling of her breath and roundness of her breasts. Once searching ecstatically, clamping her body to mine with one arm, I slid the other down behind, below her sinuous, silky back to the welling round of her buttocks. I gripped as a bruin in death throes all the while thrusting against her wolfish mound. I possessed all of her. She enwrapped my bruin-tail with her legs, which through each lunge she contracted lifting to meet me in air. My hug sometimes forced Mary's breath out in a cry. Then against animal desire, I loosened my grip and raked her back and hindquarters, tearing at them with abandon until she howled.

When we left our spirit-masters, expiring the bear and wolf in panting breaths to the bedroom ceiling, we became again tender humans, shedding our fur coats, stroking skins oiled with sweat, steadying placid gazes through each other's eyes into our human, passion-spent souls. We smiled. We kissed.

Love was all more wonderful than I had imagined, but in my enamored innocence I did not realize that the passion that Mary released in sex was blown by the same wind that drove her, time and again, to cross into the horror of vehemence as she had that night in the kitchen. Love and destruction in Mary came from the same place.

Less than a year after destroying our kitchen, we quietly lay together on the lawn of the quad—thankfully away from our favorite untainted sycamore—when a nearby knot of rowdy men began to razz us about our kissing. One said, "Hey, now, don't get too hot, there, babe."

Mary raised her head, lifted off my chest on her arms, and said, "Come here and say that." She lowered to kiss me full and long.

The next thing I knew, the fellow was there, standing above us. "Hey, now, don't get too hot, there, babe." He accented the "babe."

Mary jumped to her feet before I could say a word. I watched from the ground. He towered above me and looked a good head taller than Mary who now faced him at arm's length. "You butted into the wrong kiss," she said.

"Sorry," he said, "but what does your boy have to say about it?"

He grinned and began, I think, to repeat his statement. He didn't finish. Mary leapt. Her left leg kicked out, fast and high—her form like a ballerina, but with the power of a striking snake. Her heel met him square under the jaw. He went down in a heap.

His two companions' smirks fell to the lawn. "Shit," they said in unison and started to back away.

"Come on, Tatty," Mary said, "this is no place to be." Her calm seemed unearthly.

I followed her unhurried gait up the quad. Just before we turned past the performing arts building, I saw his companions had the student sitting up, hunching over his knees, looking dazed below their loud derisive banter. "You sure showed her!" they shouted.

That incident left me amazed and ashamed. It scared me. I worried we would be targeted as some sort of "Indian troublemakers," but I still pilloried myself for not taking the lead in the melee. I was as shocked as our tormentor by Mary's power. I couldn't imagine how it had sprung up so suddenly. Either of us should easily shake off a little student banter. Her impulsiveness sprang up fiercely. I had just that day finished reading a fictional death whose only evidence was a small bruise under the chin from a blow received in an auto accident. That, I knew, could have happened on the quad. This time I had to say something.

"You could have hurt that guy," I said.

She kept walking. "I know what I'm doing."

"People have died being hit like that."

"You don't understand, Tatty." She would not elaborate.

I lacked Mary's swagger. I could see that it would land her in trouble, and it did.

The next spring semester, Mary had to pay a fine and restitution to one of her teachers. I thought she would be expelled.

He had somehow crossed her—I hadn't known how—and she retaliated. She argued with him, yelling loud enough to be heard in the adjacent classrooms, I was told. She followed him to the parking lot, where she pushed him down and broke every window in his sedan. She stood on the hood and hopped over the roof to the trunk to kick in first the windshield and then the rear window. She pried a landscaping stone from a wall bounding the lot—it weighed nearly thirty pounds—and pummeled each of the passengers' and driver's windows in succession, all as the awestruck and horrified instructor looked on. She left the stone sitting on a pile of beaded glass on the driver's seat.

Mary would not tell me what had gone on before, but the rumors spread were that the instructor had tried to seduce her. He left at the semester's end. Mary refused to reveal the source of the argument to college authorities, who hushed the story. She paid for the damage and served a year of college probation for the incident. The city cops were never called. This time I made Mary swear she would walk away or talk to me before acting out again.

Mary's demons moved into her painting. Often she depicted the lake that lay solid and deep within her memory, sometimes scenes of hunting there, animal gore often spilled abundantly. One, most effective, showed a native man raising hands to ward off an attacking eagle, another, a hunter beneath a deer hide with horns tied to his head, squaring off with a huge, rut-enraged buck. The hunter seemed clearly overwhelmed. A winter scene showed an Indian maiden, naked against the cold, reaching arms out to a light glowing before silhouetted pines. This she named *Pietà*.

Though she never sought to explain the themes of her art or the outbreaks of wildness, we came to tacit agreement that this was part of her personality, troublesome and fearful, that was to be accepted with the rest, most of which was lovely, enchanting, and enthralling. Despite haunted misgivings, I stayed on, determined in my affections and love for Mary. Our pairing filled the emptiness that Mother's death left.

I had heard of Mother's death only after her funeral. In a long and thoughtful letter from Elsie, her sister explained Mother's wish that I keep on at school and memorialize her through my studies rather than by appearing again in Nova Scotia for a funeral she knew would only haunt me forever. She died in late January, when travel there was at its worst. Elsie assured me Mother's last thoughts were of me and my welfare. My aunt sent me a box of keepsakes—three pieces of Nakamura china Mother had collected before the war, a rose-colored, glass pitcher I had seen on her dresser every day of our life together, and a carved wooden-framed photo of the three of us in early, happy days, showing me straddling my parents' laps, all of us smiling at the camera.

The letter was more comfort than the objects, but I kept all in plain sight in the apartments Mary and I occupied over the years. And though Mary voiced sympathy and asked me to move in with her, her real help was her strong, quiet presence going about the daily duties and acts of mundane life. I had little appetite for love-making during that time, but Mary did not take this as an affront. She persisted: gentle, voluptuous, and persuasive through almost a year of my depression and mourning.

In our early years, we steeped ourselves in our Native heritage like a blanket wrapped around sheltering us from the cold, abrasive world outside. We attended lectures sponsored by AIM through the Seminole tribe, and each of us delved into our own expressions of Native culture—Mary in her art, and I through story.

Mary painted at times without stop. Sometimes her other studies suffered. She continued to draw her best work from her little clear lake tucked in the glaciated, bowl-infested geography west of the giant Lake Superior. Her canvasses were admired by the Natives who befriended us but were criticized by her teachers, who probably did not understand their importance to those of Indian blood. They appreciated the technical aspects, not the subject matter or sentiment. She worked, not oblivious but in defiance of their slights.

I turned to Native stories like that told by Nebe, the old woman my grandmother brought me to, but

I felt less magic in the stories of the Mi'kmaq. Perhaps my abandonment of my father's heritage blocked that connection. I delved instead into Ojibwe legends of Mary's people. The differences were really minimal, since the Ojibwe are fairly close relatives of my father's nation, both Algonquin, but the remove freed me to explore.

Several times I was invited to read or rather tell stories that were supposed to be of the oral tradition though I had gleaned the ones I knew from books and tribal literature that came through AIM. I followed through a couple of times. But the telling proved uncomfortable and troubled my sleep. It brought Banook's voice to my ear. Finally, I left my story-telling behind as impractical. Though I continued to study and read the stories of the Algonquin peoples—learning ever so little of the language I had heard only when my father was drunk—I kept them largely a private affair. My Native research was a link with Mary. That was enough for me.

Mary's activism itself waxed and waned. At first, she joined protest after protest, worked on committees without cease, and then, suddenly, she would stop cold. After a little while, she would pick it up again. I didn't understand this cycle or what caused the starts and stops. She went gangbusters for a while then dumped all activity. It was as if she were of two different minds in a single body.

Through it all, we pursued the college curriculum, transferred to FSU, and finished our degrees in Tallahassee: Mary in art, I in literature. We married after graduation, set out to earn livings, and spent our time peaceably, productively. Mary turned to gallery work, which was spotty and lean. I worked through soulless struggles in a land development business my college friends had started. Imagine: an Indian in land speculation.

I left that job and moved into something more solid, less filled with conflict for me—the hurricane shutter business. Storm preparedness held another irony, but it supported us and was practical and helpful. It was something I thought I was good at—until I traveled north again.

Up in Minnesota I had no shutters to protect me.

THE LAST LEG OF THE TRIP up here to Thief Lake that I had thought was almost finished was taking longer than I had hoped. The plowed one-lane highway, so clear after my stop at Bobbie's, became increasingly fainter and masked with snow as I moved north. The swirl of heavy flakes spanked the windshield and stuck against the glass, splattered like a swarm of wintry mosquitoes. They smeared and obscured the view of the road, which itself began to look like a tunnel with a crumbling ceiling.

I drove. I mulled over my encounter with the two men. Even this close to my destination, it seemed odd. What were the chances that out of sixty people anyone at the counter of Bobbie's would know the very folks I had traveled 1400 miles to meet? Or would recognize who I was? Or would be able to guess why I was going? The unexpected interlude left me feeling stripped bare. I prefer the anonymity of city life.

Something Danny said particularly bothered me. The nicknames he used seemed too familiar. Had I known him? No, that wasn't it. It was his wording "know, knew both." He might have been referring to Mary's parents, whom she said were "long gone." Why not just "know?" Then he had said, "I grew up with all three of them." If he meant Mary and you, Tiny, that accounted for "both," but maybe he was counting Windsong, though he most certainly did not grow up with her. She was a good fifteen years younger. So why "know, knew both?" It did not add up. Ultimately, I had to write off his comments to backwoods inexactness. Anyway, I would not likely see Danny again. I did not need to probe the issue, and since I had fallen victim twice to day-dreaming, I dismissed further speculation and continued the last leg of the journey focusing my attention on the road. I drew my will around me like a winter coat, buttoning it over the need to reach Hongisto's Implement.

The confines between the drifts and banks imparted the same eeriness to the road that years before had hemmed me in on narrow tracks to Nova Scotia. On that dismal pilgrimage, with frost on the coach windows and chilling thoughts coating my mind—thoughts of my father's body riding behind me through the night, coffined in the cargo car—my senses had tensed and stayed alert to rasping claws of strangeness hovering near the nape of my neck. The boy I was then felt that should he stir or make any motion to look behind, scaly fingers would close around his throat. I had not dared turn.

Now, alone on the highway, those weird memories drained me. Parched, I swallowed with difficulty. Despite the dryness in my mouth and a thickened throat, I sweated profusely inside my jacket, layers below its cotton shell. I sensed a gloaming djinni emerging from the dark around me, taking shape in spaces outside in the howling storm, threatening to invade the hood of my sweatshirt swathed around my skull. I knew nothing was there, yet in an odd trick of displacement, the Jeep seemed like a coffin and I, like my father returning home, felt dead to earth, stiff with fear, heart-cold, defeated, and much too young to die, even though life had made me old. That black, chill solitude settled over me.

The single-track road I drove toward Mary became the rails my family had ridden north through Montreal on to Truro. My father had withdrawn from life but advanced into his past, toward the land of his birth. His death initiated me into that world.

Alone in a moving sarcophagus, I felt insignificant in a northern Great Plains storm that rattled the chassis of death itself. The blizzard blew in defiance of my progress but also led me into a past more obscure than the mysteries that had been posed to me in Tatamagouche by my Mi'kmaq ancestry. Somehow, the storm, the buried track beneath the snow, images of decease, and shadowy memories all called forth those old talons of dread. What lay ahead of me now? I feared what I might find at Thief Lake—entanglements with a past I had no part in yet felt captivated by. There shuffled the walking dead at which, like at the corpse of my father, willing or not, I would be made to look.

My heart kept pace with the *thrum-thrum* of the wiper blades. Just ahead, figures swirled through the headlight beams, pulsed between distinct pictures and scrimlike images with each swipe that cleared away the spattered flakes. As if incarnating before my eyes, dancing phantoms appeared then dissolved in my vision again and again. These dancing imps beyond the glass took on more and more solid, active form, sometimes seeming to peek inside the cab, to grin oddly, sometimes beckoning me outside, only to fly off left or right, sucked into the dark storm. In the headlights everything but these figures was black or white. The gnomes took on color, chimera. They sparkled like whirling atomic rhinestones, like prisms in the vacant night. They tossed handfuls of snow into spangled arcs that spelled out a message momentarily across the windshield, letters erased by the wipers before I could decipher them. The imps spoke, too. Above and between the howls of the wind and the rumble of the road, I could nearly make out their mouthed words, words that whirled in sound just as the figures and snowflakes themselves swirled in sight. It was impossible, but I thought I heard a twisted "we" once. I tugged my hood away from my ears but too late. Then, a syllable, "go" fell on my senses. I gave no thought to the impossibility of hearing anything through the windshield or beyond the thudding of the wiper blades, now heavy with snow in a *hump-a-hum-hump* cadence. It was as if those voices had moved inside the cab. I jerked around as I suddenly heard words whispered from behind me. I practically felt on my neck the breathy word: "Windigo."

My spine contracted. My kidneys stabbed me sharply. I lost my breath. A flash of white light immediately followed that aural clarity and certainty of this singular word. Then swirls of yellowish orange and a sustained, mechanical roar drowned the swimming sprites and their speech in a surging avalanche.

At once, the grip of my imagination slackened. The storm loosened. The road widened. And off to the right, I saw, through a filter of gyrating snow, a road-grader fitted with plow that had swung across the roadway, taking a pass at a spacious intersection.

I tried to settle down. That accounts for the flash, I thought.

The eerie spell dissipated in twin lamps beaming either side of the machine's cab. Those nothings I had seen and heard fled from the spinning amber beam on the plow's roof. I skidded to a stop thirty yards ahead and stabbed the button of my flashers.

A memory sprang forth, suddenly splashing in the glitter of Penn Station in New York, emerging from the blackness of the solitary rail line that carried my father's body toward Nova Scotia. Then, as now, similarly fantastic dervishes vanished before bright lights, their incantations silenced, the weird sensations they had engendered steadied. This Minnesota intersection was neither Penn nor Montreal's Central Station but condensed my road-dreams to solid stuff. No crowd greeted my arrival, only the presence of one flesh-and-blood human. It was the grader driver who broke my spell. Having dropped his window, he leaned out and waited for me to trudge back the distance.

"Whoo-ee. Quite a storm we've got out here tonight," he shouted over the diesel.

His cheerful voice heartened me. "It is," I replied. He seemed to be as relieved to see me as I was to see him. "You probably know where we are."

In the middle of my query, I saw a mechanical crane's arm soaring above the drifts to my left. Next to it stood a snow-covered sign, dark without its power, and a lineup of drifted-over harvesters, looking like ghost-tractors plowing tundra fields.

"This here is Hongisto Road."

I already knew the answer but asked anyway, "The implement dealer?"

"That's right." He swept an arm toward the cherry picker and tractors.

"Do you think I can get through to the lake?"

"Maybe. I plowed down as far as Tillie's an hour back. Shouldn't have much trouble with what you've got. Where exactly?"

"Martin . . ." I shifted to local names ". . .Tiny Bassett's."

"Well, past Tillie's is a Phillips station. Take a right there. I don't know if you'll drive much further. It ain't plowed, but if you need to, you could walk the rest. It's half a mile. You can follow the lakeshore."

"I'm lucky to be this close. Thanks."

"I'll be coming down there in a couple of hours if I don't get pulled off. I'll look for you. Watch them curves."

"Thanks."

"Good luck."

It seemed that luck was the common currency in the north. I picked up on it and returned the coin. "You too." "Good to see you" came to mind. I held that back.

A little luck was all I needed to complete what had become a thirteen-hour gauntlet. I had departed Saint Paul six hours back and home seven hours before that. The prospect of warmth, food, and what I hoped would be welcoming embrace of my wife made the suffering seem almost worthwhile. Unless something else happened, a short drive and a snowy walk would bring me there.

The conditions were treacherous. After leaving the interstate, the main road had climbed for some time. Now Hongisto Road descended steeply toward the lake, weaving its way along hillsides, between house-size blocks of stone, and around sharp bends as it followed the river gorge. The road carried narrow shoulders, crowded here and there by dark barreled pines and a few huge white-barked birches that stretched naked to the wind atop the granite outcroppings. Though the road had been plowed an hour before, some of it was drifted over deeply. Crooks in the road gave shelter from wind, and in those places the road remained scraped bare to the gravel. Some of that gravel had been pried loose by the grader and lay atop the road's frozen-solid shoulder, like marbles on a dance floor. It was at the first of these curves I received another winter driving lesson.

Anxious to get to Mary, I had crested a hill and came down much too fast through the wind whipped snow, finding a sharp turn at the bottom of my descent. I downshifted but slowed insufficiently and had to brake, something I knew was risky and wrong. The tires gripped the snowy middle of the road but slipped and rolled laterally on the gravel kicked loose by the grader. When the Jeep skidded around, I frantically turned to follow the direction of spin. The Jeep raked the snowbank, continued to spin, though more slowly, turned twice, and jolted to a stop, the engine dead. I restarted, carefully righted my direction, pulled over, and breathed.

Out of the car, I saw the gash I had made in the banked snow and examined the right rear of the Jeep. It looked undamaged.

"Goddamn it." I swore at the storm as much as at my luck. I kicked some of the gravel out of the roadway. Having to come north was enough. Having to beat a storm was too much. "Damn it, Mary!"

Disgusted, I returned to the Jeep. "Watch them curves," the grader driver had said. Well following advice, even my own, had never been my strong suit. But getting back in the car, I swore to slow down and be attentive to the lay of the land. It seemed that the blizzard was letting up. That was a good sign.

But no, it didn't, and no, it wasn't. The wind, the snow, and drifting again pressed down. The road became steeper and more serpentine. I was crawling the last five miles home, remembering that I would have to walk the final half-mile in deep snow. The brief exposure I just had checking the Jeep's quarter panel told me that I was not prepared to go very far on foot. I certainly wanted to avoid the fate of that traveler in the Yukon who set out when the temperature was 50 below zero. Sure, he would be all right, he had thought, unless something happened. Well, something did happen, and instead of rejoicing with his camp mates, he spent the winter frozen stiff as a log just over the hill from warmth, food, and cheer. The further I moved away from the main road into what Mary called "the boonies," the backwoods where she had been born, the more I realized I could make that Klondike story my own.

Mary seldom talked about this place, but when she did open up, I had visualized a quaint hamlet on the shores of a placid lake—quiet, secluded, and safe. Since she didn't talk about the winter, her descriptions of the lake telegraphed warmth into my picture. I thought of the Florida sunshine when she described home. I knew the weather grew cold up here in winter, but I never saw it that way. I couldn't imagine anything so frigid.

These "boonies" were dark, foreboding woods I now saw as forlorn and dangerous. The storm and the stark nude birches gripping granite tofts inspired anything but a warming glow. The unwelcoming foment only compounded the unfriendly, easily fatal cold and desolation of the place. How can people live here? I wondered. Until recently, Mary had refused to return. Even if she were to stay, I knew I couldn't stand the place. It would kill me. Still, I was close. That was comfort. Unless something happened.

Something happened. Since that time, I have tried to piece it all together, but other than the fact that I lived through it and was told some of the circumstances later, the whole experience seems dreamlike, oddly disjointed, and surreal.

Cooley and Danny told me later that what I saw could not have been. What I did see—real or not—was at the bottom of another steep grade, around a hairpin turn. I heeded my own advice, taking it slow, but the steep descent and severity of the bend, an outside turn, became only the background when that "something" happened. Hidden as the road veered left, then revealed instantly in the headlights of my Jeep, was a staggering shock. Broadside to the road stood a gigantic white deer. His snow encrusted nostrils steamed luminescent clouds. His antlers menaced my panicked eyes. He turned full, lowering his huge rack to charge. I had no time to think it through. I cut the wheel hard. The buck sprang, flew above the roof of the Jeep, and disappeared like the spirits that had danced before my headlights.

I was told later that the Jeep slid, then dropped off the low side of the narrow shoulder, descended out of sight in one sudden fall. The Jeep bashed the close-growing pine trunks and slid down them, plunging through a deep drift of snow that cushioned its fall. The car must have plunged off the road creating an explosion of fluff that fell again to cover even the top of the Jeep. It was as if I had driven off a lakeside cliff and had been swallowed by the water below. Hardly a trace could be seen.

Though they hadn't witnessed it, Cooley and Danny later talked about the accident as if they had.

"You were going slow," Danny said, "that's what saved you. Faster, you would'a slammed through them trees."

Cooley shook his head in disbelief. "Looks like the thing just dropped all together, all at once. Flumph! Right down in the drift."

"You got wedged," Danny laughed. "Better'n being crushed."

They could tell me less about the buck, except it was not possible.

"First off, whitetail deer ain't white. And that's what we got 'round here."

Cooley dismissed Danny's comment. "Even if he was, he wouldn't have antlers this time of year."

Danny wouldn't be daunted. "They hunker down in storms anyway. Even the bucks."

Cooley nodded. "It'd a' been strange to see one in a blizzard."

I countered, "It *was* strange."

How strange, I never dared tell them. There are things you don't tell people. White spirit deer leaping over your car roof can be mentioned, not insisted on, but voices and the things I saw—even given the sound blow to my left temple—were not for public consumption. Until now, I've told only one other person, and he's dead. I never told Mary.

"You could a' froze down there," Danny said. "When we come round that turn, all you could see was the radio antenna sticking above the road."

Cooley nodded.

"If the lights hadn't been shining underneath the drift and melting the snow around them," Danny said, "we would a' just passed by."

Cooley added, "I would a' missed the antenna sticking out."

"Salt 'n' pepper."

Cooley just glared.

Danny leaned forward, twisting that mouth of his upside his nose. "It was the strangest thing I've seen in a while. Then you weren't even there."

"We thought you'd crawled through the window and wandered off."

"Yeah, until we saw the snowmobile track down the way. Then we knew exactly where you were."

Cooley shook his head, "The skidoo track leads right here. That's why we stopped in t' Tillie's."

I couldn't have been luckier than to have those two as travel guardians—backwoods karma. Maybe that is what "boonies-luck" is: friends. They may have missed a chance to save me from the buried Jeep—something with which Danny in particular was mightily disappointed. Danny in a friendly, dense sort of way, and Cooley, keenly but in a stoic sense, saved me from much more than they knew. I figured that they both understood in the way hunters sense the presence of game. What I might have suffered had we not earlier shared a coffee counter and warm cinnamon buns, I can't say. I was grateful that my fate was not to be marked by freezing limbs extending, elongating, expanding in icy stiffness, but had those two not caught up with me at Tillie's, I might have been worse off.

Still, I did not share all the "something" with them— it would have sounded too much like insanity, even though, as evidenced by a splitting headache and the swelling above my left ear, I had taken a good whacking in the Jeep's fall from the road, probably striking the door casing. That smack might explain everything I experienced. How long I was out or semiconscious, I haven't figured even yet. It could have been a minute or an hour. The visions that welled into my mind may have been things I saw or figments of a clubbed, overworked head. Yet the clearest of these actually seemed to come in that split second before I swerved, when the white tail turned his snout in my direction, steaming the air in a defiant snort. Whether the "head-whomp," as Danny called it, added this feature or not, it was as if I heard the deer speak rather than snort, or something in between the two. It sounded something like "*Ruskh*." Meaningless to me, but by the way it sounded, the word, if that was what it was, was delivered as a message. It seemed significant. Was it a warning? Information? I had no time to consider. The buck vaulted to the sky—I could say it flew as if it had invisible wings—and vanished into the blizzard that had revealed it only seconds before. What followed made it certain to me that I could tell no one much, at least no one I knew then. I haven't sorted it out myself. You're the first I've told. The vision felt real. It was like this:

Amber light from behind me, flickering as if from a fire, filtered into the upper reaches of a cavern. I felt myself lying across an animal-skin pallet bathed in a comfortable darkness. All was distinct but so dim that I could only see by contrasts. Apparitions floated by, dark patches rose and fell, seemed to inhale the russet wavering light, expanding then exhaling darkness as they diminished. Others, I was sure they were humans, were in evidence, unseen though implied like a photographer taking a picture.

Those figures were like the woman who took a photo I have of me and my childhood playmate, Roberta Meager, seated on a blanket covering a long davenport that faces the camera. We are so small that the soles of our shoes hardly reach the front edge of the cushions and are fully illuminated along with our two entranced, round faces in the darkness. Only our shoe soles and faces catch the full light. We lean forward, our little torsos obscured in shadow yet faintly discernable. I wear a plaid shirt, Berta a frilled white blouse. Below our extended, lighted faces, our arms are hidden in shadow. We stare, mystified, into the box camera that snapped this shot. Our legs are eclipsed by the soles of our shoes, which squarely face the lens. The features of the living room disappear in darkness behind and off to each side of the couch. That unseen room betokened the unseen other, the photographer—Roberta's mother—who abides beyond the vision of the lens, beyond the foreground, a presence as certain as she is imperceptible.

This unseen other was what I detected in my vision-cavern. I could see no one, but someone, shadows told me, must have been there.

I felt movement, presence in the black recesses of the cave, shades rather than shadows, for the yellowish-rouge glow came from no single source. If there were sound, it were indistinct, like a stream curling slowly around boulders far downstream, a continuous smooth lapping. I felt secure in the darkness surrounding my bier.

I rose. The pallet became a stretcher as if unseen "photographers" lifted each of the four corners. We advanced. I was borne outside, under a sky speckled with constellations none of which I recognized. These and the pitch sky were held aloft on the even darker pointed silhouettes of conifers. As we moved, I lay, looking to the stars, though occasionally I lifted my head to see where I was carried. The vacant bearers moved my cot now faster along a wide, snow-covered path bathed like the cavern in auburn blush that crept up the trunks of pine that bordered our way. The sensation of forward motion without visible impetus created a feeling of being tied to the hood of a car that ran only its parking lights and sped through a snow-laden forest of pine trees. Though the speed increased each moment, I enjoyed a comfortable trust and contentment like a warm drunkenness. I felt unburdened in the mystifying vision.

Out of the pines on each side along the path sprang a woman. This pair sped ahead of my stretcher. Each pivoted diagonally across my path and, avoiding being overrun, leapt again into the darkness of the pines. One ran naked. Her jet-black hair streamed across the amber sheen of her buttocks. Her coppery body glistened with sweat even in the chill air. The other woman, wrapped in a white robe, ran barefoot. She loped and threw her arms repeatedly before her. These two crossed and recrossed my path, exchanging positions. I observed that they changed roles as well. One burst forth barefoot, then appeared the next time nude, as if the screen of passing pine trunks acted as a quick-change dressing room.

The two sprinted. Their crisscrossing of the path made it appear they were cinching a tall boot with unseen, tawny cords, using the pines as lacing hooks. For all the difference in their garb, alternating one to the other, from the rear they appeared just alike. The women pulled ahead, each leaving the snowy ground to run more rapidly on air. They diminished in the distance of a straightaway and disappeared around a bend in the road. Supine, head lifted, I continued to follow.

At the bend I—I say "I," though the feeling was more we, my bearers and I—encountered a man, burly like a bear, round with hairy face and hairy clothes, bulky in dress, racing directly toward us in what seemed like terror.

He ran at us, fast for his bulk and the heavy boots

he wore. He looked behind him. He stumbled, tumbled, rolled to his feet still running—all in one motion—still looking rearward. I expected him to turn around as we converged, but he did not. We did not collide. We did not evade each other. Our opposed trajectories intersected, and, dreamlike, we melded through each other—like vapors passing through a screen—without jarring or even sensation. I twisted on my cot to view his face after he passed through.

Still looking back, his fully bearded face turned right at me in his wake, and it stretched in terror. His mouth was crooked, curling back from his molars on one side. His eyes opened wide, shedding tears across the streaming edge of his lids. His pupils were fixed on something behind him and beyond me. He looked astonished and aghast. Through his thin-stretched lips, he emitted a rippling moan, a trail of dread rising and falling, quavering insanely in its own wind. Although he could not have missed seeing me, he took no notice. Terror drove him and obscured everything else. As I continued forward around the bend in the road, the forest swallowed him again.

The figure's awful moaning and certain fright did not disturb my tranquility as I flew toward the source of his discomfort. I felt disconnected with the scene, without fear. I was an observer, curious but insulated and untouchable.

Past the bend, I arrived at a clearing that rose to a barren knoll. Moving toward that crest was a white-glowing globular shape something like a translucent cloud. It scudded over the drifted snow, all the while changing shape, diameter, and height, as if it were pulsing as it moved. It seemed to breathe. In pursuit was the naked woman I had seen zigzagging the path. She flailed her arms laboring through the drifts. The amber glow that had bathed her before turned bluish beneath the open sky. She wallowed nearly waist-high in snow, chasing the orbic apparition as it crested the rise and began to descend the other side. The blue woman clambered to the surface of the snow and, as before, ran on the air above it. She seemed desperate to reach that glow. She topped the hill just as the shape was to set behind it, seemed to dive off a promontory after the lighted orb, and disappeared with it in unison, like the moon and a planet in conjunction, setting together at once.

The second woman, appearing off to my left, now wrapped in swirling black capes but still barefoot, screamed. She held out with both arms a stripped pine branch pointing in the direction of her companion's disappearance. As the orb and her sister disappeared, she wilted to her knees and beat the snowdrift before her. Each time it hit the snow the naked pine branch made a dull thud. She continued rhythmically to raise the bough and to bring it down hard.

The thudding measure throbbed in my temple. I felt my head expand with each stroke, pounding not just on the snow but also inside my skull. Then I heard the hammering much nearer. It roused me to pain. I moaned as I opened my eyes and turned in the direction of the sound. I lay on my back across the seats and console of the Jeep, my head just below the rider's side window, pulsating with the blows. Someone was thumping on the window.

A muffled voice repeated several times before I could understand what it was asking me to do. "Roll down the window."

I moaned with the movement but reached the crank. Slowly, fighting the accumulated snow on the ledge, I eased the glass down partway.

The voice was more distinct. "That's good." He pushed his flashlight inside to illuminate my face. "Man! Are you all right?"

"Did I hit it?" I was referring to the buck.

"Hit what? You went off the road, Bud."

"Where?" What could I say? In the sudden flash of his light I saw the buck slide by. I plunged into the cavern. I sped after the running women, passed through the terrified man, and gaped at the bounding orb. None of those events fit with the man calling me Bud.

An arm came inside the Jeep and cranked the window all the way down. Snow fell from the window ledge and cooled my temple. "Let's get you out of there."

The man grabbed my hat that lay below the window crank. "Let me slip this on. You got a good whump on your left side. No sudden moves."

I did as I was told.

"Okay, can you slip those arms out the window? Go easy." I took it slow. He watched my face carefully. "I got my sled right here behind the skidoo."

I had no idea what he meant, but poked my forearms out the window. He slipped a narrow board along my back and reaching over me fixed straps attached to it around my chest and hips. "Relax. Let me do the moving." He grabbed the board solidly, tipped it carefully on the window ledge and slid the board with me strapped to it up and out the window. He moved around to pivot me on the fulcrum of a sled he had positioned next to the roof of the Jeep. I'm not small. He had tremendous strength and knew what to do. He must have been there for a while, and he had worked it all out.

I lay up on the sled and could see even in the driving snow that we were above the Jeep. I had arisen from the netherworld of the cab. A snow tunnel led down to the window and fell into the dimness of the rider's seat lit by the dash lights and muffled headlamps reflecting against the snow.

"Shit! The lights are still on," my rescuer said. "Well, I ain't crawling down there to shut them off. Let the battery die."

My rescuer took control. I fancied him a midwife, delivering me from Mother Winter. "Lay back on the board, Bud," he said. "Don't worry. I'm going to cover you with this blanket and tarp. These here straps will keep you tight on the sled. You don't have to worry."

In a few minutes he had me cinched and secure. He sat past my head on the snowmobile's saddle while he took off the snowshoes he had been wearing all that time. "These fit right here by your head. I got this rig all piped out!"

In a minute we were underway. Snugged to the sled, the ride seemed like my dreamy, cruising pallet. A few small jolts jostled my tender temple, but we finally took to the drifted road after a few turns and the terrain gave forth smoothly. I relaxed. The snow fell on my exposed nose and eye lids, covered my knit hat that he had pulled down below my hood, and crusted around the turtleneck of the jacket that rose past my chin and covered my lips. I blinked snow off and watched the pines' dark rockets disappearing into the stormy sky and counted the few giant birch reaching toward rocky outcrops, spreading their impossibly huge boughs to lift piles of snow on their shoulders.

I had become the listener, hearing the nothing that is in the snow and knowing I would be brought safely away. That thought like the storm itself played on me. I had fallen under the spell of the North. I needed time within warm walls to recover my sure senses.

We were moving along the road, I hoped, toward Mary. I gave up watching the snow swirl above me, gave up confusion, gave up the fear of concussion, and closed my eyes to the storm.

PART II

Tillie's

He was quick and alert in the things of life, but only in the things, and not in the significances.

Jack London, *To Build a Fire*

I OPENED MY EYES to startle at the huge face hovering above me. It was his breath that had warmed my nose and my closed eyes. He'd carefully, gently brushed the snow from my eyelids and was working barehanded to clear the snow from the folded margin of my knit cap. He rubbed his hands together and smiled at my open eyes.

His face was close, but he spoke loudly over the idling of the snowmobile. "I knew the ride would keep you awake. It's not good to sleep after a head-whacking."

I nodded by closing and opening my eyes, which was as much as the restraints and my bulky clothing allowed. In the light of the snowmobile headlamp, his beard seemed on fire with snow and steamy breath.

He put his face closer. "Listen." He looked straight into my eyes, noted the focus and continued, "I am going to leave you alone here just for a minute. Okay?"

I gave him a deliberate blink.

He placed his bared hands on my shoulders, firmly but gently, like a caress. "Just to be sure, I want help moving you inside. I did enough wrestling back at the car. Couldn't be helped. I can check you out better once we carry you inside. Okey-dokey?"

This time I spoke through my bundled clothes. "All right." His ministrations felt good.

He smiled again as he rolled the turtleneck below my chin. "Listen. I know what I'm doing. I do a lot of doctoring around the lake here. Don't worry. I'll take care of you."

I was glad to hear it but looked a question at him.

He understood, grinned broadly, and nodded. "They call me Scummy." He patted my chest, imparting a congenial and grateful glow inside my wraps. I must have lifted a wry corner of my mouth. "Yeah, it's an odd name. I'll explain sometime."

He loosened the straps some. "It'll give you more room to breathe. But keep them on while I round up some help inside. Don't move around too much. I'm draping another tarp over you to keep the snow off." He adjusted the tarp over the snowshoes that seemed to tower above me and snapped some tabs through their webbing. He fussed with his arrangement, then he lifted the lip of the tarp and pointed at a wall three feet away. He had parked next to a building that sheltered us from the wind. "I'm leaving you some reading material." He chuckled. "Don't worry. I'll be back in a couple of minutes."

I heard his boots crunch over the snow packed close to the building. The sound of his tread faded round the corner of the structure. I craned my neck to see but rebounded sharply with a throbbing reminder at my temple. He was gone anyway.

Just below the edge of the tarp that Scummy hung over the snowshoes, the headlamp illuminated lettering on the side of the building. It was written in verse. I blinked to clear my vision. Without moving, I could see only three lines. More accurately, for the tarp sagged in the middle obscuring part of the top line, I saw only two and a half lines. I read what I could see, strapped in as I was, and then reread it. I filled in the first three words and came up with:

If you're feeling sad and blue,
Stop at Tillie's t' tip a few.
Your friends around you

Something in the triplet sounded familiar. Was it a jingle? Its carefree, sympathetic sentiment carried the rhythm. Was it the name? Tillie's? I had heard of it, somewhere. I was sure I had. But it wasn't until the crunching of more boots approached that I remembered who had mentioned Tillie's before.

"Hey, Bud." Scummy jammed his head close as he removed the tarp. "I got help. We'll do the lifting. You just rest easy." He tightened the straps again and patted my chest.

Before Scummy killed the headlight, I confirmed my first reading of the lines and was able to see the rest of the verse below as they lifted me a bit unevenly:

If you're feeling sad and blue,
Stop in at Tillie's t' tip a few.
Your friends around you
Your blues in brew
Will turn from sadness and from rue
To jolly times with our three-two.

The light went out, and Scummy removed the key.

The jingle made little sense to my tired and addled mind, but the catchy ring of the rhymes batted around in my brain far into that long evening. The rhythms receded when Scummy hollered in the quiet that had descended over the little scene, "Hey, listen up."

Once he gained attention, he gave orders that sounded kind and sure, but they were directions that could not be ignored or disobeyed. Scummy was in control.

"Jarvi, you take the foot poles. Let me snug them straps again.

"Gary, you and me will take the head poles. That end's heavier.

"Hey, leave them snowshoes behind. Let me check." He circled the sled, looking at it carefully. He made some adjustments to clamps and straps on each side.

"Okey-dokey, the stretcher should lift right off. On three, men. One. Two. Lift!"

The man in front, Jarvi, grunted at my feet. "Christ! Roscoe could'a given me a hand here, but oh, no-o."

Scummy quelled the complaint. "Jarvi, you know we're better with three. Roscoe ain't in any shape to help."

Gary agreed. "He'd be more trouble than help. You know that."

Still, Jarvi whined. "Sure, take his side like always."

"Let's go." Scummy could have said, "Forward. March." For the crew moved in step alongside the building under the sign that advertised "three-two."

I lay back, batting with my lashes the snowflakes that were still falling heavily, and tried to see as much as I could of the surroundings. The men stayed close to the wall that soared upward to short eaves of snow-hooded rafter tails. They were like birds who took refuge from the wailing storm, hiding beneath the overhang. The wall, with its single window, was plated with corrugated-pattern flat shingles—compressed gypsum and asbestos, the kind that had been used in the 1940s—and was appointed midway up by swan-necked electrical lamps, either burnt out or turned off, for they were dark below their conical shades. Three of these lamps hung in an array over the verses I had read. The words were painted directly on the siding. They now were imprinted on my consciousness. They rolled around in my mind like a mantra.

What does "three-two" signify? I wondered.

I didn't have time to ask. The banter among my stretcher-bearers precluded questioning from me. I was an observer, and I didn't feel like breaking in.

The storm blasted us as we rounded the corner. Jarvi hefted his two stretcher poles above his parka-padded hips. "Up with your end, guys. We got the steps."

The two at my head lifted me up. I saw the front of Tillie's flying even higher above the adjacent eaves, a reticulated façade capped with wide, thick boards decorated at the right angles with simple but evident carpenter's ogees and scrolls. Tipped up as I was, I could see the steps below where brick met the asbestos siding under a pipe rail. I wondered if the brick were solid or faux-brick composition shingles that could fly off in hurricane-force winds. A pair of double-hung windows several feet each side of the door we were about to enter emitted a faint amber light, like that from a fire, flickering through deadened neon tubes that spelled "Hamm's" and, the local brew, "Fitger's." A solitary and quite-dead swan's-neck lamp confirmed the power of the blizzard. The storm had knocked the lights out.

Once or twice the litter I was strapped to canted dangerously. I gripped the rails on either side to brace myself. The three men won my gratitude and admiration—despite their grousing, swearing, and a little bit of bickering—for their careful work. I anticipated and watched—flat on my back as I was—each maneuver they planned and executed. They kept a steady hand.

Negotiating the door proved to be a chore. The

steps came up from the side to a narrow concrete landing covered with compacted snow and bounded at the far side and front by pipe railing. Jarvi stopped on the landing, looking toward the window set beside the door. He crooked his head several times, as if to beckon someone sitting by the window to come to the door. I heard what I thought was wild howling from somewhere off in the deep of the storm.

Jarvi waited. He shook his head in disgust. He set one pole of his end on the back rail, opened the storm door with one free hand, and swung it wide with his left foot while snatching the stretcher pole again. The door swung in an arc nearly as wide as the landing and plowed a tiny avalanche of fresh fallen snow off the far side. It was a tight quarter. The men at my head seemed patient and content to hold.

"Fer Christ's sake," Jarvi said, "at least Roscoe could'a got the door."

"He doesn't even know we're here," Scummy said, doing his best to keep me level through it all.

"Guess you're right." Jarvi shrugged. "Switch off to the left so's I can get closer to the door."

I felt an exchange going on behind me. Gary must have climbed outside the railing, while he and Scummy slid the stretcher along the top rail to bring it perpendicular and in line with the open storm door. Scummy chuckled from below me as he lifted to keep his end up.

"You still with us, Bud?" he asked. I smiled with an eye-nod he couldn't see.

Jarvi bent a bit, holding the left handle, and balanced the right on his thigh while he turned the knob. Scummy supported and slid his end forward in accord with Jarvi's move indoors. Gary, now on the door side of the rail, hefted both head handles himself and followed Jarvi inside.

In a gush of heat and close, beery air, the lantern and fire-lit interior of the barroom fought for a minute with the power of the storm outside. The howl of the fierce whiteness echoed, then melted. The blizzard rushed at the door but veered off as if it feared the orange glow that glinted in the polished wood of the bar. The storm fled before soldier-like bottles of liquid fire in files before the spotted, molted silver of the huge mirror that doubled the rows of liquor bottles. The kerosene lanterns and the open stove fired at the wind's gusts. The storm faded and the heat swelled.

Scummy swung the storm door shut and secured the entry door against the drafts. Like a giant animal, the frenzied blizzard butted the windows and, even more forcefully, bit at the corners of two large rooms at the building's front. Timbers, boards, and beams creaked against each other.

"Set him 'cross those chairs I put by the fire. Don't move 'im closer yet. We'll inch 'im forward." Scummy was taking charge again.

On the right side of my face, I felt the heat radiating from a large metal flue. As if alive, the heat sent shafts of golden radiance from the open door of the large wood stove similar to the one in which my Finnish grandmother baked bread. Someone shoved three pieces of cordwood through the oven door and clanged it shut.

"Yah, that's good. Not too much right off," Scummy said. He pulled up a low stool near me.

"Listen, Bud, we're goin' ta warm you up, but gradual. In a minute we're goin' ta start taking layers off bit by bit. Just rest easy. I'll get some things and be right back." He patted my chest again. The warm feeling I first encountered at this gesture swelled now in the shadowy warmth of the pungent barroom.

Scummy disappeared at the back of the far room somewhere behind a draped doorway. Flat on my back, I saw part of the room reflected in the mirror—the bar itself and the shadowy space behind me above the doubled images of the bottles beyond my extended feet. I felt the stove on my right churn out its heat.

In the light that escaped spaces around the stove's ports and lids, flickering on the worked filigree of the tin ceiling, I saw, again, the cave. The rectangular vaults between crosshatched beams coved in fanciful stamped metal vines supported a thin relief of grapes that wound its way through light and shadow. I traced it with my eyes, trying to find its end, but the effort only tired me and returned me to my starting point. I floated as in the dream toward the firelight above that writhed around blades of three fans that, had they been electrified, would have sent the rising heat back down. I imagined myself drifting with the warmth aloft toward the higher reaches of the room.

I heard patrons murmuring out of sight at my head, and I saw others—three seated at the bar, two at a table nearer the fire, and a lone stubby figure perched behind the far bend in the bar. He was sitting six feet from the door on a high stool in the barroom's front corner near the windows. As we entered, I had heard Jarvi snarl at this man. Even under his breath, it was loud enough to be plain: "You useless stump."

Behind his large, shaggy profile, beyond the fur-lined hood he had thrown back, a window stood adjacent to the one facing the front. This bearish man swayed from one window to the next, glancing outside furtively, past the glass tubing that spelled "Hamm's," but without seeming to look at anything. He turned, gazed into the barroom, glassy-eyed, unfocused. With a jerk, he swiveled back to look through the windows.

The back of the chair supporting my stretcher foot restrained my view of him, but I could see enough. He wore a queerly familiar expression. Had I seen him at the truck stop? I wondered. I was confused. I watched him. His rhythmical movement—between the fogged and rimed windows beyond which he could see little but frost and the snow-crusted boughs of pines—fascinated me. I realized that he was moving in time to a slow dirge that rumbled from his slack, beard-rimmed mouth. At one point humming what seemed a continuous, hypnotic, and ever-changing melody—of which everyone else in the bar seemed oblivious—his voice rose in a moan I had heard before. It gained intensity then lessened after a moment, much like the blast of a train's horn as it passes, wailing faintly, then building insistence to crescendo and, finally, dying into a distant hum as it vanishes. Yes, I thought, I heard that moan when they carried me in. No one else in the bar took notice. At the third crescendo, an objection, a single word, sounded from the back of the room. Still the moaning went on. The voice repeated the word in a guttural, barely intelligible snort, "Roscoe."

Then Scummy stepped out from behind the curtained doorway. "Roscoe. You're moaning," he said.

Immediately, the humming stopped. The figure beyond the bar ceased his swaying. He swung around and rested his elbows on the bar edge. He sipped his beer.

Scummy came to me, pulled up a short stool, and unloaded his pockets on my chest and stomach, using them like a surgeon's tray. He had brought several jars of salves, bandages, a sewing kit, and three pill bottles. He off-loaded, then went back from where he had appeared and returned with an ice pack and a pan. He set the pan on the stove and proffered me the pack. "Just hold this on your noggin, Bud. I filled it with snow out back."

I did as he told me. I pointed toward the bear-man at the bar. "What's wrong with him?"

Scummy looked at me as if he saw me as a stranger for the first time. "It's a long story. First, let's take a look at you. Okey-dokey, Bud? Just hold that sack on the bump. Keep it tight to it."

He scurried around me, adjusting the chairs, bringing me inches closer to the roasting stove. Then he loosened my boot laces, carefully removed the boots, and set them near the stove. "We don't want to break a toe off now do we," he winked at me in glee. "I'm just going to check for frostbite and warm them up a tad." He gently bared one foot, placing the sock on my knee for safekeeping, and looked at the toes closely in the beam of a small flashlight he took from his chest pocket. Satisfied, he examined the other. He hung both socks over a wire strung above the stove, dipped his hands in the pan, rubbed them together and held them out to the stove top. Water drops from his hands spattered and spit on the iron.

After a minute or two in this ritual, he turned, positioned his stool at my feet, and began to rub them slowly, first one foot, then the other. In rounds, he increased the speed and pressure of his massage. His hands were warm from the fire and surprisingly soft, though I sensed strength in his tendons and bones.

"I didn't learn this in Nam. There you didn't worry about frostbitten toes. Rot and lead slugs were the bother there." He lightened up on the rub, added one of the salves from a jar on his "medic shelf," and slowed the rub, thinly coating each foot. He took another careful look with the penlight, nodded at me approvingly, grabbed the socks off the line, and rolled them carefully inside out, finally, back-rolling one on each foot. I couldn't help but wiggle my toes. If you were going to tangle with the northern winter, you needed the company of someone like Scummy.

"You might have a sore spot or two tomorrow, but they look fine. Now let me see that head."

He unzipped my parka, removed my gloves, examining my hands in the same way he had done at my feet, shifted me closer to the fire again and moved the stool around to my injured head. "Rub your hands together. Just lightly."

I heard the moaning from the end of the bar start once more. "Do you know him?" I asked and instantly realized the stupidity of the question.

Scummy lifted his eyebrows and pushed his moustache and beard away with pursed lips, "Oooh, yeah. Roscoe and I go way back. We're best friends." He continued to doctor me. "Take the cold sack away, could ya? Close your eyes a minute."

He beamed the light on my wound. "Okay. Here, look at this." He took the ice pack, trading it for a small mirror. "Hold that so you can see."

I adjusted the mirror and studied the illuminated area.

"You see this cut here?" He pointed to it with a blunt finger. "I can probably close that up with a steri-strip or butterfly. Might be better'n stitching it. It ain't too long. Less scarring than with stitches. You okay with that?"

I wasn't just liking his bedside manner—Scummy was fantastic.

"Okay. I'm not beautiful anyway."

"Just down this, it'll help you relax." He held my head up and brought a shot glass to my lips. "Take it easy now, it's Jack." The sharp strains of whiskey rose to my nostrils, and I opened my lips.

The light from the stove and lanterns wavered in the lift and luff of the building straining against the storm. Below the groaning of the frame structure in the wind, a low conversation fed its way around the two rooms. The moaning in the barroom rose and fell. I lapsed into the glow of the whiskey and the stove. As Scummy worked on the cut, he spoke to me in a low voice.

"This is a small place. Everyone knows everyone else. Knows everything about everyone else. So you don't have to ask, of course, except if you're from outside. Roscoe and me go back, way back like most of these other folks too. He's near four years younger'n me, but 'cause he was a great fisherman and hunter and famous for it early on, we got to know each other that way. We were fairly close neighbors, too. I delivered his daughter."

Though he used it as diversion from the stinging at my forehead, Scummy clearly enjoyed telling the story. That was plain.

"The way we met was crazy. I was out squirrel hunting, must have been ten or eleven. I never had much luck huntin', back then or ever—guess that was actually lucky 'cause, when it came to shooting in the army, I couldn't hit a target no matter what. So they gave me a kit and made me a medic. Not a safe job, but better'n chucking ammo into the jungle. People tend to shoot back when you do that. My guys always had my back.

"Anyway, squirrel hunting. I finally got in prime position on a big gray bushy tail. He was sitting on an open branch, right up in the sun, taking a nap maybe, just sitting as pretty as could be. I stayed quiet and took careful aim. He couldn't'a' been mor'n eight or ten yards away. Should have been an easy shot. I was just ready to squeeze when off goes that squirrel's head cut clean off, and he topples off the branch without moving a paw or curling his tail or anything. I watched a headless squirrel drop straight to the ground, and I hadn't even shot!

"I hear this 'yahoo' from behind me. Here comes a little kid—I think he was seven then—from about twenty-five yards behind me. It was Roscoe. He shot the head off my squirrel at a hundred feet. He cut in right behind me.

" 'Hey, that was my squirrel!'

" 'You should'a' bagged him, then,' the little squirt said.

" 'You could'a' hit me.'

" 'If I had hit you, I would'a meant to hit you. And I never would, anyway. You can have the squirrel. I just want the head.'

"He was the most daring little devil around the lake. Best shot. Best fisherman on lake or stream. Best woodsman, too.

"We've had good laughs about that day, I can tell you. I figured if someone that young had that kind of aim, he was someone I wanted to hunt with. And we did hunt—duck, geese, coots, pheasant, and deer. After Nam, I lost my enthusiasm for hunting. Birds and tiny critters seemed too small. Deer were too human."

I thought of my "dream deer" which, I would have agreed, was too human. I wasn't ready to talk about that one yet.

Scummy was bending close over my head, penlight in his mouth now. He worked carefully, stripping bandages, applying them, checking the result. He leaned back and took the little flashlight out of his mouth. "I'm going to cover that with gauze. Might keep these idiots around here from head-butting you." He tidied up the bandage remnants and unrolled some gauze. Scummy drew close and nearly whispered. "Seems like the good ones have bad luck. Roscoe had his, that's for sure."

He glanced in the direction of the bar and continued. "About a year after I came back from Nam—the second tour and the last anyone ever spent there—Roscoe was going with a real nice girl, and it looked for all like she would tame him and make a home with him. Cripes, it was even hard to get him out to the woods much. He was steady on her.

"The next winter Roscoe and Morgan, his sister-in-law-to-be, talked a bunch of people into going out in a storm, windigo chasing."

"Did you say 'windigo'?" I asked. It surprised me.

"You heard of them?"

"My wife told me a couple of stories, yeah."

"Scary, huh?" Scummy continued his story. "Roscoe and Morgan could both be as wild as the woods, and they and everybody else had been drinking most of the day. A bunch left from right here and went off buzzing around the forestry station roads in Roscoe's great big Buick. He shut the lights off. It was dark as death.

"The weather got dangerous out there, and two other carloads of drunks called it quits. The sisters and their men kept on. The sisters spotted a windigo. They wanted to run a chase. The two boyfriends fought about hunting without the car, going on foot. Both were dead drunk.

They argued, went after each other first with fists, then with sticks. Roscoe went crazy and nearly beat his friend to death.

"During the fight, the sisters got frenzied-weird and started running. Roscoe says they chased a windigo. Long and the short of it is, Morgan ran off and lost herself in the woods. The sheriffs found her later that night two miles from the scene of the fight. Frozen. Naked. Dead.

"The law had to charge someone, and since Morgan was gone, Roscoe was the only one left who had whipped up the windigo chase. He was seen as the aggressor. He could serve time. It was his car. They got him on a 'reckless endangerment' charge."

Scummy clamped his pocketlight with his teeth again. He had cut strips and carefully taped gauze over butterflies he used to close the cut. He nodded at his handiwork. "You'll be fine. Let's get you in a chair. Take it easy. Don't stand yet."

He had me scoot onto another chair while he removed the stretcher, rolled it up, and put it in the corner by the door. "For the next time," he said. He smiled and helped me out of the parka, which he hung on the chair back and pushed it up to the stove. He handed me a thermometer. "Put this under your tongue. Keep it from the fire." Scummy continued.

"A year and a half later, when Roscoe got out of state prison in Stillwater, his woman had moved. She had had the kid, like I said, but left it with her grandmother. The family didn't want much to do with Roscoe, of course, but he never went away, just kept getting crazier every year."

"Let's see that temp." He took the thermometer out and studied it. "You're a little low, but for what you went through, not bad, ninety-five and seven. You'll warm up."

I felt grateful. "I might not have made it if you hadn't come by."

He shrugged. "Maybe."

He busied himself with his supplies. Done repacking, he brought up his stool. "I didn't want to ask right off, Bud, but how'd you come to bury yourself way out there on Hongisto Road?"

I felt more like talking now. The whiskey, warming limbs, and mending loosened me up. Scummy was, if not a friend, the best man around. I told him selective bits of the story, starting with the deer in the road and working back toward Saint Paul. I told him about the two guys I had met at Bobbie's, about the babies coming, and about Mary.

When I mentioned Mary, he put his hand on my knee and said, "Shush a bit here." He was looking at me as if he had seen a windigo or a giant white deer. He leaned forward and nearly whispered without actually looking secretive. "Did you say your wife is up here now? She's tending some newborns?"

"Yes. Her cousin's."

Scummy hissed and shushed me again. He looked to the bar. The moaning was going on as usual. "Hey, let's get us to the john, heh? You can stand now slowly, and I'll help you walk. Put on them boots."

The safety and security I'd been feeling slid down to the drafty floor and an uneasy, confused concern drifted up, following Scummy's sudden hush. Given his certain care, his odd caution alarmed me.

I heard Cooley's warning, Don't mess with them people. That's where I had heard Tillie's for the first time.

I said nothing right then but gingerly put on the

boots, laced them, and rose cautiously to my feet. Scummy guided me along the wood paneled wall to the men's room.

Past the L-shaped partition, a door built from tongue-and-groove knotty pine swung into the small, dark room, partitioned to hide the commode that reeked of urine, beer, and deodorizer cakes. From somewhere above, a draft crept down the wall.

I shivered in the unheated place. A single-candle lantern burned feebly. The acrid air brought on a nauseous weakness in my gut. Scummy turned and slipped the hook into the eye of the latch and leaned against the door. "Keep your voice down," he said.

"What's all the mystery," I wanted to know.

"Listen." He came close. He looked me in the eye, then, averted his gaze. "Your wife, you said, is named Mary."

"Right."

"She's been up here about three weeks tending to Windsong."

"Yeah, that's her name." Of course he would know her.

"Her cousin."

"Right."

"Are you sure they're cousins?"

That made me anxious. "What do you mean?"

"Is that what your wife told you?"

" Sure she did. What of it?" I wanted Scummy to move away, to unlock the door.

"I'm trying to avoid trouble here."

My anxiety flash to anger and fear. "Can you let me out? I don't think I want to talk about this."

"Look, Bud, you can trust me, but there are people

here who wouldn't be happy to meet Mary's husband. It has nothing to do with you. It's all stuff from the past."

I blew out a cloud of tension. His assurance didn't calm me, but his tone was reluctant, sincere. "Okay, what's it about?"

"I don't know what Mary has told you about herself in her teens."

"Not a whole lot. I know it was a tough time for her."

He looked me in the eyes again. He did not turn away this time.

"Listen. Mary is a very decent woman. I want to say that. Since she arrived, she's spent every minute getting ready for the births. Beanie already had hers. Mary delivered her."

"I heard." I wanted to back up. "So you know her."

"Yes. From ages ago. I haven't seen her in twenty years. She wouldn't come here to Tillie's."

"I don't get this. What you are saying," I said.

"It's about the past. The past you can't change. It's just there. And Mary's past is maybe something you don't know."

"What is your point, Scummy?" I was growing anxious again the more he stalled.

"I was there at Windsong's birth. Grandma Bassett sent for me 'cause things were getting difficult, and I had lots of experience in Nam with village women and such. I did two tours as a medic."

"So you delivered Windsong."

"Yes. And I know her mother."

"So? What does that have to do with me?" Nothing was making sense.

"Listen, Bud. Listen and don't react. Just take this in. I am not the enemy."

I hesitated. The nausea grew. My legs felt weak.

"Sit on the pot, Bud."

I sat. "So?" The moaning fear of the runner in my vision welled up in my throat. Dread stopped my breath.

"Your wife is Windsong's mother."

Anger restored my voice. "You've got that wrong, Scummy."

"Well, maybe," he said.

"Maybe what?"

"I don't have the facts wrong, believe me. Maybe it was a bad time to have a child. Maybe she couldn't face it with all that was happening. Anyway, it was a long time ago and in a different life. It was pretty clear. It's understandable. She wanted to leave that life behind. Even the kid."

"No. She doesn't, didn't want kids. Neither of us did."

"Sure. I get it. But Windsong is sure hers, even if Granny Bassett raised her. I was there. I know."

The candle above lit his face, his beard steaming with his breath. A flood of rage and fear sprang up my legs past my knotted stomach, hit my bruised temple, and throbbed there insistently.

Scummy gently took my arms and raised me up. "Steady. Keep it together. I shouldn't have shocked you, but I had to tell you to stop you talking out there. There is nothing wrong in what you did or said, but the main thing is to keep this quiet while you are here, here at Tillie's."

Cooley's voice rang out in my mind: And don't stop in there, either. Now I was sorry I had. I wished I were still in the Jeep.

"That's why Cooley warned me from here."

"Probably. But nothing is going to happen." Scummy

spoke in his bedside voice again, "I just don't want folks to know you're Mary's husband until you can join her—which will be after I feel it's safe to move you. Going out in the storm is not a good idea. Okay?"

"I don't understand this."

"Okay." He swallowed and let out a long breath. "If Roscoe finds out who you are before you leave, he'll tear this place up and maybe you, too. I don't know any two men who could stop him."

Even though my whole body was churning and pulsing with fear, anger, and dread, I did not worry about Roscoe, about who he was, or about what he could do. My early fascination on seeing him held firm. Weirdly, I felt connected to him. I looked at Scummy. "Why? Why would he go nuts? Or more nuts?"

"Why? Death, jail, and the family stuff. Please don't ask me to explain it now. It has to be later. Just keep it down. Okay? You need to rest."

I felt uneasy but more comfortable trusting Scummy than striking out somehow without him. Also, I wanted to get out of the toilet. I nodded my head, "Okey-dokey."

Scummy smiled. "Take a leak, Bud."

"I don't have to go." But to humor my medic, I did what he asked.

Scummy looked around the pine-paneled room. "Hey, as long as we're here." He stood to the urinal.

I turned to the sink and after splashing icy water on my face, felt better. "I think I'd like another whiskey."

"One more, that's it. I'll get one at the bar. Let's take a table by the fire."

Scummy went to the door, turned the knob silently, drew the hook out of the eye, and opened the door with a quick pull. No one was there. He pointed along the paneled wall toward a table around the corner by the stove. He went to the bar to get my whiskey.

As I stepped out from behind the el-shaped partition, someone swung the front door open, and the storm blew in.

"Hey, Tatty, there you are!" It was Danny, stamping his feet on the doormat.

Cooley was behind him, pushing his way in. "We thought you'd be here."

I hold still. I watch what Tiny will do. Both bells are tinkling. The fishing poles are bent. The lines go taut.

"Tiny."

The big man stares. He is fixed on the burlap curtain covering the window between us. It seems as if he is seeing between the web of fibers, past the open miles of snow and ice, and on to the pine and fir forests that line the far shore—looking into the past.

I try again. "Tiny, the bells. Both bells are ringing."

With a start, he looks to the poles. Then he jumps from his chair. "Holy shit!"

He pulls the nearest pole off its ice pick. The line spills off the reel. He flicks the rig's brake. "This is a big one." Tiny tightens the drag slightly, then jerks the rod high. "Hooked him sure. He swallowed that bait." He lets the fish take more line.

"Tatty, hold this one." He hands the pole to me. "Just let him run a bit." The line spills more slowly off the reel.

Tiny jumps to the next pole. He performs the same tasks. "Got him. Got him." He dances in place. "Okay, now tighten down on that drag, like this." He demonstrates. "Now, pull up and reel down." He watches me. "Good."

We work our fish. The short poles welt the air and wobble under the power that stirs their lines. Tiny instructs me. "If the line goes slack, reel in."

In a minute he says, "You're going to have to brace both poles for a bit while I work the gaff." Tiny hands me his pole and grabs a long wooden-handled hook from the corner by the door. I prop a pole on each knee and clamp a hand above each reel.

"Just hold on. They're going to tug hard when they see this thing," he says.

Tiny slowly slides the metal spar of the gaff through the hole nearest him. Both fish pull frantically at their lines.

"Hold tight," Tiny says. He lowers the gaff further, letting the pole slide through his hand. He pins the last two feet of handle to the side of the hole with one stocking foot. "Okay, now hand me my pole."

I am careful not to cross the lines.

He reels in, keeping his eyes fixed on the hole. "There he is. A lunker." Tiny seizes the gaff handle. One-handed, he draws his pole up, positions the metal spur, then lowers the fish as he pulls up on the gaff. Up the walleye rises. Coming through, the fish nearly fills the hole.

"Look at him. Fat and sassy." Tiny presses on the wood handle to hold the fish to the burlap carpet. He kneels to unhook the fish, but failing that, instead, cuts the line. "That barb is way down in his stomach."

Sliding the fish to the door like a flopping mop, Tiny opens the door and flings the fish off the gaff. "He'll be just fine out there."

He turns to me. I'm still holding tight to my pole. "Now, let's bring yours up. You work the pole. I'll tend the gaff."

We try twice to land the fish. The third time, Tiny draws my walleye up through the ice. "He's bigger than mine," Tiny says. "We'll fry him up instead of that shrimpy one I thawed and eat at least part of him."

I kneel to the fish and run my hand over the silvery blue scales. "Taken to a world you can't live in." I stroke the fish again.

"Can't go back. He'd die down there," Tiny says. "The hook, the gaff, or being touched up here will do it. Any of those would fester. We should cook him up."

"Or eat him raw, like windigoes do?"

Tiny laughs. "We aren't related to fish. It's okay."

"I am hungry."

Tiny takes the fish up with the gaff. "I thought you would be."

"Listen. While I clean these two whales, pour us a whiskey and dry off that little guy I thawed on the newspaper over on the shelf." He stops at the door. "You got me hooked. I can listen while I cook."

Afternoon light springs into the shack. Tiny slips into his boots and slams the door.

I busy myself with the thawed fish and the whiskey. I sit and pour. While I wait for Tiny to return, I hum a little tune.

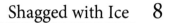

Shagged with Ice   **8**

STEPPING OUT OF THE CHILLY, sharp air of the toilet into the sour heat of Tillie's bar did nothing for the nausea that had turned my pounding head light. All I could think about was getting to the table, sitting in that chair. I felt weak.

When I moved from behind the partition that screened the door to the toilet from the barroom and turned to Danny's loud greeting, dizziness whirled around me.

Danny approached, doffing his mitts and hat. "We saw the Jeep! Then the skidoo tracks. We thought we'd give you a lift the rest of the way to Bassett's."

Prickly anxiety crept into my belly and rose to my head. I wanted escape.

I felt like I was sleepwalking—floating along sunny Tallahassee streets, past people I may have known but barely recognized. I moved without willing it, a somnambulist walking in the brightness of day. I imagined that I trailed a hand along the shop window ledges to keep balanced. I watched my reflected self—my real self it seemed, the one free of a body that dragged me through fear toward pain—the self free of the physical tomb that moved toward unconsciousness and fading release, the one living solely in photon-spirits just below the molecules in the surface of window glass. My reflected self looked on unaffected by the burgeoning

171

density of flesh infused with dread. Confronted by dangerous reality, I wanted to meld with that chimera within the safety of an imagined glass and away from a dark approach of pain.

Cooley came up behind Danny. "I guess that Mary will be up at Grandma's cabin. We can take you . . ."

He froze in the middle of his sentence. He glared at the space behind me.

Behind me, Roscoe spoke. "Maybe I'm the one who should be taking him."

I knew the voice. I saw his bar stool empty at the end of a conical, rotating tunnel of black, telescoping away from me as I receded. I was now a figure reflected in a window, watching what happened from outside myself. As if plunged into a darkened room behind a glass wall, I watched and overheard everything from far away.

As I tumbled backwards, I heard, "I've got him."

Roscoe stopped my fall. He had me under the arms and dragged me to the chair I'd been headed for.

He propped me there, moving the table edge to my belly. I still felt far away yet was aware that Roscoe had sat down beside me. "Grab that bar rag, Danny," he said.

A cool cloth on my forehead condensed the airiness and brought me back from behind that glass wall. Roscoe removed the cloth from my forehead, folded it, and held it out to me. "Take it. Might need it."

Roscoe turned to Cooley. "Grab some chairs."

Cooley set chairs around the table. Roscoe sat and stretched his legs aside. Danny and Cooley sat across from me. They both looked uncomfortable and concerned.

"Sounds like you all know each other," Roscoe said. He sounded reasonable.

Danny looked to Cooley. "Ya, we met down at

Bobbie's when we were fetching Uncle Joki."

"So, Joki's here too?"

"Naw, we left him off home."

Roscoe, who had been rocking and moaning last time I looked, was surprisingly cogent. None of the groaning babble he had released before came through now. "So, I'm the odd man out." He waited, but neither Danny nor Cooley said a word.

Finally, he said, "You should introduce me, don't ya think?"

Danny relaxed in his chair at Roscoe's congenial tone. "Sure. This is Tatty. . . ."

I helped him out. "Langille." It was all I could or was ready to say at the time.

"Tatty, this here is Roscoe Lucci." After a pause he added some friendly banter. "He's one a' our wops up here."

Roscoe, hunched forward, raised a bent wrist without lifting his elbow off the table to proffer a handshake. It seemed polite enough. I took his hand.

I felt his grip like a wooden clamp not fully applied but powerful and hard. He didn't let go but crooked his neck to look at me closely. One of his eyes turned outward, up and away from me, the other, like it was sighted down a rifle barrel, held me directly at point. His sharp-shooter focus and grip told of robust strength in Roscoe, and I kept my hand clasped firmly and my own gaze steady.

For the first time since swerving away from the buck, I felt full, stable, and focused. Though I sensed no animosity or danger, Danny seemed to cringe at what he might have thought would erupt from our prolonged, silent regard. To me, meeting Roscoe's eye was like seeing my reflection in those store windows.

Roscoe held on. "A good hunter knows when to listen to the wind."

I don't know where it came from, but I countered his cryptic greeting. "A smart buck knows when to leap and when to hunker."

As if I had passed an initiation, he released my hand. I confirmed his acceptance with a measured gesture. I raised the cool cloth he had given me to my forehead.

"I don't know, but it seems like we should know one another," Roscoe said.

"Yes, it's a small world up here," I answered. Scummy's caution stood as sufficient warning to me, and I thought better of volunteering much of anything yet.

I didn't have to turn to know that the hand that now lightly rested on and that gently squeezed my shoulder was Scummy's. His touch was singular and imparted the same comfort it had while he was working as medic.

Scummy set my whiskey down. "Gents, can I offer you something?"

"Beer, thanks," Cooley and Danny said.

"Salt and . . ." Danny held up.

"Not now, Danny," Cooley said, then in Finnish to Scummy, "Joo, kaksi olutta, Fitger's."

"Kolme-kaksi? Or strong."

"Three-two's good."

"Roscoe?"

"Whiskey. Like my Langille friend here." His tone spelled distance. Scummy had shifted the focus.

Scummy held the conversation in check and returned to the bar for the beers and whiskey.

Into the uncomfortable silence Scummy left behind, I injected a question. "What is this three-two? I saw it in the poem outside."

Cooley took it up with a gratified tone. "Well, originally, it was something the State of Minnesota invented to keep the Indians sober."

Danny shook his head, "No, to keep the Finns sober."

Roscoe slammed the table.

I thought he would begin to moan again, but he looked between Cooley and Danny—it was hard to tell what his eyes focused on. "You guys are full of shit."

"All right," Cooley came back, "in Minnesota you have beer at three-point-two percent alcohol and strong beer at, what? twenty-four proof? Some places sell only three-two. That's the way Tillie's started. Some people like it 'cause they can drink it all day and still walk home."

"Two three-two's."

Scummy handed over two amber bottles to Danny and then put one of the two shots held in his other hand in front of Roscoe. He cued up a chair but continued standing, taking in the scene that five minutes ago he had hoped to avoid. "Here's to peace and friendship," he offered. The five of us clinked our drinks together. For a moment Scummy's ghosts of the past disappeared with the warm cheer of bottled spirits.

Danny seemed unable to stand a silence. "We were talking about three-two."

"Yeah," Roscoe took over, "we were talking about three-two. But you fellows didn't drop by for the beer. Did ya?"

Danny looked to Cooley.

"Down at Bobbie's I told Tatty we'd look out for him along the road. In case something happened," Cooley said.

Danny swallowed his sip of beer and blurted out, "Ya, and we told him not to stop here!"

Roscoe sprang on it. "Now why the hell would you warn someone away from Tillie's?" He riveted his straight eye to the center of Danny's forehead.

"I brought him here," Scummy said. "You two saw the car?"

Cooley slid an arm along the table edge in front of his friend as if to cap his mouth. "We saw the antenna first. It would'a looked like a stick without that orange ball on the end. Stopped and saw the lights still blazing away down in the snowbank."

"I left them on," Scummy said. "There was no time to go back in."

Cooley tapped the table before Danny. "We looked inside. Nobody there, but we took the luggage from the back so no one would swipe it."

Danny couldn't be stopped. "Yeah, and we took it up t' Tiny's."

Roscoe took a sip of the whiskey. He sat back. Did his hunting instincts tell him when to wait and when to move?

"Beanie said everybody was up t' Granny's."

Cooley tipped his bottle toward Danny. "That's when we figured you were here for sure. Anyway, your stuff is all up at Tiny's."

Roscoe swallowed hard. "Oh yeah, there's always a warm welcome up at the Bassett shack. Shit. I haven't seen the inside of that dump since I was a kid."

"There's no need for that kind of talk," Danny said.

Roscoe bellowed at him. "Oh, you want talk, huh? Talk is what you'll get, Mr. Daniels. What is it you want to talk about now? Your good pal Tiny?"

Scummy tried to quell it. "Go easy, you guys." Indicating me, "Old Bud here is still not in top condition.

He took a good one on the head."

"So in your professional opinion I should shut up. Is that it?" Roscoe was flaming with the whiskey.

"You know how I feel about my patients, Giaco. I'd feel the same about you." Scummy raised his eyebrows, set his eyes kindly, and creased his lips together in earnest.

Roscoe seemed to frown down his ire in the face of Scummy's kindness. "You're right, Jay. I do know."

I thought of these two hunting together, trekking the woods, building a friendship day by day. Roscoe honored the bond. For now, at least, he deferred to Scummy. I didn't know until much later that Scummy had nursed Roscoe through some of the worst years of his life, through drunken wandering in the woods, had patched him up after horrid beatings he took in the idiotic fights he picked sometimes with three or more opponents, and nursed him through weeks of fever that left Roscoe a burned-down candle of his former, sturdy self.

Even without the background, it was clear the two were connected, and I could see why. I felt a similar affinity simply from the few minutes of care Scummy had given me. And for all Roscoe's oddities, he was intriguing. I thought that he accrued his touch of magic from solitary company with the woods.

The détente encouraged Cooley. "So you think Tatty here can move on yet?"

"You saw him go down just now, didn't you?" Scummy said.

"Yeah."

"And is it getting better outside?"

"I heard there was eight, maybe ten more inches to come," Danny said. "Wind is pretty stiff."

"Well, I would rather not take the chance if we can

keep him here. We've got heat, food, and plenty to drink. I suppose it depends on you, Bud."

Since I hadn't seen any family yet, I wasn't too anxious to go back out in blizzard conditions to meet them. I didn't know where Granny's cabin was, but no one had said "near" to it. My storm legs were worn and tired, my head, even if clear now, was tender.

There were Scummy's worries to take to account, but since he seemed to handle the two outbursts I had witnessed, I disbelieved what he had said about Roscoe. Staying might give me some time to untangle his screwy story about Mary and Windsong, and I thought sleep would be a good start at doing that.

"I wouldn't mind a bit of sleep, if you think it's advisable," I said.

He intoned his medic's advice, "Long as you don't mind me waking you up every two hours. You can probably sleep on the stretcher here near the stove."

I looked to Danny and Cooley. Neither said anything. "That sounds good," I said. "I've been at this trip for, I don't know, since four this morning, might have been three o'clock here when I got going."

Roscoe's question woke me from the sleep talk, "Where'd you come from?"

Danny flared out, "Let him be, will you?"

"No, Danny," I said, "it's okay. I flew up from Florida this morning." I wanted to get into the open.

"Jesus Christ. Into this?" Roscoe sounded downright sympathetic.

"I didn't know about the storm until I got to Saint Paul. It wouldn't have mattered anyway," I said. I didn't tell him that Mary wouldn't have understood. It felt best to leave her out as long as I could.

Roscoe stood abruptly. He circled the table, tapped Cooley and Danny on their backs as he passed, and pressed on Scummy's shoulder on his way round. I heard him say, "Better get some sleep then."

Nothing else. He went to his stool by the bar, holding what was left of the whiskey, turning his back, and looking out one then the other of those two adjacent windows. He looked as forlorn as a lost hiker hunched in the snow—a snowman, shagged with ice, forever cold— waiting for the winter to put him to sleep.

Cooley sighed, apparently relieved. "Well, we got some trekking to do."

Danny seemed surprised at taking leave. He tipped his bottle high to empty it. "Yeah, we got to bring Joki's machine back."

Scummy rose. "Go slow out there, boys. Even with a wide track, you could get stuck in this weather."

He turned to me, "I'll set the stretcher up with some blankets for you. Sleep is the best cure." He went toward the front door.

"Thanks for finding me, guys," I said to both of them.

Cooley spoke low. "We'll be going up to Granny's cabin to let them know you're here and all right. It's more or less on our way home anyway. Joki won't mind me keeping the wide track until tomorrow. He's in for the night. No one's going anywhere no how. You take care. Watch Roscoe close. Don't get to fighting. He's still real mean, no matter what anyone says."

"I'll be careful. I need some sleep is all."

Danny joined in whispers. "Sleep with one eye open. See ya later."

Scummy was back with the stretcher. "See you guys around. Bud here will be ready in the morning."

Cooley and Danny moved round the room, barking farewells to those they knew, which seemed like everyone. They stopped at the door to secure their boots and wraps. I heard them say something to Roscoe, stolid on his stool. They waited for a response but had to do without. The bear-man again sat separate, listening to something in his own world, intent on what was happening on the other side of the glass or maybe within the glass. Finally, the pair pushed the storm door against the drift that had accumulated while they were drinking their beers, and they tugged the door shut behind.

In two seconds, Danny pushed his head back through. "Max, you want me to shovel some of this out of the way? You're going to get snowed in."

The bartender waved an arm at him. "Yeah. And shut that door."

I heard Danny scraping the landing and steps. Max came round the bar and looked out the window where Roscoe sat. He murmured something. Roscoe lifted a hand and waved him off but seemed to be nodding approval. Max turned down the lanterns at the bar to a low glow and extinguished the candles that shone in the mirror. He came over to the stove, opened the firebox door, rattled the ash, and added more wedges of wood to the glowing embers.

"That should keep it for a couple hours," he said shutting the door. "Closing time," he announced.

He adjusted the draft slots on the stove and twisted the knob on the lantern hung beside it. The fine shining nets of kerosene-fueled light flared, glowed yellow then orange, and, finally, thinly golden as they deadened to ashen white. Max moved on to the lanterns hung over the pool table.

"Closing time," he said again. "'Course you can stay, but the bar is closed."

He removed his waist apron, hung it on a hook, and cut through a curtain beyond the poolroom wall. I listened to him mounting stairs at the back and, in a minute, heard his steps across the second-story floor.

Danny's scraping had stopped. The borrowed snow cat hummed away into the depths of the storm. The stove creaked, expanding with the fuel Max had added. The wind moaned misery in the pines and shook Tillie's with its gusts. Everyone quieted, spoke in hushes or not at all.

Next to the stove, Scummy had made me a pallet padded with a mover's blanket. "Get some shut-eye, Bud," he said.

"Thanks." The coming sleep welled up in a glow of gratitude. "You know, Scummy, I can't thank you enough for your help. I could have frozen out there."

He crouched on his heels and spoke low, "You might have lost toes or a finger, but the car was plenty of shelter for a while. You might have lasted 'til morning."

He flashed a smile. "I'll be waking you up in a couple of hours. Sleep." He rose above me and stepped back into the darkness and quiet that had fallen within the rooms.

It was two o'clock in Tallahassee. I had been up for twenty-two hours, but exhausted as I was, sleep proved elusive. I lay, watching the flickers of light dance on the filigreed coving of the ceiling, listening to the wildness of the storm outside.

T<small>HAT MORNING ALL</small> I <small>HAD IN MIND</small> was to join Mary at your house, Tiny—partaking, though a bystander, the family celebration, and then to be on my way, back to warmer days plying my storm shutter business in advance of hurricane season. What had started as a single day's travel had grown into the running of a gauntlet. It had already become an emotional whirlwind.

What I had allowed to rest as a featureless, blank era in Mary's past—moving at peace with her opaque feints against even idle curiosity, not wanting, really, to know what lovers she had bedded or what hopes she had once embraced before we met—those hidden and forgotten days now danced in the fire-lit ceiling like northern devils scraping scales from my eyes, all the while infusing confusion and suspicion in my heart.

No, I had not wanted to know Mary's past, and I wanted her to be free of whatever lurked behind her laconic mention of years growing up on the lake. But . . . a daughter. Why didn't she tell me? Though I did not want to accept it and wouldn't believe until she told me herself, the fact explained the sudden advent of long telephone conversations with Windsong and Mary's hot desire to arrive so early to the birthing bed. A daughter. She had to know that someone would tell me. Someone besides Scummy must have known.

I traced every conversation I could recall we had had

about children:

"After what I went through," I had said, "I don't think I could be a decent father."

Now I see in memory Mary's steady gaze as I had spoken these words.

"I would rather it be just you and me, Tatty. That's all I want," Mary had said.

The subject came up when friends started families.

"You were right, Mary. Kids do change a couple."

"Yeah, Al and Sally are completely overwhelmed."

I'd nodded. "I can barely get Al to work overtime anymore."

How she managed to string me along for all those years mystified me, made me wonder as much about what I had been doing as what she had been up to.

I put myself in her place and walked through the steps she had wanted me to take. Fly into Duluth. Take the short drive with her to your place. Stay there with family. Return to Florida in a few days. Could she have concealed her truth for three more days? Did she want to? I knew my Mary. She had the strength to hold things in.

At least I thought I knew my Mary.

Afterwards, I didn't want to be told, but the family must have known. Did Mary think everyone would continue her fraud? "Fraud." The word scared me. Was it fraud or simply an omission she thought innocuous once in the Florida sunshine? That seemed to give her too much credit. There was another question I held away from the dim light in the bar's coffered ceilings, held it in the shadows of the beams, kept it from my addled mind.

My own words to Roscoe nagged at me, "It's a small world up here." I had said it, perhaps, like Mary, half knowing the implication and import of that truth.

I wondered about Roscoe sitting on his stool, fixed on the power within or beyond the window glass, still and silent. What was he thinking? Scummy warned me about Roscoe. So far everyone had warned me about him. He now seemed a man on the opposite side of my own dilemma, somehow invested too deeply in a scarred past, unable to be freed even by time, and certainly not loosed by drink or warring ways. I could not penetrate the steadfast silence in which Roscoe wrapped himself to discover his part in this or know his reality, past or present. Scummy's cautionary, sequestered talk hid more than it revealed of the shadowy past.

In my own removal from reality, from what I considered reality—the house in Tallahassee, the business, my life there with Mary—I had grown uncertain of direction and forward motion, uncertain, at times, of what I was seeing. I was uncertain of what was real and what was dream, uncertain of my ability to care, uncertain of whom to trust or who could help.

In the wilderness of the blizzard, I had lost my bearings, had delved into storm-dreams, had met gust-demons, had flown off the road, and, perhaps, now, would scud away from the sanity around which I had built my life. Lost in this maelstrom, I felt naked and alone. Hurt, a victim of hoax or cruel truth, buffeted by sharp, chilly winds, I descended into a confusion of weariness, wavering illusion, and trial. I sought the darkness and escape of sleep.

Despite this raw, grating angst, sleep did seep up from the stove-warmed blankets. I finally surrendered to it and trusted what might come. The snoring from the corners of barroom reassured me. I wasn't alone. Those northern yokels I had wanted to avoid—the ones who hadn't traveled further south than Duluth—now felt more like the cousins and uncles I had avoided all my life. Now we were sheltering together, plying our faith in what we had built against the strength to destroy. The framed timbers of Tillie's held us together, kith and kin, though keeping an ear cocked to the misery in the wind. The feeling of clannishness gave me comfort.

I shifted away from the stove. Others moved here and there in the room. I settled in the slack luff of our common sleep-sail, loose between gusts of blizzard wind.

Once, I started at some movement near me. A dark, luminescent figure seemed to tower above my head. It hovered above momentarily, then swept away. I slept again. Other figures stirred visions. Inconstant, fleeting, murmurous, they floated through an air filled with particles of saffron-colored light. Red dust motes pierced these fluctuating, wandering bodies entering and exiting in the same arc, flaring as they reappeared, while the dusky flamelike figures circled on themselves, weaving around one another in spirals emanating from a tight center of ruddy light.

"I'm sorry to do this to you, Bud, but let me see those brown eyes." Scummy held his flashlight aside. "Look up a bit."

"What is your home address?" he asked. "What road did you take to get here?"

I was clear enough. "Hongisto," I said.

"What day is it?"

I was close.

He switched off the light.

"You're fine. See you in a couple hours."

I was steeped in darkness again. This time I dreamed on the motion of the wind. I flowed along, not feeling the bluster but being carried with it.

At my feet this time, a figure totally dark but sensible in its dense blackness, flew prone at a short distance back on the air streams. As if swimming on the wind, I stirred the air with winglike arms, putting distance between me and the unknowable figure following me.

My effort brought little relief from the oppressive tailgater, and soon his shade shortened the distance between us to mere feet. He became a persecutor who chilled me with a blue-cold radiation. I banked, my arms like gull's wings, dove below, then arched my back to rise around and away from the stab of his frozen touch. I was free only briefly. In seconds, the feeling of cold and dark filtered over my torso from above. I twisted and curled away, diving, banking, and soaring then swooping toward the snowy hills that suddenly lifted high and inclined toward a moonish shimmer at their crests.

The form that followed me—now only a shadow of a shade below, like the silhouette of a raptor on the whitened ground of the hill—receded before the light, falling further behind as I skimmed the snowy terrain. At the crest, the black form outdistanced and gone, it was as if I burst through a string curtain of tiny, prismatic beads that scattered in flares of iridescence, now aside and then behind in the glare of an oval moon, the elliptical edges of which held the figure of a woman, hair streaming down her bare back, who opened her arms wide to embrace the light before her and danced inside the orb like Shiva. The intense moon-glow grew blindingly bright.

I woke chilled, sweat-soaked. I had wrestled the covers off. This time, not Scummy's flashlight but a much stronger beam struck my eyes. It came through the open door, shooting past the stove and shining directly on my pallet. A figure stepped between, covering the brilliant light and blazed with a corona. It spoke. I knew the voice.

"I'm going to plow down a half mile further then swing back. Thanks for the soup, Max."

It was the grader operator I had encountered at the head of Hongisto Road. He had told me he would make it down this far in a couple hours. The storm must have been a bad one. The bar clock showed four-thirty. I felt safer, knowing someone was out doing battle with the blizzard, keeping what for me had proved to be a tenuous connection to an outer world.

Max swung the door shut against the light and the cold. I was now fully awake. He walked by me past the stove. Seeing me up, he spoke in a low voice.

"Looks like we might have clear roads in the morning," he said. "I told Loren about your car so he wouldn't bury it more than it already is."

I warmed at the thoughtfulness everyone and now Max, had shown me. Certainly, to survive a winter here, one needed friends to combat the cold, isolation, and monotony. "Thanks, Max. I really appreciate it."

"Dawn comes late here, near seven," he said. "You can go back to sleep."

"I'm getting up for a minute." I saw Scummy stretched out on the pool table.

Max pointed at him, "You might tell him you're okay. He'll sleep better that way."

I did as Max suggested. Scummy muttered, "Okay," and continued snoring. I headed for the john.

The door was slightly ajar, but the men's room seemed even colder than when Scummy brought me there for secrecy. I moved past the drafty window into the doorless toilet stall. I stood shivering. An unnerving quiet spread over the room as the stream of my urine steamed and splashed noisily in the bowl, reverberating in the icy silence. I realized the storm's groans and wild shrieks had died. Utter silence seemed to stand listening outside Tillie's walls. My dreams flooded back—the blazing white oval, the pursuing phantom shade—whirled within the flushing vortex of water, leaving only a sharp trace in the air before disappearing.

Now, a waking dream rose like a nightmare—the kind that defies consciousness, that persists outside the boundaries of sleep, that engenders phantoms under the bed or hair-raising breathing on one's neck. Standing there, I sensed blackness at my back. I felt the fear of turning to see what my utmost horrors must be and froze with the sudden terror of knowing and of not knowing. I knew someone was there.

He spoke to me. "Sometimes I know I am about to die." I did not turn around.

Any words, even these, were more comforting than the continued silence or the wild, roaring dervish howl that my tense muscles anticipated.

Talking to him was my escape. "And what do you do then?" I said, still unwilling to turn around.

"I close my eyes. I see myself hunting, sitting on a deer stand, camouflaged, fifteen feet up in a big old pine tree. Death is a royal buck coming down the path, sniffing the wind, looking around to find me in the empty woods. There I am loaded, cocked, and ready. I won't make a noise. I'm not hiding, just sitting above the scene, listening to the sound of a few leaves rattling along the ground. I'm not going to shoot. You can't kill death. I only hope he'll pass."

I was sure of his voice now. "Then what happens?"

He took his time telling me. He waited a good while in the silence and the cold. "I sit tight. I bear down in hunter's haven with stillness and patience. The buck comes below me, directly under my platform. He paws the ground a bit, shakes his antlers and waits. We both wait. He snorts once. I know he can sense me—his nostrils must have flared at my scent—but he doesn't know where I am. I am above him. He can't know where I am. It's like I am on the far side of a glass made a mirror by the sun. He can't see me, can't believe in anything beyond a deer's earth. I'm safe in a different world, one he can't find. Then he moves on. He follows the trail up a rise, turns on the path away from me, and disappears, first his hooves, then his legs, and finally his body, head, and antlers sink below the hilltop."

"This happen a lot, Roscoe?"

"Just three times in my life."

I stood in the toilet stall, my back still turned.

He took a long time to say it, but I sensed he wanted to tell me. I waited a while. Then, slowly, I turned and walked out of the stall.

He leaned in shadow against the closed door. I couldn't see his face, but his breath plumed away and up into the candle-lantern light. He spoke with the same sad reluctance I had heard in Mother's voice when she'd said, "Your father is dead."

Roscoe spoke carefully. "First time was when I saw the windigo. The night Morgan died. It changed my whole life."

I heard him struggle to control his breathing. He didn't continue for a minute. "Second time was the day I got out of prison. I came back home and found that my woman was gone. Five months after I was jailed, she had delivered my daughter and disappeared."

I wanted to ask questions, to get a better hold on what he was telling me, but he seemed to be prying words from a hoard he had held close for years, peeling them off one by one.

He inhaled deeply. "And the third time was tonight, when Danny and Cooley stormed in, and I figured out who you were."

This was exactly what Scummy had warned me of, and I had no idea what was about to happen. I would not have been surprised if he had sprung on me, something Cooley had whispered about. He could have raged or fallen into one of his bone-chilling moans. But his story about stalking death demanded patience. Facing him in the dark, I stood tall, though inside I hunkered down.

What came was neither attack nor release. It was more surprising than anything I could have thought.

He stated it as fact. "You've seen the windigo."

In the instant he told me, I knew it was true.

I was thrown, but just as during our handshake, I held firm. How he knew (more surprising, how *I* knew) was yet another twisted, unsteadying mystery pelted straight at me by my voyage north.

"Yes, I have. It sent me into the ditch. It was a huge white buck," I said.

"It still had its antlers, didn't it?"

"Yes. A huge rack."

He spoke to himself. "In the middle of winter."

"I swerved. It leapt over the Jeep."

"Did it talk? Say something? Make a noise?"

I couldn't stop myself. It was stupid, meaningless. "Yes. It snorted."

"What did it sound like?"

"I don't know. Like a sudden release. I couldn't understand what it meant."

His voice, still quiet, grew to a subdued, choked shrillness, "Was it my name? Roscoe? Did it say my name?"

I knew he was right. I had not recognized it when the buck snorted. I did not know his name or who he was or anything about him then, but now I saw the deer again. The bluster of steaming breath shot from its nostrils as it snorted, "Ruskh." Still, was it warning, information, premonition? I was wary.

"I don't know."

He stepped forward. His face glowed in determination. "Did it say my name?"

"I'm not sure."

Now he grabbed my arms, more in entreaty than aggression. The light bathed his eyes, wide, expectant and fierce. "It said my name."

"All right. I didn't know you at the time. But yes, it could have. It sounded like it." We both waited. "Yes, it said your name."

"You're sure, now."

"It's clear now." The reluctance in my voice convinced us both. "I'm certain."

He slumped against the wall. "Then it's getting close."

I could see only his breath in the light. He was puffing short and hard like a man who had just run up a long hill. It was distress I couldn't understand, except that it felt deep and dangerous. I was silent and guarded.

Roscoe had let go my arms and seemed to be unaware of my presence. He looked up toward the candle-lantern. He spoke to himself. "It was me who should have died." He slid back against the door.

I remained silent. Only his ragged breathing told me Roscoe was still present. Then quietly, growing less in volume than in area, a swelling moan filled the tiny room, eerie in the crisp silence that seemed to hold still while the moan filled even the spaces separating molecules of air between Roscoe and me. The sound expanded, pressed outward, powerful and painfully heavy. It flowed like a tide in the Gulf, long and pervasive. Then it stopped, and the silence crashed in my ears.

Still, I waited. Even though I could feel shivers rising up my back, I made no move toward the door.

Roscoe's moan released him from whatever hell he had come from. Now he was back with me in the toilet at Tillie's. "I know you haven't told anyone about the windigo," he said.

"It's not the kind of thing you want people to hear."

He stood away from the door. "Unless you're someone who has seen it."

I made no move to leave.

Finally, Roscoe spoke. "It wasn't a deer. What I saw first. But it doesn't have to be. The Indians say it comes differently to each person. It changes the man who sees it. Touch it, and you die."

He stopped, breathed more gently, evenly. "As soon as I knew you, I wanted to kill you."

I stiffened. "I'm glad you didn't."

It was true that I was in no shape to defend myself when I arrived. I knew he was tough, but I had him by five inches, and sleep had restored my strength some. I stood taut, ready, energized with cold.

"Me too. For once I thought about something."

Though not much made sense to me, it seemed almost normal next to the strangeness of all that I had endured after leaving Bobbie's. The visions and dreams I suffered seemed to inure me to this weird circumstance—standing in a darkened toilet, talking of ghosts and goblins with a longtime local who had just shared his thought to murder me.

"When Mary came back three weeks ago, I dreamed I could get my life back, the life I lost twenty-two years ago in a storm. Then I heard about you. You're her husband."

"For fifteen years. I've known her twenty. Half her life."

"I knew her the other half. I thought her coming back would solve things."

I didn't know what he meant.

He must have sensed the disjointedness of his story. "Listen. I don't think you want to hear this, but I loved Mary. We were a couple. Windsong is our baby."

I hadn't been too weary to piece together Roscoe's scarred history. I just had not wanted to admit anything to myself, at least until I had talked with Mary. Now the story was in the open. I staggered back against the urinal. I straddled it backwards, the cold china gouging my kidneys. "What?" I gasped.

Roscoe was eager to calm me. "We had run together for years. We had plans to marry. We planned to build a cabin on the lake."

His staccato testimony made it seem normal. I separated myself from the story. It was a different Mary he had known. He had courted another, earlier Mary. She was not really my Mary. I caught my breath again. "What happened?"

"I killed her sister. Her twin. I killed Jay's girl. Yeah, killed my best friend's baby, Scummy's child, and its mother."

The brutality of what he told me hit me like rapid blows of a cudgel. The blows of his confession were visceral and heady. Rage rose to my throat. I tasted bile.

The stillness shook. A moan erupted deep from within Roscoe's belly. This time it was wound tightly with horror, loathing, and truth.

This bear-man had a child by my wife, whose life was intertwined with a soul mate, a twin, Scummy's woman. The woman who carried Scummy's child and who died. There was no innocence in the world.

I heard the moans rise anew in a foul, sickening harmony that seemed to splatter to the floor like vomit.

Roscoe grew silent before me. I realized that my own moans had mixed with his. As if to comfort me, he grasped my head below the ears and held my jaws firm, closed. "Listen. It's bad, but not what you think."

"No. I don't want to hear. I'm sick."

"Listen. It wasn't my fault. No. It was, but I didn't want it to happen."

"I can't listen to this. I have to leave. I have to sleep."

"No. You've got to listen. You're the only one who'll understand."

I pushed his hands away. Pushed him back, hitting my head in recoil on the pipes behind me. I thrust off the wall, brushing by him. He was off balance and grasped the door but went down in a slick, foul mess on the floor. I pried the door open and used it to steady myself. I pushed the door against Roscoe and staggered out, banging into the toilet partition.

There was stirring everywhere. I heard Scummy rolling off the pool table to his feet. Chairs scraped the wooden floor. Max's muffled stocking-footed steps thumped down the stair.

I pivoted around the partition, steadied myself and tottered forward toward my pallet. I heard Roscoe bang the door open, bang the door shut, and rush after me. I went down hard under him in the middle of the barroom floor.

He flipped me over like a weightless carcass. He sat on me, pressed my shoulders against the floor with tremendous strength, and pushed his face nearly into mine, "You're going to hear this."

I heard tumult over me. Both Max and Scummy yelled, "Get off him!"

Roscoe held firm and roared, "Get back! Get back!"

"Listen." He hissed heavy and close. " We chased the windigo. Jay wanted to stop. We were drunk. We fought. I put him out. Beat him with a stick. I dragged him into the Buick and laid him out on the back seat.

"The girls had gone wild, especially Morgan, Jay's girl. Both ran. I chased after them, but they ran like scared, crazy does. Fast. I lost sight of them. I tracked them. Then I found clothes on the path. They were stripping off their clothes."

A collective inhalation around us seemed to suck all the air out of the room. Roscoe and I were now surrounded by the denizens of Tillie's. Flat on my back under Roscoe, I looked up at them—Gary and Jarvi, who helped bring me in, Scummy, Max and others I did not know but had seen. They tightened the circle looking down on us, not to restrain Roscoe but better to listen to what he was now saying. Their wild, wide eyes circled above told me they had never heard Roscoe's story before.

I saw the scene unfold. I had seen it before. I told it. "They ran. Crisscrossed the road. One without shoes, the other stark naked."

Now Roscoe jerked back from me. His eyes widened. He let go my shoulders. "You saw!"

I couldn't stop. I had to get rid of the vision by telling it. "You chased them to the clearing. They ran ahead toward the light. One fell in the snow, tangled in fallen logs underneath. The other, all naked, ran to the light."

Roscoe nearly screamed it. "Yes! Toward the light. That horrible light . . ." Silence crushed us.

My voice broke. "I didn't know it was you, but I saw you." I said it with revulsion. "You ran. You ran away." It was an accusation.

Roscoe hunched stiffly. "It scared me."

He looked up at the close circle that was his jury. "It called my name."

Then he bent his head again to me, just inches away from my face. His whiskey-laced sobs intoxicated me. "The light called my name."

I took over because I knew he hadn't seen the rest. "I saw what happened. She ran up the hill, naked, chasing after the light, skittering over the snowcrust. When she topped the hill, she dove into the light. I saw her again, running within the blazing circle, opening her arms to the circle of light."

Roscoe slumped over me. He was a man confronted by all the wrongs committed in his life. He sobbed. His terrible moan rose over us all, then, at once, was interrupted by an inrush of frigid air and a scream wilder than blizzard wind through naked trees.

A FRIGID GUST OF AIR SWEPT across the planked floor. The rush of air carried—and may have been outdistanced by—a shriek even more chilling that seemed to break through that end of the circle around me to thrust the onlookers back. The cry pried the circle open. There in the slowed time of what felt like my death, my transformation, or my emancipation, a screaming figure, black-clad in leathers, booted but hatless, her arms rising above her flowing black hair and trailing a long scarf, leapt high, vaulted off an extended leg—her leading leg cocked like a Valkyrie's crossbow—and flew at me, eyes flashing and wild, mouth agape, screaming. Her coiled leg released like an arrow as she herself sailed at us direct and square. She hit Roscoe, who, dragged from his misery, had suddenly risen to his knees and twisted toward the piercing cry. The impact sent him back to the floor. Both the screaming Valkyrie and Roscoe now yelling in pain, piled over me, my shoulders pinned beneath his legs.

"You son of a bitch! Get off him!"

I couldn't help but blurt out the obvious, "Mary!"

She did not acknowledge me. She flipped onto her back, now kicking at Roscoe, screaming, "Get your worthless carcass off of him, bastard!"

"Mary! It's me. Tatty."

She turned on me. "Didn't they tell you not to stop

here?"

"Christ, Mary!" Here I was—I lay on a barroom floor, beaten—travel fatigue pounded me; visions and dire dreams had ransacked my mind; my gut was in turmoil; my head, knocked and bumped, was achy and light; I had been attacked by a weeping lunatic, then by a screaming dervish. "That's all you can say?"

Mary whirled toward Roscoe. "What in the hell is going on here? What do you think you're doing?"

Roscoe, as wide-eyed as his visionary self I had seen escaping the windigo, was dumbstruck. His left shoulder sagged. He rolled his head side to side. "I had to. He saw it."

I rose up on my elbows.

She turned a horrid, strangled face to me, "See. He's a lunatic. This bughouse is an insane asylum!"

Deceiver flashed through my mind. You're the one who's crazy, I thought. The truths that both Scummy and Roscoe had disclosed tore at my chest. Mary had deceived me. Twice. Now she blamed me. I wanted to burn Tillie's to the ground.

"I brought him here," Scummy said without looking at Mary. He moved around Roscoe, looking at the shoulder. He slid a bar stool away and crouched next to him.

Mary hadn't looked at Scummy, and she didn't look now. "Sure you would. Do you think I hadn't heard? The whole lot of you are crazy." She seemed to include me as one of the nuts.

Wasn't I her husband? Her lover and partner for life? At Tillie's that idea seemed demented. No, not demented, diseased, sick.

Still, even here, Mary really wasn't crazy or ill. I looked at her. She was sane all right, and health thrilled in her every breath. Was she afraid? Was that why she had lied? But what was she afraid of? Why couldn't she tell me? Why now treat me like her foe? Was it the unbelievable, psychically convoluted details that made her go so far as to expunge a sister's existence from her life? From our life?

As if hearing my thoughts, Mary stood. "Let's go," she said, "you'll go nuts if you stay here longer."

I looked over at Scummy, but he seemed more interested in Roscoe's shoulder than in answering Mary's or my implied question. "I think you broke a collarbone," he said, "Can you lift your shoulder?"

Roscoe stared blankly at Scummy.

Mary extended her arm to me and braced herself as if to wrench me from the floor. I looked at Scummy again. "What do you think?"

"Yeah, Jay what do you think?" Mary echoed in rage.

Scummy looked to me and raised his gaze to Mary. He was calm and quiet. "Give me a couple of minutes with this shoulder. Then I'll tell you what I think. Okay?"

Mary stamped a boot. "Okay." She turned to me, "You can just lie there if that's what you want," she said. "Max, you got coffee?"

"Upstairs," Max said, "it's made." Without another word Mary stomped to the steps and banged her way to the second story. No one else made a move.

I sat up and looked around. Scummy tended his new patient. Roscoe groaned with the attention. They murmured with one another against the knotty pine panels of the bar stand. I heard something about an X-ray, then a clear and certain "no."

The clock said five a.m. It was pitch as midnight. The others had slunk back to their various sleeping spots. I was no longer the center of their attention. I forced myself to my knees then rose up gingerly. I grabbed a chair to steady myself and waited for some strength to return. I was alive but felt at least eighty years old.

Mary moved about on the floor above. She was right. This was no time to give in to lunacy. If this were a bughouse, I wouldn't be one of its inmates. I had to get things straight.

I had to go upstairs. I had to confront Mary. I glanced at Max, who was pouring whiskey for Roscoe. Scummy was about to set the collarbone "by feel." Max pointed me toward the stairway. I shuffled to the back.

I negotiated the narrow steps, careful not to trip on the overshoes and bottle stock that Max kept there out of sight of the patrons. It was dark. Dizzy, I felt my way along the walls to the door above, which opened out over the stairs. Nothing was easy. I had to back down three steps to negotiate the door swing and since there was no railing, I had to hold onto the knob as I climbed the three risers. Mary was no help. I entered a short hall, stepped over a fallen broom, and nearly stumbled on stray liquor bottles. Beyond was Max's kitchen.

Mary sat at the table weeping, her head in her hands. She swept back her loose hair and watched me enter. "I don't think Windsong is going to make it."

It took me a moment to comprehend. I had brought questions to ask. I had demands to make. But Mary had more immediate worries.

"The babies are fine, but I know something's wrong. She's bleeding too much. Granny took charge. She told me to come for you."

I struggled to move from what had just happened and what I was feeling below to this. "Is that why you flew at Roscoe?"

"No." She was sudden and firm. She shook her head. Her hair fell over her eyes and hands again. "Maybe."

She paused as I waited, "I suppose," she said, her mouth muffled behind her hands. Then she pushed her hair back and looked up at me. "I need you with me, Tatty."

I moved around the table and crouched beside her chair encircling her with my arms. "What can we do? Can we get a doctor to come?" I kept my knowledge about her daughter to myself for now.

"No one can get out there in time. The hospital is too far." She raised her face to look at me. "Tatty, I'm afraid."

I stroked her shoulders and kissed her face through veil of her hair that smelled of fallen snow and cedar smoke. "It'll be all right."

She managed to compose her voice and vision, swept hair from her face again and looked at me squarely. "I needed you with me. I waited. Then, when Danny and Cooley came and told me where you were, I couldn't stop myself. Granny said, 'Go' and I ran out to the wide track they brought and drove like mad the shortest way I knew, most of it off the real road. Tatty, why didn't you listen to those guys?"

"I had no choice. I went in the ditch."

"And Jay found you. Always the hero. He would bring you here. He didn't know."

"Didn't know what?"

"He wouldn't have known you were my husband."

"No, he didn't. I told him later. He may have saved my life."

She nodded and touched a finger to her lip. "Jay would do that."

I pointed to my temple. "He patched me up. He warned me about Roscoe."

Mary sprung alert. "What about him?"

Despite my urge to confirm or disprove what I had been told, I knew Mary well enough to let it out slowly, to have her grasp it, hold it before saying anything. "At first, he said that Roscoe had done time in prison for his part in a death."

"And then?"

Slow, go slow, I told myself. Seeing Mary as she was, I no longer wanted to wreck the place. I now worked to salvage what I could from this storm in our lives, yet I didn't know if I could get past Mary's lies. I wasn't sure exactly who she was, but my practical side finally demanded openness. To continue, we had to clear the air of every last thing.

"He told me about Windsong," I said at last.

Mary turned away, looked out the window. I watched her reflection in the glass. The image of Mary, her head propped above an elbow, curled two fingers over her lips, another two just aside her high cheek. The waver of the glass made her look sadder. I waited and watched.

She sighed. "I don't know if I would have told you." She pressed her lips tightly together.

I caressed her cheek. "I think I understand. I'm not sure, but I think so—at least that part."

"What part?"

"About Windsong." I met her eyes. "She's yours, no? She's your daughter."

Mary looked to the window again, then she shut her eyes. "And now she's dying."

Though her anguish shook me, an awful strength welled up my chest, exhaling warm comfort and steadying power.

"Mary, we may lose ones we love. Yes. But we don't will it or want it." As I said it, I understood in a new way what Roscoe had been saying.

She lowered her head toward me. I rose higher to meet her. "You did all you could. It's not your fault."

Mary sucked her breath. She shook her head slowly.

"Tatty. I wish I could believe that. You don't know. You don't know."

"I know about Roscoe." I immediately regretted saying it. What did I really know?

"What?" Her voice rasped. "That he's Windsong's father?"

Especially with Mary, I wasn't ready for such honesty. "Well, I . . ."

"He's not," she said. "He only thinks he is."

After what I had been through in the last full day, nothing surprised me. My hold on reality was as tenuous as snowflakes under a warming sun. I had had to shift my view of the world, of my life, and of Mary too often in the last eight hours to be either certain or shocked.

"He's not?" I wondered if Roscoe, half-crazy already, would fall further into madness if he knew.

I wanted her to answer the question of paternity, but I felt sorry for Roscoe, too.

Perhaps Mary caught sympathy in that tone. She said, "I don't plan to tell him."

"I won't either," I said. Suddenly, we were back on the same side, together against a world conspiring to unseat our happiness. I stood and guided her up into my arms. We held each other for a long time.

Eventually, she let loose. We both sighed.

"Your coffee's cold," I said.

She laughed and brushed her face with an open palm. I took her cup to the sink, dumped and refilled it. I pulled the other chair around to her side and set the coffee at her place. We sat down facing each other as we had hundreds of times.

"Look," I said, "I don't want to go forward on half-truths. Maybe it doesn't matter anyway, but I don't understand why."

"Why I didn't tell you about having a child?"

I waited, prepared to watch her face. "No. About having a twin."

She looked unsurprised, ready, but a little resentful.

She looked to the window. "These bastards have no decency."

Whom she meant was unclear. I waited.

"There hasn't been a day, not a minute in the last twenty years that I haven't thought of my sister, and every time, I've wanted to tell you. At first it was too fresh and hurtful. I was running. She was gone. I didn't want to bring her with me to the south."

"You didn't trust me?"

She smiled faintly. "I trusted you," she said, "but would you have fallen for someone who told you she was half dead? That half of her had died in a bizarre teenage stunt?"

I wondered. "Would I?" I admitted it. "Maybe not." I said.

"Well, it isn't something you bring up on a first date."

"No. But later?"

"Tatty, it's even more complicated than that. There are things I should have told you, yes"—she paused a moment—"and I will, but here, right now? I'm not sure this is the time."

Just then a snowmobile roared into Tillie's yard below us. Mary scrambled to the window to look. She grabbed the sash, "Hell, its Cooley," she said. "I know it's about Windsong."

Mary was around the table, pushing past me. She ran to the stairway and threw the door open, nearly leaping down the flight of stairs. She disappeared into the steep blackness before I could get out of my chair. I followed to the top step and stood looking down into the darkness.

I picked up that broom and glanced back at the lighted kitchen table. Spilled coffee was trickling over the metal edge. I went back, mopped up the coffee with a rag from the sink, and sloshed water around the cup under the wall-mounted faucet.

I stood at the sink, rinsing the dishrag, squeezing it out, and rinsing again. I stared dumbly at the pitted chrome of the ancient spigot handles. I studied the broken tiles on the backsplash, an alternating checkerboard of green and cream. One tile was missing. The teeth marks of the trowel arced through twenty-five-year-old mortar behind its place. I guessed the tile had broken when it fell.

How long I stood there stupidly, I don't know. I waited to hear something from the barroom. The rooms below had quieted like the storm itself. Silence crept into every corner. I wrung the rag one more time. A few brownish drops plunked onto the porcelain sink. I folded the rag and hung it over the faucet.

I turned to the stair head again and listened. It was absolutely quiet downstairs. I looked out the window above the kitchen table. Over the snowscape below fell a luminous silver glow, the moon shining through the scattering storm clouds, stringing silver ribbons over drifts and snow-laden pine boughs.

The scene was overlaid with my own image, reflected in the light that spilled from the kitchen lantern onto my face. I looked like a cold and lost kid in the glass. I stood looking into that boy's chilling gaze filled with the silent moonlight beyond his eyes. I looked for something. I strained to hear any sound of the land below, anything beyond myself—beyond the boy's self—something to hold on to. It was only light over glass. Nothing was there.

I turned down the steps. Slowly, I felt my way into the darkness below.

When I came to the turn of the stairway, I saw, over the rod that held heavy curtains, the flickering of a fire stirred up in the big stove. The heat did not carry up beyond the closed door on the stair; it barely penetrated the stairway through the heavy drapes that separated public space from private. I lingered there for a moment and listened to the crackle of wood in the firebox. The heat would be intense on the other side by the cast iron range.

I paused at the curtain. I heard low conversation. Several voices intertwined just above a murmur. Words rumbled in bass tones but were not plain. Others joined as if responding, like a chant, like, "Amen." The ineffable feeling of a wake flowed from beyond. The somber sounds hushed when I stepped into the room.

Five people sat around a bare wooden top table that had been brought toward the stove. Roscoe and Scummy sat together. Mary, who was furthest from the stove, was on their right. I couldn't see Cooley's face but suspected by his girth it was he with Max beside him who sat facing the others, their backs to me. Cooley's big parka hung off his chair. He extended one hand, his arm bared to the heat, across the table, holding Mary's wrist. His other hand toyed with an empty shot glass. A bottle of Jack Daniel's stood open in the middle of the table, and all but Cooley held shot glasses filled to various levels with the suede-dark liquor.

Like Cooley, all had shed their jackets and sweatshirts; the first time I had seen Roscoe or Scummy in anything but puffy, quilted coats. They looked diminished, stripped to an inner core like leafless trees in mid-winter. They stared at what looked like a pendant on a rawhide strip Mary dangled over the age-groved wood tabletop. The gathering looked like a solemn family meeting.

Cooley turned in his chair and solemnly nodded to me. He tilted his head toward the empty chair between Max and Mary. There waited a full, untouched glass on the table in front of the seat. Even so, I felt like an intruder. Not that I was unwanted, but I simply felt disconnected from the grief that weighed over the table and the deep history that connected each of these mourners to the others. This table was the lake that I hadn't yet seen, joining opposite and far shores into one continuous strand. I had been called here from an alien coast.

I stood behind Mary's chair. I placed my hand gently on her shoulder. Then I reached over for the glass, an island in the lake's center.

Cooley held the pendant up, turning it over in the dim yellowish light. The bob was the tip of a deer antler, about three inches long, deeply grooved and ridged, an ivory color streaked with variegated ridges of tan and brown. It had been carved into a dome shape at its wide end and was fastened to a silver ring through which ran a well-worn string of rawhide. Mary took it again and ran her thumb over the horn's surface.

"I hadn't seen this for over twenty years," she said.

Roscoe gazed at it, apparently entranced by what was dangling before him. "Morgan wore it all the time," he said.

Cooley took Mary's wrist once again. He squeezed gently. "Windsong asked Granny to get it from her hope chest. She wanted you to have it."

Mary wrapped her hand around the amulet and turned the other over to grasp Cooley's hand. "Windy," she said.

Cooley spoke low. "She was a beautiful woman."

I downed the shot.

Max grabbed the bottle, stood, and, refilled each glass. He held his aloft. "To all spirits. The departed and those with us, still."

Every one drank.

Mary was finished. Her face shone sallow and drawn in the firelight. Her shoulders slumped over her arms like the pine boughs weighted to ground by snow. She had been up all night, first with the births, the babies, and then with Windsong and tearing down the trail to Tillie's to find me. What had happened to her seemed the worst that could ever occur. She had lost a child. She had lost her only child. One she had, in truth, abandoned and, at last, recovered in her own middle years, only to lose her again. Mary looked defeated.

This hurt was something I could not comfort. She had moved back in time, seemed far away from me. Right then, I would have forgiven her all if it would mend her life, but forgiveness was not what Mary needed. What lay beneath her worn features was even more potent, more deadly than Windsong's loss.

Without turning to me, still holding Cooley's hand,

she said, "It's time to go back. I have to see my child."

Roscoe roused, returning from his far off reverie, pushed his chair back, scraping it across the floorboards. "I'll go with you."

"No." Mary's denial resounded. She slapped her glass to the table. "She is my child."

Roscoe's shock registered gravely in his eyes. "She's mine, too. I always loved that girl."

Mary raised her voice. "You don't know what you're talking about."

"Easy, boy," Scummy said. I wasn't sure if he talked as a medic, a friend, or a judge.

"If I don't know what I'm talking about," Roscoe defied them both, "I do know what I'm doing. I'm going up there. Those babies are mine as much as yours, Mary, maybe more."

Mary cut loose from Cooley's hand, stood and, pointing a sharp finger at Roscoe, yelled, "You go near that cabin, and you'll have neither arm to knit with."

"You surprised me once. You won't do it again. I'm ready. It's my right. She was mine."

"She was not yours," Mary seemed to have taken a step away not only from me but also from Roscoe and every other person at the table. I looked around. Scummy glared and shook. Everyone else was dropped-jaw surprised. Roscoe looked for a second like he had been punched.

"Don't pull that woman-bullshit on me," Roscoe sneered. "You think I don't know better?"

"I think you know nothing."

"Well, I'm going whether you like it or not." Roscoe stood. Despite his braced shoulder and broken collarbone, he set himself solid, defiant.

"No." Mary turned to ice. "You're not."

"See if you can stop me then." Roscoe hoisted his parka with his good arm.

Scummy tried again. "Hey, Giaco, think about it."

Mary stood. She reached across the table for the bottle. With one deliberate, deft, and powerful swing, she smashed the Jack Daniel's across the table edge. Shards flew up and away. She was left holding an ugly-looking bottleneck, jagged and sharp. Mary dropped into a crouch, waving the dangerous weapon at Roscoe.

"Don't," was all she said.

Despite his broken shoulder, Roscoe pivoted, dipped to snatch up the broken bottle bottom, and swung around in a circle, spinning to a crouch face to face with Mary.

No one moved.

"All right," Mary said. "Tell him, Jay."

"Mary," Scummy appealed. His was voice desperate.

"No. It's the only way," she said. She hissed at Scummy, "Tell him."

Scummy shook his head. He took a step away.

"You aren't Windsong's father, Roscoe," Mary flatly stated.

Roscoe grinned crookedly. "So who do you think is? I know you never had anyone else before."

Mary crept up from her crouch. "Yes, that's true. You're right about that."

"So she's mine."

Her voice was scraped and husky. "No," Mary said. She turned to Scummy who had backed up to the wall beside the stove. "Go ahead. Tell him, Jay. Tell him."

Roscoe held his crouch. He watched Mary. "Tell me what, pardner? Tell me what?"

Scummy looked again at Mary. "I'm sorry, Giaco. I

never thought she would come back."

"What the hell!" Like lightning, Roscoe crashed Mary against the far wall, pinning her bottle hand with his hip and bringing the bottom shard up to her throat. His fierce eyes burned a singeing glare. "What's he talking about?"

I couldn't move. Horror unfolded before me.

Mary moved only her mouth. "You'll be killing the wrong one, Giaco." Her calm assurance in the face of Roscoe's threat shielded her.

Keeping the weapon to Mary's neck, Roscoe looked at Scummy. "You tell me or someone is going to die here. She's saying I ain't Windsong's dad. I'm not granddad to her girls. Now how can that be? Friend?" He let the last word explode from his mouth. It sounded like a verdict.

Scummy came forward. "I swore I wouldn't tell. The sheriff was hot to jail her along with you."

Roscoe waited.

"We figured it would be safer for the kid and for her."

I looked around. We were all mystified. Roscoe was clearly confused. He waved his glass knife under Mary's throat.

"Cut the crap. I'm serious," he said. He raised his elbow higher as if to slash.

"Put it down." Scummy sounded resigned. He moved carefully closer and twisted the chair around. "I'll tell you." He looked defeated, sad, the loneliest man on a storm-torn earth. He slumped onto the seat.

Roscoe lowered the bottle shard but kept Mary and her weapon clamped to the wall. He faced Scummy. The heat in the room grew intense. Sweat beads stood out on every brow.

"Mary died that night, Giaco," Scummy said. "It was Morgan who lived."

Tiny slams down the frying pan. "If I had been there, that guy would have been lying on his own jagged bottle."

I look at him. Tiny, one hand on the frying pan, the other holding the dishtowel, appears more a domestic than a fighter. "Are you saying I should have done something?"

Tiny lifts the pan. He wipes it and places on the shelf. "I'm saying I've had problems with Roscoe. Any of those so-called Viet Nam vets there that night could have acted."

"Well, I hadn't fought in a war," I said "I wasn't a soldier. And what we all were going through at that moment inside Tillie's in the middle of the storm of the century was closer than I ever want to get to battle. It was hard to tell who the enemy was. To me we all seemed like bad guys—two held lethal weapons, one wallowed in his past revealing unforgivable sins, and the rest of us just cowered. I felt like an enemy, a comrade, an aggressor, and an innocent, all in one."

Tiny hangs the dishtowel on a peg, and sits. He folds the leftover fried walleye fillets in newspaper and slides them under the tarp into his refrigerator. "I'd say you were Roscoe's victim."

"Maybe. But at one moment, I was Roscoe's nemesis, the husband of the mother of his child, and the guardian of his grandchildren. At the next, I'd lost the same woman he had. I was nearly his twin."

Tiny is shaking his head. "You two're nothing alike."

"Again, maybe, but we were tied together by sorrow and by visions full of spirits, mystery, and fear. We both were touched by the windigo."

Now he waves a finger at me. "Sure but he had your wife by the neck."

"We should have been on opposite sides," I say. "He was threatening my wife, but I felt nothing but sympathy. I had a singular understanding of his suffering, and at that moment, I hoped my goodwill could help—him and us all."

"You were mixed up," Tiny says.

"That's it," I say. "The paradox confused me. I froze as he threatened Mary's life and did nothing to avert the danger."

"I would 'a' been in his face," Tiny says.

I draw in a deep breath and let it all out. "I know it's strange, but I am sure at that moment I would have bolted to the rescue had Roscoe been the one attacked."

Tiny recoils. "The hell you say."

"It was like being caught together in a hurricane, being swept into the waves, being lashed together over a barrel. Roscoe and I felt that same fear and that same determination telling us, 'If you act as brothers, you've got a chance.' I knew Roscoe's suffering—the jolt of his irredeemable loss. He lost a daughter."

"He never had one," Tiny says.

"He thought he did," I say. "He thought it for twenty years."

Tiny crosses his arms over his chest.

"Look," I say, "it's like he was in a plane that suddenly drops a thousand feet. What he thought was sure turned to nothing, not even thin air. I felt that way too, like I was in some kind of a vacuum."

Tiny looks at me like a judge. "Maybe it felt like loyalty or some sort of love to you, but it was just guilt. I watched him all those years. I know."

I'm going to be stubborn. I lean over the table. "You do know. So, you tell me."

Tiny carefully places his elbows on the table's edge. We are nearly head to head. "All right," he says.

"In the twenty years after prison, Roscoe acted a role. He pled guilty to reckless endangerment for his part in my sister's death."

"He paid his debt," I say.

Tiny holds up a hand. "Roscoe served only fifteen months of the sentence. And, really, two died, since she was carrying a child. Anyway, he was out. He played the part of a patient, waiting lover. What a joke! 'You'll see. Mary will come back.' He even told me that. He must have seemed right to himself, but ha. What an idiot."

"He didn't blame Mary for splitting?" I ask.

"Roscoe thought he knew her reasons. He told me once that he forgave her for leaving the kid. At first he looked for her, but no one could tell him a thing. Her whereabouts? Unknown."

I spring on this. "But you knew. All that time you knew that the woman he loved who had carried his child was not gone—but dead and gone."

Tiny sits back. He examines his hands as if he looks for guilt on them. "I knew. Yeah, I suppose I knew. How can you not know your own sisters, even if no one else can tell one from the other?" He grows tall in the chair. "Damn right I knew."

"And you said nothing."

Tiny grips the table edge. He rises and leans in. "Hey!" His voice rattles the house. "He killed my sister!"

I hold on. I need to understand. "Even when he was leaving the garden stock and wild strawberries on the doorstep, you gave him no hint."

Spelling it out, Tiny says, "He wasn't welcome." He lifts his palms to the air and shrugs. "Granny felt differently, but I said 'no way.' I didn't let him in."

Uneasy silence taut as a fishing line extends the length of the room. Tiny snaps the line.

"Okay, there was more. Yeah, he shared fresh-butchered game that he packaged and quarts and quarts of blueberries. True, he left them at the door. We ate the wild rice he harvested. We don't believe in wasting food. It's too hard to get. But let him near Windsong? Not on your life. That would have been wrong. You can see that."

"No," I say. "What harm would he do?"

Tiny grabs his ears as if to tear them. "What? Do you think the man isn't a killer?"

I open my hands for peace. I motion Tiny to his chair. "Okay. Okay, I'm not saying you were wrong. I get it, but at Tillie's that night, I felt sure of Roscoe's generosity."

"Generous? More like dangerous."

"Maybe it was buried under a ton of suffering, but his caring came from love and loyalty, not guilt. I sensed a wild goodness in him. In the short intense time I had known him, Roscoe was not moved by a twisted briar of regret. He suffered loss too openly for that."

"You romanticize things too much," Tiny says.

"I probably do." I rush on. "Look at all the waiting he did. He didn't know better, and no one who knew told him."

"You make it sound like I was the guilty one," Tiny

says. He seems angry.

"No. You're not responsible," I say, "but Roscoe gradually lost hope, gave over little by little to his moaning, drunken despair, chained in place, waiting.

"I saw him, a staked bear unable to touch a berry bush he could see and smell but that grew too far away. He could neither openly feed his love nor leave it behind."

"Well, boo-hoo," Tiny says. "He earned every minute of pain. G-o-o-d."

I ignore the jab. "I'm not trying to justify Roscoe, really. But think about it. As horrible as his life was through those years, the truth, revealed in that split-second damned any trickle of joy that had filtered through before that evening at Tillie's."

Tiny drops his fists on the table. "Hey. It isn't my fault. He watched Windsong grow up. Nobody tried to stop him doing that, not as long as he kept a distance. There was some joy in that. So it turned out to be false."

"Yeah, watch her. Watch her like a hunter from in a duck blind on a faraway shore. He figured he could wait for the push of winter to bring Mary home. Like circling in to a decoy, she would come for the girl. But it was Roscoe, the hunter, who was completely fooled. In a moment, the stark, naked truth of an unfulfilled oath shot them all under a winter sky, the girl, the mother, and the waiting hunter."

Tiny shakes his head. "If his woman and child were dead, it was because he killed them long before."

I look to the fishing holes now skimmed over with ice. "I can't help feeling for the guy," I say. "I see Roscoe, the migrating mallard lured in by decoys, lowering to the water, getting close to the blind. Suddenly, something is wrong. Buckshot sprays the air. Truth is horribly, bloodily revealed."

"You make it sound like he was a hero."

"No, he wasn't a hero. In some way, though, he was noble." I get up. I stand over the table, ticking off items on my fingers. "He watched over someone else's child for twenty years. He waited on the return of a woman dead for two decades. He spent his love on the dead. His loyalty spent for a lie. In a second, his life drained of hope. Roscoe's crime, if that's what it was, gaped black and self-mortifying. His wild escapade had not brought a careless fate to the untamed sister but against his own girl, against his own child. His recklessness had led them both to death. Roscoe was a walking tragedy." I sit down with Tiny.

I am not done. "He was like a snowman," I say. "He had kept alive a frost-family, a family he had brought to its own frozen end. It lived only though his cold, coal eyes."

Tiny goes to the door. He stomps his feet into his boots. "Jesus. You go on. I'm not listening to anymore."

I get to my feet. "Martin, please, I am not blaming anyone. Not you, not Granny, not Mary, Scummy or Roscoe, either. I'm just telling what I saw. The secrets Mary forced out of Scummy that night changed Roscoe."

I reach for Tiny's sleeve. I gently grasp his shoulder. "Right or wrong, I was his partner. It was horrible to see Roscoe ripped to shreds. I watched the truth slam him to the ground. It was ghastly. It drained me, body and spirit."

I let go of Tiny. He steps back to the table. "You're confusing him with Scummy." He leaves his boots on and sits. "You came in on the end of it. I suppose it looked different to you. Some of us had already checked our losses over twenty years."

We're both at the table again. "Yes," I say. "Scummy suffered, I know, but the same truth that gnawed at my gut tore at Roscoe. It ate at my loyalty to Mary. Roscoe had none of that left."

"Well, you've got a point," Tiny says.

"Roscoe was betrayed. So was I, by my wife and by myself."

"How's that?"

"Oh, I had been so satisfied with my life. I was real comfy. Then in a moment, I was in a dangerous storm. It defiled my existence. At the end, I lived Roscoe's pain."

"Okay. You deserved better. Yes."

"Deserved?" I say. "I don't think so. I made my own life. I lived with eyes closed. I shut them when my father went to his grave and sealed them when I sent Mother after him. What I had over Roscoe was that I had pieces I could put together."

"I'm glad you can see it that way," Tiny says.

"Well, partly. I couldn't define myself anymore by who Mary was or was not. Neither could Roscoe, not even through decades-long love. We each lost a woman we loved. Loss froze us. Looking at Roscoe, I wondered if my love had really existed any of those twenty years."

Tiny shifts in his chair but says nothing.

"Both Roscoe and I waited two score years to discover the hollow core in the trunk of our family tree. Mary's death—two decades ago for Roscoe, moments before for me—tied us together. It was as if Mary, chasing the windigo or whatever it was, reached across eight states to skewer my heart on the same stake that chained Roscoe. I could only hope that my suffering would be shorter than his had been. That's how we were different."

"So you blame Mary?"

"Who do you mean?" I say. "I'm calling her Morgan now. It was really Morgan who lied all those years."

Tiny shifts again. "I suppose that Roscoe had Scummy to condemn."

"He did. That's the shame. I couldn't quarrel with Scummy. Jay Lahtinen had done nothing wrong by me. He left out some truth that was too complicated and embarrassing, yes, but I felt nothing but gratitude for him. Scummy meant me no harm."

"Could you have protected him?" Tiny asks.

"I don't know. I had no idea what was about to happen."

Tiny's eyes flash. "You were told. Time after time you were told."

I bite my lip. It's true.

Tiny moves in on me. "You were fooled." He hits the table. "Twice," he says. "Anyone could've told where blame would fall. You just didn't heed those warnings about Roscoe."

"You're right. There was something from the beginning. Even before I met Roscoe." My voice sounds thin. "What do you think, Tiny? Did Roscoe know what he would do? And when?"

Tiny knits his brows and sneers, "He knew all along."

Tiny's look burns my face. I hide behind my hands.

"I'm not done piecing everything together," I say. I bring my hands to the table and look Tiny in the eye. "Maybe I was his patsy. I suppose it's true. It happened so fast."

We sit. Tiny brushes crumbs off the table. He tests his coffee, finds it cold, and sets the cup down again.

I keep trying. It's why I'm here. "Listen, Tiny, I need

to know what went on the night of the windigo chase. Tell me what you know?"

Tiny stokes the stove and makes another pot of coffee.

He takes his time. The coffee begins to perk, and he talks.

"Everybody at Tillie's knew. Enough of them talked. The case against Roscoe started with their stories. They all said that it had been Roscoe and Morgan, always the wild ones, who pushed the thing.

"Scummy was against it. Mary always went along with what others decided. So, it was three to one. Scummy lost the argument. They all headed out for the forestry station. Eight more followed in two other cars, but those turned back to the bar before things got hairy. The weather was getting bad."

I urge Tiny on by adding what I know. "The police didn't need much from the folks at Tillie's did they? Roscoe testified against himself. Didn't he tell the cops the whole thing that night?"

"Yeah, the whole story," Tiny says. "When the going got dangerous, Scummy dug in his heels. The three couldn't out-argue him, but Roscoe used fists. That fight made the sheriff zero in on Roscoe. He admitted he cold-cocked Scummy. Roscoe knocked him out with a pine branch and loaded him in the back seat. He'd covered Scummy with a sleeping bag. He wasn't a bad friend. Just a bad drunk."

"I imagine," I say, "that saved him from more counts, from more time."

"It did. Anyway, the girls took off on foot. Roscoe followed. The prosecution accused him of three wrongs: One, he got everyone out there. He assaulted Scummy, and then he disappeared."

"What about Morgan?" I ask.

"Well, the law would've loved to have Morgan. Morgan had tangled with the sheriff regularly, but always slipped onto the rez or teamed up with her sister to fool them. People told the law she got the chase going. Everybody said it was her own fault. The idea of the windigo set her off big time, and this wasn't her first escapade."

Tiny moves the coffee off the burner to let it finish perking. He continues. "We didn't know then that he'd run, but he did leave Morgan to search for her twin.

"After getting lost, she found the car with Scummy in the back. She kept up the search along the forestry station roads until the gas tank was nearly empty. Then, she drove to Lake Community Hospital. She might have saved Jay's life.

"As soon as she arrived at the clinic, she heard that a naked body had been found along a forestry station road. The whole place was jabbering about it. Morgan knew who it was. She automatically used Mary's name with clinic nurse. They didn't know the difference. Mary hadn't wanted to chase. She was always the innocent one."

I examine Tiny's face. I'm wondering.

"How do I know this?" he says.

I nod. "I just want to keep things straight."

"So did I," he says. "When Scummy was nursing Windsong through the measles, I had some time with him. I got most of it out of him. He and Morgan had been lovers. He knew pretty much everything."

"Is that when you found out? About Morgan?"

"That's when I knew for sure. Granny knew right away but didn't admit anything to me until Morgan was coming back. She had raised those girls and could tell them apart even with her back turned. I had put it to

Mary before she left. She just stared at me and shook her head. I thought she was lying, but I wasn't sure. With the way Scummy talked later, I knew."

I have more questions. "You know what I saw in that vision, but I don't know what actually happened after Roscoe ran."

I have Tiny on a roll. "Morgan said that she searched for Mary," he says. "Of course, when she talked about it, she switched the names. It wasn't only the gas tank being low that made her stop. There was no heater in the car, and she was getting frostbite. She nearly lost toes."

"What about Roscoe?"

"Six hours went by after they'd skidded out a' Tillie's. Late that night the sheriff heard Roscoe was raising hell in Orr. How Roscoe got there no one knows. It's nearly thirty miles away. They put him in the town lock-up. He babbled crazy stuff. That didn't help his case."

"Didn't anyone suspect Morgan's con?"

"Sure. The sheriff was suspicious, but, for one thing, we were born on the reservation. Records were made scarce. Those two were so much alike, only Granny could tell them apart every time. If they wanted to fool me, they usually could. After that night, Morgan kept out of sight."

"So they issued a death certificate for Morgan Bassett," I say.

"Yep. Took their sweet time, but then Jay and Morgan were off the hook. Of course they couldn't be a couple anymore. Not here. Anyway, Jay had to grieve."

"So Scummy lost his woman, too."

"All three of you did." Tiny shakes his head. "If he hadn't been so drunk, they could 'a' got Roscoe for manslaughter. At least they thought he was drunk. He was either drunk or crazy. He babbled about the windigo constantly."

Tiny's words make me smile. "I know they believed nothing of that."

Tiny grins. "Well, I've never seen one," he says. "By the time Roscoe was released, Mary was gone. Windsong stayed with Granny. Granny never tells anything."

"I suppose Scummy figured he could keep quiet too," I say. "Did Morgan tell Jay she was leaving?"

"I think Granny was the only one she told. I came in one day, and no Mary. Granny said, 'Now both sisters gone.' I was the one to tell Jay."

"Poor Scummy," I say. "To admit anything would have brought on more heartache. He'd tell no one. He might have promised Morgan he would, but he couldn't tell Roscoe. He'd allow Roscoe to continue thinking he had killed Morgan. Scummy accepted the risk. He knew holding back could drive Roscoe and him apart like nothing else. Still, he couldn't let Roscoe know he'd killed his own Mary."

"I'm the one that had bad times with Roscoe," Tiny says. "He and Scummy stayed friends."

The dust motes stream along sun rays piercing the burlap. "Yes," I say, "only because of Scummy's chicanery. Roscoe would think his friend had forgiven him. And because Roscoe thought he had killed Scummy's girl, he'd never bring it up. He wouldn't rub salt in wounds. That helped Scummy cover for never talking about the windigo chase. Each had his own motive. Roscoe and Scummy never talked about the sisters."

"Jay was too soft to tell Roscoe anyway," Tiny says. "He took care of everyone. Every person on the lake owed him a life, if not his own, a family member's. He did not hurt people. He just couldn't do it. He was a medic. He was that way before he went to Nam."

"Scummy was like a doctor," I say, "choosing to do an emergency appendectomy. He must have seen small chance that all would fall apart. He had weighed the alternatives and concluded it was the reasonable choice."

Tiny puts it bluntly. "No. Jay didn't think it was a gamble to keep quiet, but he was wrong."

I slump back in my chair. "I felt close to Roscoe, but I made the same mistake Scummy did. That night showed me how wrong I was. It showed me how wrong we all were."

I WAS FROZEN TO MY CHAIR in Tillie's barroom. The full situation of that moment, I knew fully, understanding Roscoe's pain, Morgan's deception, my own loss, and both Scummy's reluctance and release. At the center of it all was Morgan.

Morgan's stamina for emptiness mystified me. She must have culled that fortitude from deep inside this forbidding northern landscape, sinking so deep down that it was preserved by slowly consuming her own self. Emptiness left her a skeletal Morgan beneath an outer shell of Mary.

Her deception explained the wild, nighttime outbreaks of destruction and despair through which, I had thought, we struggled together over the years of our marriage. Who, even in the presence of total strangers alone, could subsume a personality forever below another's? Not even a twin sister. Who would not break, burst forth suddenly at times in the face of being crushed from within like a black star?

What must have been Morgan's suffering over the years—much of which I suffered as well without knowing its source or reason—drew scant sympathy from me in that instant at Tillie's. Even her position, staked to the wall under the power of Roscoe's torso with a razor-edged bottle shard at her throat, gave me no qualm. Somehow, I trusted Roscoe at that moment more than I could my own wife.

Years of strife and yearning came to a head in a decrepit Northern Minnesota tavern, shuddering in the natural and human carnage of a once-in-a-century blizzard. Piercing me on the power of that storm was something far greater than even the Canadian half-continent could spawn. Something blew in that released me from the ties of marriage. Now I knew storms. I didn't know Morgan.

It had always been easy for me to ignore damage and turn immediately to rebuilding, to face away from the hurt, even as it scabbed over and scarred. That ability brought me success in my trade.

Even as a kid I stood ready to turn from the shock and haunting rattle of my father's death. I bricked up his memory, mudded, sanded, and painted the wall, and shifted my attention away. My source of comfort was my future with Mother.

When she approached her own end—she knew my isolate leanings perhaps better than I—I shunted her off to her sister. It was at her request after all, but I threw myself into college life to shut her out. Then Morgan appeared to fill that void I refused to feel, and I wrapped myself in her life, away from Mother's grim reality.

Now that half a lifetime was turning upside down, as if the old oak floor of the tavern had tipped drastically, shifting me along with it. I instinctively turned my allegiance away from a wife buried already twenty years to a man I had so recently met in this ill-fated excursion into the north.

My encounter with the windigo had unhinged all connection with my marriage. It was as if a great hand had slipped the top linchpin of a storm shutter. It strained away from its jamb on its lower hinge, inevitably tearing away by its own weight at the slightest hint of a storm. I might never speak of the windigo outside the confines of Thief Lake, but it left me the wreckage of a hurricane.

So when Roscoe spoke to me, I took it as a new direction. I was ready to turn away to build something out of disaster. I moved at his insistence, intent on saving him and myself if I could. I didn't question where my actions would lead.

Scummy sat with his head in hands before Morgan who Roscoe still pinned to the wall. Roscoe, shard in hand, regarded Scummy with that same horrid, lip-lifted grimace I had seen in my vision of him escaping the windigo. Scummy was sobbing. His shoulders shook.

"Tatty," Roscoe said, using my name for the first time, "take this woman's weapon so I can let her loose, would ya?"

Open-mouthed, I nodded.

Roscoe sounded kind, almost polite with the patience of an experienced hunter. "Hold on to her when I let go, please."

She struggled. Knowing her power, how Roscoe kept hold, despite his broken collarbone, I could not imagine. She was like a fierce moth on a pin.

I circled the table to get to the bottleneck she held in her left hand. As I passed Cooley and Max, I placed my hands on their shoulders as much to steady myself as to assure them things were going to be all right, to maintain calm, no matter what happened. As I passed him, I touched Scummy's shaking shoulders, doing my best to telegraph comfort and calm down my arms, using his own words "It's going to be all right, Bud." I patted him twice.

Morgan was still struggling. "Don't trust him, Tatty. You don't know him."

The words sounded familiar but pronounced in such a voice that I couldn't conceive of any truth to them. It was Morgan who was speaking to me. She rose now to the surface of the woman I had known. She spoke in a strange tongue. She uttered lies.

I nodded as if I understood. I found my voice. "It will be all right. You know me."

"You don't understand, Tatty. This is deeper than you can know," she said.

Like a figure in a dream, I moved toward her through a stilled landscape.

Roscoe held firm and calm. "Give him the bottle." Then he glowered at Scummy. "All this time . . ."

Scummy only rolled his head in his hands and swayed in his chair as Roscoe had on his bar stool.

As I approached, Morgan cautioned, "Tatty, he's crazy, don't you see? Haven't you seen what he can do? Don't."

I reached out, thinking that for the first time in my life—maybe since "being brave" for Mother—I was taking charge, leading instead of following at a distance. I grasped her wrist gently, avoiding the tips of the glass spears. "Please, Mary," forcing myself to use that familiar name, "let go."

I spoke in the same comforting tones I had used when I found her at midnight, bloodied, bare foot, standing in the middle of the kitchen floor surrounded by shattered china. At both moments, a deep tranquil power steered my feelings. I was in emotional command.

I couldn't see her eyes for Roscoe's body in the way, but I imagined her look, desperate but deterred. I pressed my fingers to her pulse lightly in reassurance. I felt her heart beating hard all the way down her arm. Then her left hand's grip relaxed. I slid the fingers of my hand along her palm and dislodged the bottleneck from her loosened hold. It fell to the floor.

Even before the bottle hit the floor, Roscoe whirled and dissolved from between Morgan and me. I held her, as a husband—and as a hunter capturing his quarry. Morgan, now disarmed, accepted my grasp. I hugged her upper arms and shoulders, at once holding and soothing. She resisted only in her despairing tone. "Fools, fools," she muttered.

With Morgan in my arms, I touched my forehead to the wall. I heard Roscoe's steady, slow intonation, like a dirge, "You knew all the time, friend. You knew."

Scummy replied, but I couldn't make out the words.

Below the words Roscoe spoke I heard the beginning of that low rumble I had come to associate with his despair, that unworldly moan I had heard first in a dream, then from the bar stool, and later filling the putrid atmosphere of the men's room. "I got nothing. Empty hands." His moan swelled. My own chest expanded with the breaking of his heart. "I should have left you to sink into the swamp."

Again, Scummy spoke, but it didn't come through.

Roscoe uttered words surrounded by moaning, "Stand up, Jay. Let me see your face."

I held Morgan. I couldn't turn. I heard the chair scrape as Scummy rose, then a shocked "hey" from Cooley and Max together, followed by a low-down grunt and two chairs clattering back from the table.

I let go of Morgan and spun around with the crash of chairs. Roscoe's right arm, driven into Scummy's gut with the strength of a twenty-year rage, raised him entirely off the floor. "No more," Roscoe said. With that, he flung Scummy to the floor, whirled, and fled through the door before either Cooley or Max could tackle him. A peculiar flapping sound stopped us all and drew our eyes to the man on the floor.

Scummy rolled side to side twice. Blood soaked his shirt where Roscoe had driven the bottle bottom into him. Scummy held himself up on his elbows. The square bottom of the whiskey container plainly showed at the center of the freely flowing stream of blood.

Scummy struggled up and said, "Shrapnel. Seen it before."

Morgan had collapsed against the knotty pine wall and slid to the floor. With everyone gathered around Scummy, no one moved to the door. The roar of a snowmobile could be heard starting, sputtering, then speeding off from the side of the building. Max was on the phone. I heard "Hurry, it's Jay Lahtinen" and "Not much hope." Cooley bent to Scummy, doing the only thing that could be done, patting his shoulder, saying, "It's going to be all right, Bud."

I staggered to the door to follow Roscoe. I flung the door wide and peered into the darkness, but in a new eerie glare, I could see nothing. Sometime during the last minutes, the electricity had been restored, and the lamp over the door blazed, blocking out by contrast all that lay beyond.

I listened intently. What I was listening for, I didn't know. I pushed my senses beyond the curtain of light. I heard nothing. Morgan had been right.

Max, off the phone now, stood behind me, took my shoulders in his large hands, turned me away from the door, and nudged it closed with his foot. The barroom was ablaze with neon signs and overhead bulbs that lit the wake of murder. I knew without looking that Scummy was dead, a fatality of the windigo he had argued against chasing over twenty years before. It had finally come to him.

Twice, outside noise cut through the morbid hush in the barroom. Once it was the passing of the grader, at which Max went out. He spent ten minutes, judging by the idling of the diesel, telling the driver all that happened. The second sound that came much later was the insistent whirr of the sheriff's and the ambulance's intertwining sirens, feeling their way down Hongisto road.

We all crowded out the door on to the porch. The sheriff, standing in front of his car looked at us—a forlorn group—and said only, "All right. I suppose there's no hurry, but let's go inside."

Without a word being spoken, the scene had been tidied up a bit, some chairs righted and moved. Max swept up the pieces of the bottleneck Morgan had grasped. He emptied the dustpan somewhere behind the curtain, perhaps outside. Someone—it might have been Cooley—mopped up much of the blood. A bucket on wheels stood nearby. Scummy lay covered with one of the blankets off the stretcher.

All of us who could bear witness seemed to have come to a tacit agreement that what had happened was a horrible accident between arguing, drunken friends. Let the authorities level charges and accusations. During the sheriff's visit, I held to calling my wife Mary. The rest followed my lead. As far as the law was concerned, Morgan was still dead.

During the questioning, I learned that Scummy and Roscoe owned Tillie's and that Max ran the place for them. Sorrow pervaded the rooms. The ambulance attendants wrapped Scummy up and removed him to their vehicle. Coming as far as they had to the lake, the medics would be on their way to retrieve Windsong's body as well. Father and daughter would travel together to the grave, their unannounced blood ties buried with their bodies.

Morgan and I would lead the way on the snowmobile, towing the stretcher as Scummy had done. The ambulance would follow only as far as the end of the pavement half a mile ahead. Cooley, with one of the two medics, rode the skidoo. He was after Danny, who, he said, would want to ride back to the ambulance with Windsong. I got the idea that Danny was father of the twins, although, as far as I knew, Windsong had never been explicit about it. According to Morgan, even while we were in Florida together, the babies were just her cousin's, no father named.

The sheriff said Roscoe would be found by nightfall. They wanted to talk with him before making charges. "Not many places to go here, especially, in fresh snow. He knows that as well as anyone."

As our two snowmobiles and the ambulance set out, thin light whitened the sky.

At the sheriff's order, Max had scrawled and hung a notice beside the door "Closed for Now."

PART III

Visions

Suddenly he found himself with them, coming along the trail and looking for himself. And, still with them, he came around a turn in the trail and found himself lying in the snow. He did not belong with himself any more, for even then he was out of himself.

Jack London, *To Build a Fire*

I RODE BEHIND MORGAN on the snowmobile Scummy had used to rescue me. It was difficult to talk above the din of the machine, and neither of us had anything to say. We were both completely bundled up against the sharp cold that followed the storm south out of Canada. I was beginning to understand what can happen in deep cold, when even spitting is a chore. Saliva freezes on lips and snaps in the air. Even through layers of clothing, I felt the frigid danger splayed against the cheery, brightening landscape.

We left the ambulance on the road and cut through the trees to the lake just past the gas station. We skimmed over the drifts of snow the blizzard winds had piled along the lakeshore. Everything was white. This low-lying side of the lake was ringed with willow at its edge, and birch farther up on the first hump of the land's rise. Both species wore white bark and were heavily plastered with snow along their trunks and atop the major branches of their windward side. One cabin roof nestled amongst the birches peeked above a snowdrift. The chimney puffed white smoke against a brightening dawn.

Early light and smoke drifted over the blanched expanse of the lake. But for engine noise and our slow movement through fresh snow, all was coldly languid and still for miles around, hushed by the undulating berms of blown snow which covered everything: lake, forest, cabins, and hills.

The splendor of the land's beauty could not diminish the horror of Jay Lahtinen's death. Nor could a new day remove the sorrow over Windsong, her body—spent giving birth—now being readied at Granny's cabin.

My own mood was a brooding one, despite the passing of the snowstorm and the wonder it had spread over the land. My world had changed as radically as the lake and its surrounds after the nor'easter smothered it in three feet of snow. I began to wonder if the cabin ahead would hold any contentment for me but pushed those desperate thoughts away as soon as they presented themselves. I felt as if I were trying to shovel snow with a pitchfork, attempting to open a path all across the lake in order to reach the point in my life, in my marriage, and in my world from which I had started out just the morning before. As concerned as I had been then about my reunion with my wife, I was now far beyond alarm, beyond fright or flight, and nearing despair.

Even though Morgan handled the snowmobile expertly as we moved past the shoreline, I held a horror of hidden snowcaves hollowed out by the warm agitation of springs active all the year-long. They could work below the surface, thinning the ice. I flinched mentally at the possibility of breaking through the crusted lake, fatally drenching myself in the killing, subzero cold. I feared even this adventure that had already proved ill-advised and stupid could be deadly for me.

At least I was not alone. An ambulance stood by a mile back. We had company. I hoped keeping close to the shore that we were running over solid ice. It may have been the close proximity of death—two deaths now— that brought morbid thoughts of a freezing demise to mix with my old phantoms of postmortem lengthening nails and hair inside my father's coffin. I sought what comfort I could.

Just to ride the snowmobile, I had to overcome estrangement. I found myself clasping Morgan around the waist—I became more comfortable thinking of her as Morgan now that we were away from Tillie's. In the light of dawn, she seemed less a stranger. Like the times I let her lead me, as in our studies of Native lore, I once again leaned on her for support in a treacherous, whitened world she knew much better than I.

I sensed she accepted my cinching arms with some relief, and in this way we moved across the lake's ever-brightening surface, communicating with limbs and torsos rather than words.

I tried to feel her hurt, as I had been able to do with Roscoe, but could see myself only as someone she needed to count on. I could not feel her loss, but since she clearly needed me, I buried my rasped and tender hurts below a stalwart caring with which she was familiar.

The winter air, as frigid as it was, refreshed my mind and spirit and cleansed my judgment of murky alliances that had confused me in dreams and in Tillie's torpid atmosphere. I even thought, perhaps things can turn out right after all. With the coming dawn, a little hope welled from the warmth inside my layer-wrapped body.

Ten minutes into our ride on the lake, a section of the forest ahead of us separated from the background trees to stand out as a defined, linear arc, a point of land jutting into the expanse of white lake. The trees on the point swept past the background forest as we moved abreast of what would prove to be the small cove beyond that I had seen in my wife's paintings. At the base of the point the land rose forty feet above the shore, reaching toward hills that rolled further above the lake. Eventually, the far ridge of these hills, I knew, would drop into a valley where Granny lived. Higher hills beyond looked shadowy and dun by contrast with the intense brightness that sparkled on the ridge before me. The shimmering, snowcapped lake flattened below it all.

Morgan turned her head to shout through the scarf and high collar that hugged her hood close to her head. "Granny lives up there in the valley," she said pointing up the spine.

She turned the snowmobile toward the hills and mounted a trail that after last night was only a shallow snowy depression between the trees leading upwards from the tip of the cape. The going was slow. Our weight on the machine packed the snow down over the buried trail. Cooley and the medic followed a hundred yards back.

We gained a promontory that was clear of trees overlooking the lake on one side and Granny's valley on the other. From her cabin in the valley below, a single column of white smoke rose from a stovepipe, much of which was covered in rooftop snow. The plume widened only slightly as it rose in a narrow funnel, then was whisked south by the drift of frigid air cutting high across the valley. The plume bent sharply and flattened horizontally on the airwaves like a wake left by Canada geese flying south in autumn. Morgan pulled over close to a tall slate outcrop festooned with snowy beards. She killed the engine. Cooley pulled up alongside several feet away.

Morgan was in control again. "Take this machine," she said, "so we don't have to unhitch the sled."

Cooley nodded. The stretcher was fastened to the sled behind us. "I guess we can do that."

"Tell Granny that as soon as you get back here, we'll go down."

Cooley nodded again.

"Granny will have her ready, I know."

He said nothing but hoisted himself out of his crouch and stood tall on the broad seat. The medic did the same.

Stiffly, I rolled off the side of my perch to make room and stepped off onto the snow between the snowmobiles. I went down nearly to my neck, catching myself, spreading my arms wide to prevent a deeper plunge into the chasm beneath the crust.

The men, standing seven feet above me on the snowmobile seat, stared. Morgan rose and turned. First Cooley, then the medic, then Morgan and, then, at last, I erupted in laughter in exhaustion of the gloom and the grief we had held in.

Soon we were roaring with belly laughs, and those three were wiping their streaming eyes. Mine crusted with freezing tears. I had to stop. The jiggling of laughter was pulling me further into the snow. With each slip of my body downward, the trio above pointed and laughed.

Cooley said, "You look a nail driven into a board. Only your head's showing." They chortled some more.

I was buried above my armpits in the drift. I wallowed furiously against the snow, reaching, sinking, and then swimming upwards toward a handhold on the snowmobile tread. They roared once more. I could only smile at my predicament, a Floridian rube surrounded by Minnesota pioneers.

With a spring deft for a man his size, Cooley vaulted over me across the space between the snowmobiles, landing squarely to stand on the broad seat where I had sat. Morgan jumped across to the seat vacated by Cooley. The medic also sprang over me and took my former seat behind Cooley who moved forward to the driver's bench. All three straddled their seats again. Reaching down, they twisted me around to where Morgan sat and helped me pull myself up behind her on the other machine. I clambered onto the seat, plunked down, and looked at each of them. We burst out laughing again.

"Brush yourself off before that snow starts melting in your collar and cuffs," Cooley said. "And don't step off the skidoo until she tells you to."

I loosened my collar and boot cuffs and shed the snow that had been driven beneath my clothing during my plunge. They were still laughing. I could only shake my head.

"We're going to be at least a half hour," the medic said.

Cooley pointed at the sled. "Take that blanket back there." The medic handed the blanket to me across the hog-wallow I had created in the snow. "Keep bundled up," Cooley said. "It's got to be at least twenty below." He started the machine and moved forward down the hill toward Granny's cabin.

Morgan and I watched them descend the hill, making switchbacks, moving slowly in the fresh snow. The sled, riding empty, followed easily over the banks at their turns. Gradually, the noise of their machine faded.

At the cabin below where the chimney poured out white smoke the two were tiny figures. When they dismounted the machine, they sunk into the snow as I had done. They floundered down the embankment to a shoveled path, keeping the stretcher from the sled between them. I found out later that Danny had shoveled that path between the cabin and the outbuildings during the watch over Windsong.

First Cooley, leading the sled, and then the medic disappeared into that narrow crevicelike path that led to the cabin door. They would return nearly an hour later.

I moved a bit back from Morgan, sat cross-legged on the bench seat, and wrapped the blanket around me. I was feeling the first shivering tremors rising up my spine. Morgan lifted her legs and pivoted around to face me. It was the first time we really looked at each other since Max's kitchen.

She loosened the tie of her high collar, then the scarf that bound her chin. Hanks of her shining black hair flowed out from behind the unfurled hood. Against the now brilliant white of the hills, she appeared dark and noble. Her eyes flashed in a momentary warming ray, then closed to wash the cold away behind the warmth of her eyelids. She pointed with her bare chin up and behind me, then said, "Look, Tatty."

Golden shafts of the rising sun's light split the tree line on the opposite side of the lake into a hundred blazing fingers. The rays raced across the sparkling drifts on the ridge above us, creeping down the banks toward the saddle where we sat. In a few minutes, we would be bathed in sunshine.

"It's like magic," Morgan said. She pointed to the sunrise. "No matter what happens to people or what they do, this rolls on."

She sighed.

I turned to her from the glory of sunrise that filled her eyes with gold. "I'm afraid I've had about as much 'magic' as I can take in one day, even if it is beautiful."

She spoke simply and directly.

"I betrayed you, Tatty." She did not sound defensive.

Maybe she didn't mean it as an apology, and I wasn't ready to accept one. I needed time. "It's hard," I said and looked toward the rising light.

In the stillness of the hundred square miles surrounding us, our words sounded like stark whispers breaking through the frozen crust of thought.

"We've both been betrayed," Morgan said.

I thought of Scummy, of what had happened, maybe because I had disarmed Morgan. I had run the scene scores of times over in the four hours since it unfolded. I was sure that no other result but death could have occurred. Who killed and who was murdered might have been other people had I acted differently—either could have been Morgan or me. Roscoe might have died. The shadow of this kibosh was destined to darken Windsong's wake.

Someone had been about to die. I knew that with the same certainty that I knew no one could have prevented Mary, the real Mary of twenty years ago, from chasing and catching the windigo. It was as if the events of that long past night had broken through like the storm, covering everything present, not in snow but in blood. About that, I had already come to a conclusion.

I told Morgan, without rancor or self-righteousness, "I disobeyed you. I did not betray you."

"I didn't mean you, Tatty." She sighed, looked toward the sunrise and then off to the hills rising beyond Granny's cabin. When she turned again to me, she wiped her cheeks, her eyelids lowered.

"Jay was supposed to tell Roscoe after he came out on parole. I couldn't face him without anger, and maybe remorse, but Jay told me he would ease it by him. It was what I wanted to hear. He never did, though. When I came back, it was like everything had been frozen in place for twenty years." She looked at the lake once more.

I waited for her to continue. "The mess I had left behind was the mess I walked right back into. Now you know why I had to come. I would have come for Windsong, even if I had known that Jay had kept the secret.

"It sounds strange, I suppose," she continued, "but I know Windy's parentless beginnings couldn't warp her. She was strong at birth. Granny raised her well."

Morgan looked at me. "I don't love Jay. We were young. What happened back there at Tillie's was bound to happen anyway, maybe in a so-called hunting accident, but both Scummy and Roscoe lived by the same code. I hate to say this after what I've held back, but a twenty-year secret is fatal to a friendship."

A light, frigid breeze curled Morgan's hair from her cheeks and collar back to her shoulders. Her averted eyes, her profile against the snow, and her lips set firmly to each other all spoke of a rising inner strength, a decisive motion about to unfold.

I clutched the blanket closely to staunch the unsettling tremors my wet ankles and wrists ignited. I was helpless on that frozen hilltop, exposed, and threatened. My teeth began to chatter. I had to pee. I strove to control my body that wanted to buck and shake.

Morgan didn't look at me when she spoke now. She continued to gaze toward the trees that bordered the side of the cove opposite the point on whose spine we waited.

"I'm going to stay, Tatty."

As if to confirm the rightness of her words, the

sunrays reached us at that moment, reddening Morgan's lips and cheeks, warming the blanket at my back. My shivering subsided in that warmth.

This was the fear I had sensed lurking in that dark space both behind me in the Jeep and at the back of my mind years earlier during my father's burial. Revealed in the sunlight of that moment, Morgan's decision seemed natural, correct, and inevitable. The long time I had feared it—maybe back to those first extended phone calls to Windsong and Granny Bassett, months ago—seemed wasted. "For the babies? For Windsong?"

She bit her lip hard and squinted at the blaze of the sun like she was doing penance. "I couldn't save her. She slipped away right before my eyes."

"Childbirth is cruel," I said, nodding.

"No. I mean Mary. I couldn't catch her. I couldn't save her." She searched the snow as if to look for her. Her voice was a whisper, "I couldn't save my sister."

Suddenly, the crashing of the dishes in the kitchen years ago took on a new and desperate meaning. Back then, Morgan was reliving the scene that first introduced me to Roscoe—the windigo chase and Mary's death. Morgan had run from her past, but she had dragged it behind her like the sled tethered behind the snowmobile. It was like my father's coffin I had pulled along all my life.

Her return to face the wreckage those broken dishes symbolized was unavoidable. Like a lodestone to the magnetic north, Morgan was pulled, perhaps by the windigo's power, to this ridge, full of despair, full of certainty, full of vain hope.

As irresistible as my wife was in her domineering moments, she was more so when vulnerable. Despite the antipathy Morgan's lies brought on, I could not stop myself from folding her in loving comfort.

I opened the blanket, slid forward to wrap my arms and legs around Morgan, who now was infected by the chills and shaking that had just minutes before left me. I wrapped her shoulders, drew her body to me, and embraced her. "I know. I know."

I held her hunched against me, stretching the blanket around us both, while her shivering rose then subsided. Part of me wanted to lead her down the trail, as I had through the shards of dishes in the kitchen to the bedroom, to tuck her in a bed the fire had warmed down there in Granny's cabin.

I said nothing more. As near as we were, I felt still a chasm between us. Though I was twice tempted to apply the comfort of Scummy's healing mantra, instead I simply patted her back and shoulders from time to time. Might everything be all right? I wondered. It was only a hope.

Over her shoulder, I saw Cooley, the ambulance man, and a figure that had to be Danny preparing to hoist the sleigh back over the embankment. They did it with all the decorum and grace they could manage. Danny seemed in charge while packing their path with his snowshoes. He ceremoniously hooked the sled to the machine. In a moment, they would start the engine and head our way with Windsong on her bier.

Morgan hugged me close. She breathed deeply. "Stay with me."

That was all it took. In the warmth of the sun-heated blanket, holding Morgan felt suddenly true and right. She slid her arms beneath mine. At that instant, I could have promised her anything.

THE MOMENT AND THE IMPULSE PASSED. Below, Cooley fired the ignition of the snowmobile, and the three men began the slow ascent with Windsong's body.

Morgan turned toward the sound, moved away from me along the seat, and let the blanket drop from her shoulders. Then she couldn't look.

Tears spilled over her cheekbones, froze to her ruddy skin in defiance of the feeble warmth of the sun's rays. She brought her gloved hands to her face, wiped the ice away, and bit at the leather to quiet her turbulent anguish. Still, coils of grief sprang from her belly. As if she were pressing out her hurt, she broke forth in a cipher of a rousted hawk, like a solitary falcon, crying upwards, cutting the frigid silence with alarm.

Though the shrill outburst startled me, I slid along the seat toward her, offering again the comfort of the blanket and my embrace. She said, "Don't," and flailed her arms like tormented wings beating outward and back.

Then she retracted wholly into her grief. She sobbed into her knit scarf, leaning over the handlebars of the snowmobile. Her gloved hands wiped away tears. She doubled over convulsing as if she needed to spew out her sorrow before Windsong's body reached her.

For the first time since I had met her, I found it impossible to comfort my wife. She alone bore the grief for her child of a twenty-year absence, and alone she cried out from atop the hill that she had two decades before descended to leave her baby behind. Now that child—grown a woman—left her who had nursed her at infancy and at death. I was a stranger. I could not enter that place.

And she was a stranger to me. I saw it was Morgan who wept for loss. She was someone I did not know, someone whose world was separate. I could not conceive that Morgan would wash out the grief she had suffered for twenty years and return to be my wife. I did not know, either, if I would be there to find out.

I sat behind her. Her shoulders shook. I watched the progress of the little funerary train coming up the hill. Danny trekked on snowshoes behind the snowmobile that carried Cooley and the medic. He trailed the sled on which Windsong rode, wrapped in what served as blankets. When they neared, I saw that her body was covered by wide strips of birch bark.

A blanket had been folded behind Windsong's head and trailed over her shoulders leaving her face open to the sky. The birch bark blanket was tightly wrapped around her arms, binding them to her torso. As the entourage pulled alongside, Morgan staunched her tears in the presence of her dead child. She carefully traversed the space between our snowmobile and the sled to kneel at her daughter's feet.

Morgan spoke to her in low, familiar tones. Windsong's cheeks had been rouged. The resemblance of the mother to daughter was shocking. The two, the young mother gone cold and her mother of her first months and her last three weeks faced each other, mirror images of the same face, as if suddenly Mary and Morgan were together again.

Danny came up, breathing heavily. Like Cooley and

Morgan, his face formed a mask of stoic determination. "Granny won't let them take her off the lake," he told Morgan, "not until we hold the funeral."

Morgan nodded.

Cooley killed the engine. "We'll bring her to Joki's, where there won't be any kids."

Morgan again assented.

"If it were on the res, you could have all the time you wanted," the medic said, "but we're going to have to come back to bring her to the coroner."

Morgan looked to Danny. "Stay with her, Danny. I have to see to the babies."

"We'll spread the word around. It's still early. There'll be a crowd," Cooley said. "We'll tell them to come an hour before sunset."

"Sun sets around five," the medic said.

"Come early, but leave that goddamn wagon you got way down the road," Danny told him.

"Done, my friend," the medic replied.

Cooley started the engine. Morgan spoke again over Windsong as if she were telling her things, giving her instructions. What she said was lost in the roar of the snowmobile.

Morgan lifted herself to our sled, started the motor, and without looking back, slid into the track Cooley had made leading down to the cabin. By the time we made the first switchback, Cooley was down the other side of the hill. I could see Danny's head and shoulders above the rise. He looked toward the distant glitter of the January sun.

Without speaking, we descended to the cabin, to the newborn twin granddaughters, and to Granny Bassett.

After the expansive, dazzling snow burning under the cloudless sky, the inside of the cabin was close and nearly black. The fireplace flame, whose smoke I had seen from above, was the first thing to reveal itself to my sun-glazed eyes. Then appeared the fainter glows at the windows, where the drifts had been partially flung back by Danny's shovel-work. As my eyes adjusted, I saw a white-draped bassinette standing away from the fireplace. Over this hovered a tiny silhouetted figure singing words I could not make out.

Morgan took my hand. It felt like joy trembled through her fingers. "Come see them."

We made our way to the newborns and the small, dark figure of Granny who was tending them.

I had never been much for babies and felt foolish and useless around the children of our friends in Florida. These two brought to mind nothing I could say. I was more shocked than charmed. Each little face—sisters, side by side—was a scrunched-up prune. Each forehead showed a thumb-sized black smudge.

Morgan touched the tiny woman tenderly. "Granny," she said, "you can clean the marks now that they took her from the house.

Granny said something I could not understand and patiently shook her head no.

Morgan looked to me. "The spots protect them from being led away by spirits. Babies are trusting. They wouldn't know good from evil."

Where spirits were concerned, I understood the difficulties.

Granny came to me, took my hands to her face, and looked up at me. She could have been Banook for as much as I could picture my own grandmother after nearly thirty years—older than old, eyes beaming in the firelight with a wisdom gathered and stored through firm planting in a single place.

"It is sorrow you come to," she said. "For that I am sad."

I tried to muster what graciousness I could. "Still, I am happy to have made it."

Morgan fussed over the babies, and Granny took charge of me. "You are hungry," she told me. "I have fixed you some rabbit stew and a good tea."

"Thank you."

Granny led me to a corner of the room near a cookstove nearly identical to the one at Tillie's. A single place was set at the table, a worn spoon, a thick-sided bowl, and a cup without its handle. "Sit," she ordered.

At the stove, she ladled the stew into the bowl and brought it to me. "Eat." She leaned on a corner of the table and filled a cup with a peppery-smelling tea from a coffee pot. She sat on the chair across the table corner from me. "Drink."

I did as I was told. Even though I had never tasted wild rabbit before, I relished the stew—meat oily and succulent, small potatoes and chopped carrots steeped in a grain-filled broth.

Granny watched. When I looked closely at my full spoon to identify what I ate, she said, "*Manomin.*"

Morgan, still working at the bassinette, explained, "Wild rice."

Granny nodded, "Yes, we say '*manomin.*'"

I raised my eyebrows and nodded, "It's good."

She watched me eat, took the bowl before it was empty and ladled more into it. She handed it to me with an approving nod.

I was grateful for the food. It was the first real nourishment I had had in a day. Whiskey, cinnamon buns, and airplane food were not nutritious. Apparently, being hungry was my corollary to her welcome, and her eyes gleamed.

"You are tired," she told me. "Drink the tea. You will sleep." She pointed to a pallet to one side of the table near enough the stove to be cozy.

Morgan looked over once more. "It's fine, Tatty. You're exhausted. I'll lie down with you in a while."

I finished the tea and fended off the edges of a warm sleep. "Maybe I should find the toilet first," I said.

Both Granny and Morgan pointed to the door. "The outhouse is behind the shed. Keep going left," Morgan told me.

"Throw on a jacket," Granny said. I would be thankful for the advice.

Even with the jacket zipped all the way up and the hood flopped forward, the cold gripped me as soon as I closed the cabin door. Indoor plumbing came to mind.

I stood under the sky in a blazing white corridor so bright it stung my eyes. Snowwalls rose a foot above my head, carved straight and smooth by Danny's strong, steady shovel. I moved toward an intersecting path ahead that angled to the left. I was already nearly frozen. I scurried thirty hurried steps past the turn in the snow hallway to a building. The roof and walls had been drifted over, but the door and window had been cleared. I looked in. It's a shed, fool. I swore and followed the path that went around what must have been the back corner of the building. The path ended some twenty feet farther at a plank door planted squarely in a snowwall.

Off to the left, Danny had fashioned a ramp at the top of which stood a large scoop with a hoop handle. Around the scoop, hills of snow were piled higher yet. At the base of the nearest pile, he had taken care to clear snow from a stovepipe. This better be the outhouse, I thought.

I tried the door pull with my heavy mitt but couldn't get a grip. I jumped up and down while I removed the glove to manipulate the latch handle. The door released. Thank God, I thought. I left the door ajar to admit enough light to see and hurried to finish peeing before I froze.

I thought, imagine sitting here. I couldn't think about baring my rear over frozen toilet holes. As it was, all my exposed parts numbed in that minute. I stuffed all back in and hurried to the cabin.

Somehow, I expected a welcoming committee. I felt I had run a northern gauntlet and survived, but neither woman acknowledged my entry. Each was intent on the newborn she held.

I found, though, that my tea cup had been refilled. Grateful, I warmed myself at the stove. After sipping the tea, I barely remember crawling beneath the warm blankets that were covered by a tanned deer hide. The weight of the hide, the tea, and the blankets pushed me down to oblivion.

At one point in heavy slumber, I was aware of Morgan beside me. The alienation I had suffered had not dulled my body's response to her warmth, and I stiffened, hard enough to hurt. The weight of my exhaustion and Granny's presence in the cabin, however, held me quiescent beneath the skins and wool. Nor did Morgan reach for me. Later, she moved away and rose from the pallet.

Was there talking in the room? Still, I could not rouse myself. Even later, it seemed as if a greater darkness pervaded the already dusky room, as if I could sense the setting of the sun outside even through log walls and closed eyelids. Soon, I knew Morgan was talking to me, giving me directions in an oddly familiar but foreign language. I was to sleep. The family would leave for the funeral. Beanie, Morgan's niece, and her own newborn would stay with the twins. I mumbled assent through tea-numbed lips. Immediately, I sank deeper into sleep, content to be left alone in warm envelopment.

In dreams I received more direction. I heard words I couldn't mouth, pronounce, or remember, but I comprehend them as one understands pictographs or the designs in beadwork.

I rocked in a cradle made of stitched birch bark. It was like a tight-fitting canoe. Voices spoke to me one at a time, intimately, quietly, as if imparting secret knowledge, bade me look to the setting sun, move to the west, travel for days. I sensed provisions being placed at my head and feet, *manomin* for the journey. Plank doors, mounted in the blank wall I faced, opened, revealing a glorious sunset, thin on the horizon, spread across a snowy landscape.

As directed, I willed myself, in my canoe, through the doors and on to the open plain ahead. I moved by floating forward toward the sun. Behind, stars began to appear in a dimming, velvet sky. One brightened and shot across the darkening east. It disappeared below a rim of pine-sentineled hills. I felt sadness descend with it. As the dusk gathered, I enjoyed peaceful warmth, steered a steady course, and followed a path I knew would lead me home.

The tranquility of the dream impressed a meaning

in my thought that I could never articulate. Its peace released a flow of well-being I had never felt as strongly before. It was honest, open, and true. Still, its meaning was obscure, and I was reluctant to accept it. The message, though, was final. I could not reject or forget it.

From within the dream, I couldn't tell how much time passed or when one vision began and a previous one ended. Perhaps I still cruised the landscape in my canoe. Perhaps I lighted afoot amid that snow-covered plain. This may have been a separate dream altogether because the peace I had enjoyed was broken.

As I stood in this dream, the flat world tilted as if to throw me off. I felt jarred, separated, threatened. The plain shifted impossibly on a hidden axis, moved straight up and down from horizontal. I grasped the upended edge, clinging on ice to a world I thought I knew. Voices spoke from a long-past dream—or were they new voices from this separate dream? They spoke forth visually—words becoming pictures—showing a petroglyph-man opening stick-figure arms wide to a radiant sun. He bent skinny knees in obeisance and held his antlike body in waiting. In this way, I was instructed. I trusted the dream. The picture was set cordially in my sleeping thoughts. It filled me with love. I followed the instructions planted in my mind. I let go of the edge I was clinging to and slipped down the steep, icy wall past the lower edge of the world.

I woke, but maybe not quite fully. I rolled to my side. My eyes were crusted shut. I didn't dream but wrestled with what I'd seen. Again, I sank out of thought in to fuller sleep.

The dream that finally threw the blankets off led me round a sharp corner to confront a dark, bearded figure hunched and angular, not as much menacing as unavoidable. My initial surprise and resistance relaxed before the figure's first words when I recognized Roscoe. His friendly voice staunched my first instinct to flee. "I'm here to talk," he said in the dream.

The tea's effects drained from me at those words. I heard stirring in the cabin and sought it with eyes I struggled to open.

Shuffling sounds followed a hunched-back figure that swayed as he walked, leaning one way and the next. I saw in the firelight two gleaming eyes, narrowly set, following me from one sway to the next. I sat up. Gaining a better perspective and rubbing sleep from my eyes, I saw that the eyes were those of a child, a baby bound to a woman's back. She carried a similarly bound child in each of her arms.

This, I found out, was Beanie keeping the newborn twins and her own baby quiet while I slept. Beanie was tall. Her long, loose blond hair spread on each side of her back-bound infant gave the child the aspect of a wizard.

"I'm awake, Beanie," I said.

She turned, swaying with the babies, "You're Tatty, I know."

"Yes. Are the others late?"

"Some will arrive in an hour. Granny and Morgan will come first. Would you like something to drink? Coffee?"

"Not yet. It will just send me to the outhouse again."

She peered through a window now dark with night. "It is nearly thirty below zero. It might hit forty below tonight." As if she had been waiting for me to awake to effect her plan, she said, "We'll need more wood." She stood over me, insisting kindly. "The wood pile is to the right under the canopy. It's all split and piled. All you have to do is bring it in."

Though barely awake, I accepted the invitation to be helpful. "How much do you need?" I asked.

She pointed to the pegs at the door where jackets and hats hung. "If you fill that sling four times, that should last 'til morning."

I didn't relish lugging wood in from outside, but I was happy to be useful after having lain through comings and goings and having missed the funeral train. My dreams left me confused and unsettled in the waking world. "Let me wake up a bit more before I get myself frozen." I added a rakish laugh at the end of "frozen."

"The hauling will keep you warm. Take the lantern with you."

"Maybe I will have that coffee. I'll get it. You've got your hands full."

I busied myself at the stove, found a jar of milk in a cabinet that had been built into one of the walls, like a natural refrigerator. There was a thin film of ice on the milk. "Should I leave this out? Will it freeze in there?"

Beanie jiggled the babies with her laugh. "No, it's fine. You know freezing isn't so bad. It preserves things." She laughed again.

Even though it was only a cup of coffee I was preparing, I felt a domestic contentment. The simplicity and directness of the cabin was charming: heating with wood that grew nearby, cooling with snow, drawing water with the hand pump at the sink. The homey surroundings chased away concern about the freezing world outside. They overlaid the danger with cheery warmth. I can see myself surviving winter here, I thought.

Some of the radiance came from Beanie. Other than Morgan, she was the first woman I had talked to since leaving Saint Paul. I had met Granny, but we had hardly conversed, and age had turned her sexless.

I watched Beanie moving about with the three bundles. "You grew up here, didn't you?"

"Not at the lake, if that's what you mean. I lived in Eveleth, eighty-five miles away. Anyway, I'm used to the cold."

I risked a personal question. "You're not Native, I guess."

She laughed. I thought she blushed though it was hard to be sure in the light. "No, my kids are half," she said, "but I'm Finnish. One hundred percent."

"You've got to be kidding." I knew Finns lived there. Beanie was the third I'd met. "My mother is Finn. I'm half."

"*Suomalainen? Miten menee?*"

I looked dumbly at her.

"I guess you don't speak the language."

"No. My father forbade it in our house. Other than Mother, he didn't like Finns much."

"Nobody likes Finns much," she laughed, "even Finns."

"Nobody likes Indians much either," I said.

"That's why we get along so well."

Beanie delighted me. For all the children she carried, she seemed bright and airy. Her centered, cheerful banter lifted me from darker dreams, heavy thoughts. Even surrounded by a fierceness of struggle and the stark suddenness of death that had settled around us, her golden hair and raspberries-and-cream cheeks imparted a gaiety, a beauty like the sunrise I had seen chase the dark from the lake that morning. I envied her freshness and light.

I finished my coffee and began preparing for my

duties outside. I was eager to pile up some credit with Beanie and with the others when they arrived. I layered my legs and feet with long johns and socks from the suitcase Cooley or, perhaps, Danny had delivered earlier. Somehow it had made its way there. I plied my body with cotton and wool layers and stuffed my head into the tightly woven wool cap whose earflaps tied under the chin. I stood at the doorway, struggling into my hooded parka and looking down for my boots.

Beanie laughed. "Are you going to be able to move in all that?"

I tried to look over my bulk to my toes. "No, but I'm going to stay warm."

I sat on the stool to one side of the door to pull on and lace the heavy boots. I stood and zipped the parka. I pulled on the mitts. I took the sling and turned to Beanie, "Okay, four loads coming up."

"Remember the lantern."

I had to remove the mitts again to light the kerosene lamp. It took three matches for me to get it, and I was already growing hot inside all my clothing.

"Better go out before you sweat in there," Beanie said. "You'd freeze all the faster."

Despite her banter, once I was out the door, I was glad I took precautions. It felt thirty below. The air jammed icy fingers up my nostrils, and frigid inhalations flew into my lungs before my chest could warm them. How cold can it get? I wondered. Fifty below? Could I tell the difference? It could have been sixty below. I tried to imagine it. Was that twice as cold? Did the body freeze twice as fast?

I crunched over the snow of the shoveled path to the right and found the framed wooden canopy. The firewood had been split and stacked neatly underneath, but the snow had blown inside and lodged between the pieces. I had to loosen each piece, pull it out, and knock the snow off against the chopping block that stood to one side. In all my layers, movement was an effort, and before long I was hot and sweaty. I worked the first load and the second. I was learning how to survive. Thirty below zero and I was warm. I was doing useful work. That was what I had longed for since leaving Florida, and it felt good.

After I brought the fourth load in the house making quite a large pile next to the fireplace, I asked Beanie if more was needed.

"No. George will probably bring some in when he gets here anyway. Leave it at that."

"I'll brave the cold one more time, then. 'North to the outhouse, I'm going north, the need is on.'" I sang.

"Don't get frozen to the seat, now." Beanie rejoined my levity.

I didn't freeze to the seat, though I was gone long enough that Beanie might have wondered if I had. After I secured the door and picked up the lantern to return to the house, I turned, and directly in my path, hunched close to the ground, Roscoe blocked my way.

I wanted to back off, but I didn't have any place to go except back to the outhouse. He had killed Scummy. I didn't know if he was after me now or had ever been after me. Even in his obviously weakened state, I relied on the bond that dreams had woven between us. I wanted no trouble.

"Roscoe. I tried to follow you, but you were already gone."

He sounded as tired as he looked. "I came to talk."

"Out here?"

"In the shed." He pointed toward the door.

"In the shed?"

He reassured me. "I'm not armed. I'm not angry. I just want to talk."

He hobbled to the door that I now saw was slightly ajar. He opened it wide. I followed him in. Despite what he had done, I trusted his words and felt all right in his presence. After seeing him in the dream, I had half expected him. The shed was fairly warm inside.

"I wouldn't be here if it weren't so cold, but no one will look for me at Granny's. Anyway, I don't have long."

"What do you mean?"

"I think you know. You've seen it, whether you realize it or not. I'm not going to prison a second time."

I understood about incarceration. I wasn't sure how he had survived his first stint in jail. Murder, even manslaughter, would bring a long sentence. I waited for him as he stirred a small charcoal fire glowing in a castoff hibachi he'd found in the shed.

He started speaking at once as if answering an unasked question. "Jay wanted it this way."

"He wanted to die?"

"He had a knife in his belt."

"You mean it was self-defense?"

"No. I mean I had the first move. And Jay couldn't kill me or himself, anyway."

"Why did anyone have to die?"

"I was already dead, man. I should have died the night Mary did."

"No. It wasn't your fault. I saw Mary dive into it."

"That's the way it looked, but the windigo came only for me. Mary knew that."

I marveled at his logic. "She knew?"

"We heard it call my name. Even you heard it call my name."

"You're telling me that Mary sacrificed herself to save you?" It surprised me. "How long have you known this?"

"Only since this morning. Jay figured it out years ago, but he didn't tell me. I guess he was protecting me from myself."

"Why? What would you have done?"

"I haven't had much time to speculate, but probably I'd have cut my own throat."

His tone shook me. Was this the code of the north-woods hunter? Roscoe couldn't have lived with the sacrifice of a woman's life on his spirit. Her accidental death was hard enough for him to swallow. His need for Mary was not built on being protected. He was the hunter. In his world, he endangered himself and stood ready to pay.

The windigo had changed his mind. It was not from his world. All the laws that bounded his existence, the laws of the woods, he knew, understood, and obeyed. But something from outside? That was different.

"I thought it was just another kind of game. A wild thing that we could hunt down. A crazed buck in rut."

"Is that why Scummy was against it? He knew this was different?"

"He didn't know it had called to me. He wasn't there when Morgan and I heard the buck speak."

"She was there? What about Mary?"

"Morgan told her. I wish she hadn't."

I came to understand that what I had seen was not a wild, drunken romp in the woods but a hunt and a sacrifice. What Morgan's sister had in her mind I could not know, but I felt certain there in the shed that she had been following instructions from somewhere. Still, I wondered whether or not the voices that whispered them were evil.

Roscoe crouched over the coals, then leaned further back on his haunches to sit on a pallet he had prepared from cardboard and cushions stored in the shed. Two deer hides were heaped at the end of his little bed. He carefully pulled off his left mitt with his good hand, then held the other in his teeth and wiggled his right hand out. He rubbed his sling-hand held over the coals with his good one. Roscoe looked tired and old.

"Jay and I hunted forever together, starting as kids. A good hunter avoids hunting alone. Not that he wasn't one of the best, but he started tramping the woods solo a whole lot when he got back from Viet Nam. That's how he owed me his life."

Roscoe added a few black coals to the glowing host. "He never knew that I had been tracking him, just to make sure he wouldn't get himself into a jam. This was Minnesota, not the Kontum he always talked about. Lots of veterans, even some of the Finns, who are usually pretty solid upstairs, were doing weird, dangerous things right then.

"The last time I tracked him, he was following a doe someone had wounded bow hunting. I found him nearly up to his chin in swamp water. He was less than three feet from a solid path beneath the water—some submerged trunks and branch tangles we all used to cross there—but had stepped or slipped off into a mud suck following that doe. He worked a stick he carried as a lever to help him out but wedged it into the wood tangle beneath him, and it snapped in two. He had been sinking for a good while before I got there."

I hunkered down closer to the warm coals beside Roscoe. I didn't want to miss a word.

"I didn't have too much trouble getting him out, but he had no chance without help. I got him back to town. He'd lost his boots in the suck, and he was a mess, all covered in leeches and swamp muck. That's when everyone started calling him Scummy. He was always Jay to me."

I tried to make sense of it. "Is that why he didn't defend himself? Because he owed you his life?"

"No. I saved him the trouble. There's no other way out for either of us. If I went down last night, he would have had to shoot himself. We are bound to one another. Been that way nearly our whole lives. I know he meant well toward me, but once I found out about Mary, he knew he couldn't live with me or with himself."

"And you?"

"I won't last past dawn." He stated a fact. "But you have a chance. That's what I wanted to say. Morgan will be the only one left, and I don't know how long she's going to last. But them babies are important."

As if to emphasize the point, he pulled himself as tall as he could, like a seated Buddha with one slumping shoulder, and looked at me steadily. "Do you know what you're going to do?"

I shifted my weight. Put a mitted hand to the floor. "I'm not sure. It's too confusing right now."

Roscoe rocked back and forth where he sat. It seemed an affirmation. "We are not made to know." With one hand he folded one of the hides twice over, then pulled the other hide over his legs and reclined on his good shoulder, giving up a strained, tired sigh. He was retreating. He was going back to the barstool. He was finishing his solitary twenty-year-long musing. I sensed our talk was over.

"I'll look in on you in the morning. Want something to eat?"

But Roscoe had sunken into his own troubled dreams, to his own tilted worlds.

The man was changed. He had first appeared to me as a raving lunatic, a drunken bar brawler, even though Scummy had colored him in an understanding light. Then he turned engaged and assertive, controlling the conversation at the table, pounding his fist. In private, he opened up to me gently, to a stranger and adversary, then pursued, hunted me and my knowledge, searching for his own obscured truths. Finally, I saw him as a mourner, bereft and sorry, humbled by a shared loss, as an entitled member of his tragic family, who in an instant traversed from tenderness to embattled, helpless disbelief, then to decisive action and murder, brother killing brother. How much can a man endure?

Being on the periphery, I had time to mull over the revelations we both witnessed, and they tolled heavily. Standing at the center of disaster, Roscoe bore the tonnage directly. His sturdy trunk and broad shoulders could not support this realization. It crushed him.

I put a few more coals on the fire, slipped out the door of the shed, and gently closed it behind me. I returned to the outhouse for the lantern I had left there. It stood dark where I had encountered Roscoe.

A silvered light spilled over the high banks, leaving gray shadows along the shoveled paths. Above the piles at the head of the snowramp, a rising moon dwarfed me. Not yet full but magnificent, the moon sailed up behind drooping pine twigs, their sprigs of needles weighed down with the snow. The frigid air condensed the sharp moon-glow and played it over the prisms of a few icicles that had formed along the eaves of the cabin in the afternoon sun. The stillness of the clear winter light cast new meaning over the radiance of the scene. I recalled Beanie's claim, "You know freezing isn't so bad. It preserves things."

Tiny seems restless. "You think I should have told Cooley and Danny where Roscoe was hiding."

Tiny nods. "That's what I would have done."

"You would have," I answer. "I know, but the dream told me otherwise."

Tiny rubs the sides of his head. He sighs. "You put a lot of stock in those dreams of yours."

"I tried to ignore them, but I learned that they guide me. Dreams bring me confidence I hadn't had before."

"That's good, I guess," Tiny says, "but maybe these were leading you off track."

"How could you explain those dreams?" I ask. "Who could say I shouldn't act on them?"

"On dreams?" Tiny said. "You might as well fish without hooks."

"Maybe," I say. "But once I got close to Thief Lake dreams—visions is a better word—became more than the jibber you ascribe to them. I was lost up here. Visions connected me to a world that seemed more familiar to me than the actual Minnesota. I knew by instinct."

Tiny frowns. He looks at me blankly. "You got answers from these dreams?"

"At first I had only questions," I say, "but as crazy as my visions were answers seemed just a step farther. They were stuff, for all their oddities, that suddenly seemed real, more compelling for sure than what I had experienced during the previous twenty-four hours in Minnesota."

"Where did these visions come from, do you think?" Tiny asks.

"How do I know? Maybe they were evil," I say. "Maybe they would drive me insane."

Tiny laughs. "You'd think growing up with Granny's mumbo-jumbo about dreams and such that I would take them seriously," he says. "I never have."

"Yeah? Well, let me tell you about Granny and visions," I say. "She made me a believer."

I STOOD OUTSIDE THE CABIN DOOR, ignoring the frigid air seeping beneath my cuffs and collar. I listened to the swish of the night wind shaking loose snow from the white pine's needles overhead. What I was hearing was not what I was listening for. I wanted answers, comfort, not misery. I felt swallowed by troubles—troubles that I hadn't made. I was frozen, held in place, still, amid barrens as empty as my heart. I wanted to run, but there seemed no place to go. I wanted to flee, just as I had before, to ignore the mess of living and the horror of death, but I was frozen fast, my boots rigidly stuck to the earth, blocking flight.

I stood witness to the moon, the wind, the pines and birches, the drifted snow, and the simple expanse of dark, argent sky. I knew there was something more here than I could see, more than I could hear. I peered into my shadow that the moon cast on the wall of snow, as if in that cold eclipse of moonlight, that sieve of the unreflected, I could perceive what I could not see looking within. But there was nothing. Nothing but lunar shade, stretched across luminous, packed snow. I felt like Roscoe, worn and empty.

I turned to the cabin door, which opened as I reached for the latch. Danny loomed in the doorway.

"Hey. They sent me to look for you." Though he spoke in his ordinary, affable voice, he looked drained. The funeral must have been both strain and relief.

The tension led me to try a weak joke. "I got stuck to the toilet seat," I said.

Danny was quick to counter the humor. "That and broke your mantles."

I looked at him dumbly.

"The lantern mantles. Here, give that to me. Get in here."

Danny and Cooley had driven Morgan and Granny to the funeral in Uncle Joki's wide track, which they called, with affection, "the snowcat." I would see it in the morning, Danny promised. They returned with Beanie's older children, two boys, eight and five.

"Carries six, even eight, if you want to crowd in or if they're kids. Got a heater, interior lights, everything," Danny said. He seemed comfortable talking about the machine. Cooley looked on but said nothing.

Morgan came to me, draped her arms over my shoulders, and laid her head on my chest. "Windsong is home now," she said. There was none of the angry force left in her muscles and bones. I felt only slack weariness in her arms. Her languor swept into the emptiness I had felt just then outside. I filled with her need for comfort. I drew her closer. "I'm sure her journey will bring peace."

Morgan pushed away and looked queerly into my face, "Journey?"

"Doesn't her spirit travel four days?" I asked.

Granny spoke from the stove where she and Beanie were finishing dinner preparations. "You see, he knows."

Morgan shook her head. "Since when have you turned Anishinabe?"

"Leave him be," Granny said. "We eat now."

Morgan wiped a gentle palm across my cheek and

smiled at me. "We have venison, Big Chief."

Despite her sorrow, drained fury, and twisted emotions, Morgan treated me with an alluring gentleness and generosity reminiscent of our early years together. She guided me to my place at the table ahead of Danny and Cooley.

I realized from the progress of the cooking that I had been outside longer than I thought and glanced at Beanie to see how much she had noticed. She looked at me—I thought knowingly—but refused to say anything about my long absence.

"George is out plowing again," Beanie said. "He's still cleaning up after the storm."

Danny broke in, his usual enthusiastic, newsy voice booming over all, "Yeah, he's gonna pull your Jeep oud'a' the ditch."

Cooley added, "It'll probably need a battery charge at least."

Danny was being his helpful self. "We'll beef it up, and you'll be back on the road in no time," he blurted out.

The possibility of my leaving became suddenly real. Morgan and I locked eyes.

I looked down at my plate. I wasn't ready to stay or to go.

Cooley poked Danny and frowned. Everyone else ignored his gaffe.

Granny brought a platter of meat to the table. Beanie, still with the papoose strapped to her back, served a dish of steaming carrots, some of the soup from the morning, and a hot dish fluffed up with what I recognized as *manomin*.

"I brought the venison," Cooley said, "from a young doe. Trailed her a mile before I got a shot off."

"We don't wait for bucks here," Danny said, "too many deer anyway. A doe is smaller but tenderer, I think."

Beanie asked, "Since when do you stop at one, anyway, Danny? You're not allowed, but you take more'n the game warden could believe."

"Yah, and eat it all, too," he said.

Granny lifted her hands. The chatter ended.

She stood at the head of the table, swaying, her eyes focused somewhere beyond the room. "This house sees many passing. Now, two have come here, one has gone. It is sorrow, but it is the way." She seemed to reach into the darkness behind her black eyes. "Who will paddle the little ones' canoe?" she asked the darkness. Turning to Morgan and me she said, "Now we eat."

"Try some, Tatty," Cooley said, passing the platter my way.

The meat was savory, deep and rich, peppered liberally, and gave off a wild sweet flavor punctuated with the sharpness of pine. I nodded my approval as I chewed.

"This is the best venison. The meat in the south tastes like corn. In the west, like wheat," said Danny.

Cooley explained. "Here, there are no real cash crops, only garden stuff, so the deer eat whatever they can find, dandelion greens, wintergreen mint, berries, sweet grasses, even pine twigs. Gives the meat a great flavor. They even eat poison ivy and goldenrod."

"Makes you itch for more," Beanie said with a smile.

"The rice tastes like the muck it grows in. The kind Scummy got stuck in." Again Danny spoke out of turn, and Cooley shook his head.

"We'll be having a memorial for him tomorrow," Cooley said to me. "I'll take you if you want to go."

I told him yes. And even though I was sheltering his

killer out in the shed, I genuinely wanted to go. Scummy had saved me. He was a friend.

We finished the meal mostly in silence, but giving the food and the cooks due praise. It was not a glum party, even for a funeral meal, but we all tiptoed around death, afraid maybe that too much talk of it would be bad for the kids. Granny had, Morgan told the table, gathered them all together and placed with her finger a new black smudge in the center of each forehead, babies and children. "She says it keeps spirits away."

Cooley, as knowledgeable as ever, said, "You have the bark-snake over the doorway, too, Granny."

"Spirit afraid of snake. Don't come in," she said.

Cooley pointed to a narrow, corrugated strip of birch bark tacked over the doorway.

Beanie said, "She folds the bark to make it look like a snake. I had to put it up before the kids came in."

"We are safe here, inside," said Granny. Without a break in her sentence, she went on to introduce dessert, "We make pan bread with syrup."

They fried the bread in a cast-iron skillet in a thin pool of oil. Slathered with your maple syrup, Tiny. Beanie said it was from your grove of sugar maples on the north side of the lake. The bread sated us. Granny joined me drinking a sweet tea made from dried berries—she wasn't specific what kind—but poured everyone else the soporific tea she had given me early in the day. Only Morgan demurred. "I'm tired enough," she said.

We lingered over the tea. They spoke of the storm. The winter. Ice fishing was about to begin. Danny praised the snowcat again. "Uncle Joki may not get it back," Danny said.

No one mentioned Windsong or Scummy. No one

spoke of Roscoe. I was thankful for that. It was as if Roscoe already belonged with the dead. It made me edgy that he was asleep just forty feet from our door.

At the end of cleanup, Morgan came over, touching my shoulders and face tenderly. "I know it's still early." It was eight o'clock. "But I didn't get as much sleep as you did today. I imagine you'll come along later. Gives you a chance to get to know Granny." Right then, it was as if she were handing me over to Banook.

I kissed her goodnight. She went off to the pallet by the stove.

Beanie put the kids down, and the twins were quiet in their bassinette. Beanie was acting as wet nurse. I thought that the Native blood mixed with Finnish milk made the infants settle quietly. Beanie climbed to the loft that straddled the stovepipe. She brought her baby with her.

Danny and Cooley took some of the wood that I had stacked inside and got the fire blazing again. They bedded down in an alcove away from the fireplace. They spoke to each other in low rumbles. Soon they like all the tea drinkers were breathing the air of dreams.

Next to the fireplace opposite the alcove, Granny and I sipped tea, a stimulating earthy taste with the aroma of blueberries. We watched the flames dance along the split logs.

After a few minutes in which the only sounds were the crackling birch quarters and the light snores of the sleepers, Granny rose and stood before me, barely reaching to my head even though I was seated. She looked at me curiously, as if she were searching my face, my eyes, for something she had misplaced or something she thought she had seen there. Although I felt uncomfortable, I let her go on without speaking or moving, trusting her aged wisdom and stalwart senses.

I watched the light from the flames move across her cheeks and forehead. Then, with a sudden snort, she thrust her head at me, peering closer and directly into my eyes. Then, still without a word, she sat once more on the stool across from me.

I thought that when she spoke, I finally would be relieved of the discomfort her inspection had engendered, but her words, too, were piercing, too incisive to do anything but penetrate. "You see from afar," was all she said.

I knew what she meant but didn't want to admit it. Granny Bassett was every bit as obtuse as Banook had been. Now, though, I understood more than I had with Nebe and my grandmother. My denial of my Mi'kmaq connections and understanding so many years ago danced in the light, firebrands newly ignited.

"No, no. I'm just a regular guy, a shutter salesman. I can barely see beyond the next hurricane season." My own words sounded wrong in my ears. Excuse and evasion were familiar friends, but they failed me now. Granny breathed the patient confidence of the old whose time is so long that minutes tick by easily in silence.

Her chest rose and fell, rose and fell like bellows, inspiring my own lungs each time she exhaled. Her nostrils flared softly, but that only increased the strain on me. Her breath relaxed in outward flows that brought me no respite from tension. I believed my lungs would burst if I did not relieve the pressure, but I felt as if I were drowning. I held my breath.

My mind flashed to a time, years before, when I had nearly drowned. It was summer:

Mother and my father had brought me to a lake north of Tallahassee. Swimming, my father slipped under the dock where I was standing and came up growling on the other side, startling me from behind. "Watch me go under," he ordered. I went to my belly, lying flat on the dock, watching the water—just out of reach below—for signs of his dark head breaking the small waves. Up he came like a breaching whale. Then down again, under and up the other side. Four times he did this as I craned my neck to watch him go beneath the dock, inching forward bit by bit to better look underneath. The last time he surfaced—he told me later—he asked, "Where's the boy?" Yes, where was I?

My tumble from the dock surprised me, probably so much that I can barely recall sinking like a sodden leaf to the sandy bottom, which is where I sat. I had never seen the underwater world before. Its beauty was stunning, a golden glow from the noonday sun filtered in columns and rays all around as I watched it shimmer and light the fine sandy sediment the swimmers had stirred up. I felt content, light, comfortable, and at peace. Instinctively, my mouth closed, my lungs refused to breathe, but my eyes were braced open by the glory of the submarine sun. Somehow, I smelled and tasted the pungent, amber water. Soon, though, I felt pressure to breathe, to talk, to release.

My father spotted the white of my shirt against sandy bottom of the lake.

My rise to the surface was sudden and frightening. From the peace that could have been my final thought, I broke the surface in my father's arms, squalling like a newborn. Now, now back in the airy world, terror rose with me from the bottom of the deep side of the dock. All eyes and ears were on me. A boy had been saved.

This time, I knew I must surface under my own power to overcome the press of Granny's gaze, the piling on of her breath, and the leaden weight of my refusals. The rush, when it came, was like being carried to the surface in giant arms, like exploding through a screen that separated worlds, bawling in fear and relief.

"Yes, yes. You're right. I have seen things. Scenes come to me, play before my eyes." I was desperate to let it out. "I know things I couldn't have seen, dreams, visions, more than mere thought."

Granny was nodding. She looked grave.

I continued, but the old reticence returned. "But I don't know what I am doing. I don't understand what I see."

Again she nodded. She encouraged me with silence.

"Then later, someone says something about it—what I couldn't have seen—and I know it is true. I understand it then." I hoped it was enough for her.

Granny nodded again, once. Then like an owl sensing a mole breaking the surface of the soil, she sat alert, still, waiting. She had tracked me down, cornered me, and she was in no hurry. I had surfaced with nowhere to go but to the truth.

"I saw Mary, the real Mary, leap into the windigo," I said. I nearly choked on "the real Mary" but immediately felt relief and lightness.

I was afraid it would hurt the old woman who had raised both girls, Mary and Morgan, but she remained still, intent on my eyes. She spoke gently. "I felt you at the funeral. You saw it."

I was unsure. Dreams swirled inside visions in my mind, becoming a maelstrom of echoes and changing textures. I struggled to separate them from each other, first to sort which came before and which after Windsong's death, then which was telling of death, of wakes. One word Granny uttered steered swiftly to it, like the owl who hears the munching of a single blade of grass between the field mouse's teeth. "Journey," she said.

I blurted out, "Birch bark."

"Is that what it was?" I asked. "The canoe? The directions? The journey and coming home?" They were questions, but I knew the answers before I asked.

"You heard the words?" Granny seemed alarmed.

"No. But I understood what to do. They brought me pleasure, peace."

The old woman nodded once again. "We speak to the dead, to guide them to the next world. No one should hear the words."

I wondered if Granny intentionally left me behind on the family's way to the funeral. Did she manipulate me? Was it a test? My new feeling of honor mixed with old suspicion.

She still held me in her gaze. Again she jutted her forehead toward me and fixed my eyes intently as if probing them, as if reading on my face the news she wished to know.

"You saw the earth tip," she told me. "You let go."

Again I searched the churning funnel of dreams.

"Yes. It was the only thing to do."

"Then you are wise," Granny said. "And the man?"

"What man?"

"You have seen him?" This time it was a question, one I did not want to answer.

She saw my answer, unspoken on my face in the firelight.

"Yes, you have seen him." She nodded and said

nothing more for a long time.

Her statement was not accusation but something of resignation to what she already knew would come to pass. I thought of running out the door—in shirtsleeves, no less—to sound a warning to Roscoe, to help him to a snowmobile, to assist in his escape. But the little woman made no move to sound an alarm. She knew better than to interfere in affairs that had been foreboden.

Granny squatted before the fire, rocked lightly back and forth on her bare feet, and swayed side to side with the rise and the fall of the flames over the birch logs. Although her black eyes were open, reflecting the firelight, she looked at nothing in the room nor, I thought, at anything beyond the room. She began to speak rhythmically, in concert with her movements. I had to strain to hear her voice, so quiet and low that it seemed to come from somewhere far away. I sat down on the hearth by her side.

"Long ago on Thief Lake, before Granny Bassett, before her grandmother, the *Anishinabe*, the People, came to the lake to fish, to harvest *manomin* in their birch bark canoes, to gather the seeping juices of the trees, and to hunt deer. In the winter, the *Anishinabe* moved away for fear of a *manidoo*, an evil spirit, who lived on an island in the middle of the lake. It was a windigo, a spirit that ate people. Even in the summer when the warm waters kept the spirit in its cave, no one paddled close to the island.

"A year when the *manomin* harvest was lean, little sweet syrup had flowed, and deer were sparse and more secretive than usual, winter came very early. People awoke one morning to see that the lake had grown an ice-skin in the night. All began preparations to move that day. They took down *wiigiwaams*, stored food and medicine bags in their canoes, and heaped deer hides over everything. They built litters to bring all through the forest paths away from the lake.

"In one family lived a small girl. She asked her mother, 'Why must we move so quickly? Why today?'

"Her mother told her about the *manidoo* who lived on the island.

" 'It cannot chase us away. I will find it and kill it.'

"The mother shook her head, 'No, little one, it is too powerful.'

"As the mother hurried about collecting her skins, her pouches of food, and the family's clothing, the small girl walked away to the shore. When her mother looked for her, she was not in camp. She looked out across the newly frozen lake, and, there, far out on the clean ice, she saw her daughter nearing the island of the windigo.

"She yelled across the ice, 'Come back, little one.'

"All the people ran to the shore. 'Come back, little one,' they called.

"The sounds carried across the sheet of ice to the girl and to the island. They awoke the windigo, who stormed forth to the island shore. When he saw the small girl, he roared, but the small girl kept walking to the island, growing larger with each step until with her last step onto the shore, she was as big as the windigo itself.

"Now two giants, the windigo and the girl, fought. They landed many blows, but in the end, the *manidoo* was cagey and sly. It lured the girl over thin ice where a spring fed water into the lake. When the giant girl broke through, the windigo seized her. He bit her in two. Then he dragged the carcass to his lair."

Granny rose. She took three split logs, one at a time, from the stack near her and laid them on the fire. She stirred the ash with a stick. She roused the flames. They wrapped themselves around the birch staves like animal tongues. I did not understand the point of Granny's story, but I waited for her to continue.

"The Great Hare, fearing for the *Anishinabe*, sent his beloved brother, Ghost Rabbit, Chibiabos, to kill the windigo before more damage was done to the People. But water spirits who lived with the windigo swarmed forth and killed Ghost Rabbit. Sorrow of sorrows to the *Anishinabe* and to Nanabozo, the Great Hare.

"Chibiabos sank to the bottom of the lake, but with his last breath sent a huge wave that raised the island toward the sky, then dashed it through the ice, smashing the water spirits. The water surged over the frozen lake, knocking down the *manidoo*, washing that windigo toward the People on the shore. They fell upon its stiff body with axes and knives, pulled it apart and found inside a little frozen baby, the body of the small girl.

"That is why the lake has no islands and is called Thief Lake. It is now the grave of Ghost Rabbit, Chibiabos, keeper of the underworld."

Granny looked at me with eyes that seemed sightless, which the firelight made all the more mysterious. She stood. Then watching me intently, she said, "You see from afar."

She went to the ladder that Beanie had climbed. She left me by the fire and joined the papoose and mother in the loft above. She said nothing more.

Granny clearly had told me the story to illustrate something. It was hardly a local history lesson, though I knew she believed that it explained some things about the lake. I wondered if in Granny's mind in some measure the small girl was her lost granddaughter, Mary. Would I play the part of Chibiabos and challenge the windigo? Did she think that I would close out the story? Save the people? I certainly felt now that I had reached some sort of underworld, an unasked for juncture that would be difficult to escape.

I thought of the Jeep. Danny said it would be ready the next day. I had a return ticket for Atlanta in my jacket pocket. This northern world into which I had been drawn loomed sinister, dangerous, and implacable.

I looked over at Morgan, sleeping peacefully on the pallet. The bassinette stood nearer the stove. Some sort of sacrifice would be needed. But me? I thought of my childhood resolve to turn my back on the north, away from the Mi'kmaq. I thought of Mother's encouragement to stay south and pursue my education. How could I believe—as did Granny, Roscoe, and, probably, Scummy—in destiny? It was too difficult. It would cost me something, maybe Morgan, but I could still get out.

After I fed the fireplace and the cook stove, I slipped in next to Morgan on the pallet. Sleep would not come. Too much had happened. I began to wonder whether I would or could leave. Even though I had thought I was on the sidelines, at least initially, everyone and everything worked on me, drew me further and further into this story, into a life I had no idea had existed just a day before, when Scummy brought me into the men's room at Tillie's.

What I had seen of that life, I did not like. It was rife with violence on all sides. Death seemed to define its existence. Visions and ghost stories whipped its atmosphere like the blizzard wind that had scourged the lake. I thought I had come north to humor my wife, to play the role of the dutiful husband, to make an appearance, and then to return with her to our secure life in Florida.

Morgan wanted to stay. She had said it. She wanted

me to stay, and up there on the hill, I had nearly assented. That seemed long ago. Could I stay? The cold that pressed in from all directions was only one aspect, a single, disquieting element. Still, I had been out in that "damn refrigerator" and hadn't died. Actually, I had been warmed by my wood-carrying enterprise. Under the hides and blankets, nestled close to Morgan, I was warm now. The deep winter cold I could conquer, but Morgan, who was not in some sense my wife anymore, was another worry. I turned from her on the little bed.

How could I live with a woman I had not really known? How much of my Mary was actually present in Morgan? Did it matter what she called herself?

She was still the artist and lover with whom I had shared my days and nights. She had been my companion for twenty years. How could that be washed away in a day? How much change did she want?

One could accustom one's self to geography, but parenthood, caring for those twins? I feared it would open me to the destruction my father had wreaked as a parent. I rolled onto my back and stared at the wood flooring of the loft above.

I had always seen us as a couple safely childless by choice, two people moving through life together, dedicated to each other. I knew now that it had never really been true. Morgan had a daughter and now was intent on raising her granddaughters as she was raised, as Granny Bassett had raised her and Mary. Even though they were mixed like me, the girls would grow up on the lake as Ojibwe people.

I had fled, or at least had tried to flee, my Indian side, though Morgan, my studies and, now, this trip to the other extremity of the Algonquin diaspora, Minnesota, brought me back to Native roots. Parenting these children, though, seemed too big a change.

I had not wanted it. Mother had taught me calm, caring ways, but this was something I had decided long before was too risky. It called for too much change. My arguments wove themselves with the warp of my sleep, now over, now under slim threads of dreams and waking.

I lay struggling with the dilemma, shifting in turn toward and then away from Morgan. I moved to, then from, her physical presence and the heat of her will. I lay on my back, on my stomach, on either side. I sought the refuge of sleep, but it eluded me. If I entered it, I was unsure I had slept at all. I rose quietly, careful not to disturb Morgan, and put more logs on the fires. Later, I sought out the night pot they kept in an alcove near the door. Each time I returned to Morgan, chilled and eager for her warmth. Each time she stirred in deep sleep but did not wake.

First Roscoe and then Granny encouraged me to stay —how did Granny know, as I knew she did, Roscoe was so near? "Those kids are important," Roscoe had said, and Granny's story was more than simply late-evening entertainment. She did not have it in her to raise two more children. She had done that twice already as a grandmother, first with you, Mary, and Morgan, then as great-grandmother with Windsong. Though I might seem a savior to Granny and a competent caretaker to Roscoe, I felt needy and incapable.

Neither Granny's mysticism nor Roscoe's confidence seemed likely to fill my shortfalls or staunch my cravings to return to Florida. Yet I was not sure that I could turn back to Tallahassee and take the time I needed to work things out. I had done so twice before and had prospered by it, but the stakes were higher this time.

Even if I could persuade Morgan to return, she would insist on bringing the babies with her. It might work. Maybe I was fooling myself, but that solution soothed my restlessness and worries. Content that I could leave the horror and mayhem behind, still have Morgan—albeit shared with the twins—and be able to pursue my business, I drifted beneath the heat of the deer hide throws into a comfortable, dreamless sleep. What woke me was Morgan's soft touch on my cheek and, beneath the blankets and skins that kept us warm, the press of her naked body to mine.

"Are you awake, Tatty?"

I struggled to answer, "Almost."

She pressed closer, swinging an arm and a leg across my body. "It's not quite dawn yet."

"It's still dark," I mumbled.

Morgan lifted herself atop me and resettled the blankets. The sudden spurt of cold air prodded my senses awake just as the intoxicating heat of Morgan's skin and supple weight of her body aroused me. "This is how the Indians did it in the old days," she whispered, "quiet in a roomful of people."

She pulled herself below like turtle into her shell. In slow, salacious movements she removed the last layers of clothing I had worn to bed. She wormed her way across my legs, crotch, stomach and chest, finally kissing my lips as she sank in lascivious wetness to mate my pelvis to hers. She rolled and twisted with slow abandon, laying her cheek to my shoulder, murmuring my name in the lithe rotation of her hips. The thought that this was life in the northern climes emerged like an encouraging lisp in a current of passion.

It was only later that grave suspicions pulled to reverse the heavy tide of sated love. Still, our long overdue reunion that morning stood solidly in favor of our life together. Was it a sentinel to a future?

We curled into and nested in each other's arms, listening to the stirrings in the cabin. It would not be long before the breakfast fires would be whipped up and practical day would begin.

Morgan gazed into my face, "I love you, Tatty."

I felt secure under our love-heated covers. Outside, though, it was cold.

"I love you." I didn't use her name.

My ideas from the night pursued me. "Morgan, I've been thinking. I want to take you back to Florida with me. You can bring the girls with us if you want."

She drew closer. "Yes. I do want to raise the girls, but I'm not sure I can go back, at least not for a while, and maybe not at all."

I waited for her to explain, an acrid taste trickled down my throat.

"They can't travel when they are so small, and, well, I don't know if I can actually, legally, take them. This time I want no questions left over. Then there's Granny. She is near her end, and taking the babies away seems unfair after all she has done for Windsong and me."

I heard her litany like a voice receding on a train, growing farther away in distorted waves. The echo of "Windsong and me" played back from a distance of miles. If my solution was to go south, I might be going alone. Our lovemaking and confessions took on the pall of the same bare place I had left Banook and later, Mother.

Our talk, my thoughts, and any argument I could have mounted were interrupted by the roar of the engine of the snowcat.

Danny rose up in a shout. "For Christ's sake. Who's that?"

Both he and Cooley bounded to the door, jumped into boots, and were out in long underwear and caps hastily jammed on their heads. They didn't bother to look for gloves and left the door open behind them.

I had only seconds to pull on my own long johns but not time enough to get to the door before they were back. "Christ, it's Roscoe. He's headed for the lake," Cooley grunted as he pulled on his winter leggings.

Danny was struggling into his one-piece snowmobile suit. "We'll catch the bastard in no time. The cat isn't as fast a snowmobile."

The kids looked down from their loft. Beanie moved toward her ladder. "Shush, you two. The kids are here."

Danny blushed as he noticed the boys. "I'm just excited. Forgive me."

Granny had already climbed down and was at the stove. She turned her pressing eyes and insistent breath on me. "Go," she said.

Morgan came to me. "As bad as he is, he is worth saving. You're the only one who might be able to do it."

"I suppose, now that Jay is gone," I said.

Morgan placed her hand on my chest. "I saw him in the shed."

"You knew he was there?"

"He's the last one besides me," she said, "the last one from the chase."

At this moment, Morgan amazed me as she often had.

"Watch out for him, Tatty."

I didn't have to think about going but had no illusions.

"He doesn't want saving, but I will be there."

I looked to Danny and Cooley, zipping themselves into their gear.

"You have room for one more?"

Cooley shook his head, but when Granny crossed her arms, he grimaced and said, "You ride behind Danny."

By the time we raced up to the spine of the overlook, the snowcat was moving across the drifts on the lake.

Danny yelled over the whine of the engine, "He's jamming it full bore."

Cooley had already turned straight down the slope, cutting through the switch backs, bumping and jumping, at some points flying over drifts and rills.

"Hold on, Tatty," Danny screamed. He twisted the accelerator full on following Cooley down the slope.

Holding Danny around the chest, I was buffeted and beaten against him until I learned to anticipate the movements of the machine. It was the kind of thing Scummy would warn against just a day after my crash, but I had been directed to join these two, not to chase but to witness, a friend in court where Roscoe was concerned. I hadn't needed Granny's encouragement to want to see close up.

The jolts and jabs coming from the snowmobile nearly flying through the birches down near the lakeshore suddenly smoothed into waves as we rose, topped, and descended the broad drifts stacked across the lake's ice.

As we topped each drift, I could see Cooley just ahead, gaining on the snowcat where Roscoe hunched in the cab. He faced away, either unaware of or unconcerned about our pursuit.

Cooley stopped dead. Danny nearly rammed into his

machine. He pulled to the side of the track the snowcat had left and pointed. Danny moved us up to see. What was in the snow and ice before us was a fissure running across the track Roscoe had left.

Danny flipped back his hood and lifted the furry earflap of his cap. "I hear it," he said. Cooley nodded. We dismounted and stood at the edge of the fissure atop the crust the subzero weather had hardened on the snow. The ice was breaking up.

Emanating from the crevasse that had widened to the width of a foot in the minute we stood there, a groan, like a cargo ship grinding against a pier, shook the ice. The ice split the air with a crack. The slab before us sunk knee height. We all three jumped back. I broke through the snowcrust and wallowed back to the snowmobile.

Remounted, Cooley paused looking to the receding snowcat. "He's headed to Canada for sure." He spoke to me. "You can nearly see it from here."

"Should we circle round?" Danny asked.

"I'm not going on that floe. The springs come up between here about where Roscoe is now," Cooley pointed. "We've got to go around, but we can still catch him."

Groaning rose again. Both men gunned their engines and arced away from the sounds. Another splitting boom sounded behind us.

I watched Roscoe, far away now, seeming to inch across the surface, gaining more and more distance as we swung away to intercept his tangent with our arc. The cat seemed, then, to slow, but I couldn't tell how much or why. Had the wind shifted? No, Roscoe rode the cat up an incline. The ice floe he traveled over was pitching upward before him and sinking ever lower at our end. A ghostly wind sounded as it swept down to the lake from the pine forests.

Swirls of snow rose in the air, not only behind our machines but also from other quarters of the lake surface. The stiff breeze from our rear had picked up, then had shifted, lifting icy granules aloft from the tops of drifts, sluicing them onto our faces against our advance. In a minute, as if white curtains of loose weave unfurled between us and Roscoe, the snowcat disappeared behind a billowing scrim. It became a crawling animal cloistered momentarily, then unveiled for an instant as the sleet-curtain waved and swirled before the wind. The gusts now moaned through pines on shore, weaving a grim harmony with the groaning of the ice fissure. As one ice floe slipped beneath another, both pines and ice sounds were punctuated at intervals by staccato cracks of foot-thick ice. The puny engines of the snowmobiles were winter-bees to the sudden storm flowering over the ice. Thief Lake came alive, flailing snow with windy arms, rising and rolling like a spirit lifting from its bed.

Is this what Granny wanted me to see? I wondered. The hair on the back of my neck bristled. I felt that Granny was somehow watching. I wondered, "Have I become her eyes?"

Danny elbowed me gently. He pointed laterally toward the cat, which had just then reappeared from behind its scrim. It was closer, parked now off the tilting floe. I made out Roscoe's figure climbing one-armed down from the cab. "He's on snowshoes," Danny yelled to me. "We'll catch him sure now." Cooley was already curving around that way.

Roscoe, still heedless of our advance, built a high-stepping cadence on his webbed feet and struck a line angled slightly away from our path but came back onto the floating ice slab. He headed not toward Canada but toward a rising whirlwind of snow that formed a moving column, a vertical bolt of that billowing curtain that swirled between his and our paths.

I already had begun to disbelieve what I was seeing. Then from out of that whirling, twisting, gigantic chimney of driven snow materialized the same shimmering-white buck I had swerved to avoid, as if now completing the leap I had seen him begin the previous night. He landed and strode beside that howling tornado across the lake that itself groaned in fissured agony.

I had no idea if Danny saw what I was seeing.

A jarring snap shivered the ice, snow, and air. We halted. As rays of sunlight suddenly spilled across the drifts cutting between us and the buck's and Roscoe's path, a chasm yawned in tandem with the light. The sun's rays cascaded over a drop-off of blue ice that fell further down than the height of a man.

We lurched aside this newly revealed gulf and sped away, not from the other-world whirlwind or the spirit-buck that I now believed neither Danny nor Cooley could see, but from the upending ice floe. I twisted around to watch.

Roscoe faced the buck at twenty paces. The ice sheet rose at the deer's back and descended behind the man. Open water surged over the lower edge of the slab of ice, forcing the huge floe ever higher like a sinking ship upending. The wind-whipped column moved in, widening and enveloping the two figures, covering in a white mantle both the entire ice shelf, now nearing the vertical, and the open, steaming water.

Danny brought us around and stopped. The giant

floe rose even higher, then as if it could no longer carry its own weight or the weight of the two figures aboard it, flipped completely over and slapped down, spewing steaming, freezing water in a rushing torrent all across the lake toward us and the now abandoned snowcat Roscoe had left behind.

DANNY WAS OFF THE SNOWMOBILE. In one bound he jumped behind Cooley. "Take that one to shore, Tatty. We've got to save the snowcat."

I heard him only faintly. I stared slack-mouthed at the open water where there had been, only a moment before, a man meeting a windigo.

The scrim lifted. My bristling hair relaxed. Nothing was left behind.

I hadn't driven a snowmobile before, but the wash of steaming water surging toward me from the overturned ice floe that had swallowed Roscoe and the buck taught me in a hurry. Handling the machine turned out to be much like driving a car. Within a minute, I had put enough distance between the water flow and me that my rushing blood ebbed and another, all-encompassing feeling cascaded into my chest.

For the first time in years, I wept. I cried with abandon, gulping huge caverns of freezing air between choking gasps. I cried for Roscoe, moaning as he did atop his bar stool at Tillie's, as he did, when for the second time, he was bereft of his life's love. I cried for Roscoe, even though he had exploded in torment and killed his best friend. Sorrow burst forth, stopping my nose with quick frozen snot, then released like thunder the loneliness, sickness, and death that had caught in my practical-life's craw, year after year under the swelling pressure beneath my secreted distress.

Speeding against the frigid wind, away from the mist of the again freezing lake, I cried for Scummy. He, too, died at the hands of the windigo. Worse than cannibalized. He fed on good intentions, only to be horridly drained of life by his best friend. I cried for Jay, who nursed and cared for me and for the others around the lake. His error was a kindness greater than truth, a caring deeper than the bottomless muck from which Roscoe had saved him. In my panicked flight from the lake, remorse caught me. It was not so much that I had not, could not have saved Jay Lahtinen, but more that I had never been able to care as he did. Little time as I knew him, I craved the kindness that I could not emulate. I mourned his reassuring touch, his courage, his good sense.

Now approaching the high shore to which Danny had directed me, I cried for Mary and for Morgan. I cried for Mary, who had sacrificed herself for the most relentless hunter at the lake, Roscoe, who, himself, panicked at facing a mystic death that she readily and wildly accepted. I cried, too, for Morgan, for her long-buried suffering, isolation, and fear. I had misunderstood the depth of her torments that could be known only by one who had come to face loss—the loss of her sister, the loss of her man, the loss of her child. I did not know those privations, hiding as I had in what I thought was a pragmatic life. For that also, I wept.

I unzipped first one then another jacket cuff to wipe my misery-crusted face, wetted my shirt sleeves, and scraped my frosted cheeks raw on the woolen shirt.

Morgan waited with the twins at Granny's cabin. Her embrace of pulsing life, her deep-rooted and troubled past held her there. Her resurgent Native and motherly desire were frightening in their power. I quavered before her and other women in my life like the little boy before the mighty and charismatic sweep of my Aunt Elsie, at the quiet gentility of Mother, beside the sure sturdiness of Banook, under the powerful eyes of Granny Bassett, and before a transformed Morgan. The stark winter landscape, dangerously chill, replete in driven icy night, afforded no place to hide, no quarter to run to, and, no leisure to linger.

For the first time, I mourned Mother. Not my loss, not my disregard of her pain, not my unfeeling coldness at her death, but her tenderness, the isolation she endured in Truro, comforted only by her sister's love, radiant through to her last minutes. I whined and yelped a wolfish sorrow, a pain of prodigality with no return for celebration, the whimper of a son who took until there was no more. I spilled twenty-year-old tears.

I crested the hill on the western shore of Thief lake, sobbing maniacally. I stopped and killed the engine.

Down below the corridor of birches I had followed, bare as winter itself, lay the lake. Off to the north and east, hidden now from view by intervening pine-tops, came the hum of another snowmobile and the lower chug-chug of a snowcat starting. From the cove off to the right, in the southeast, rose the narrow spine that hid Granny's cabin over which drifted a faint stream of white smoke, distinct in new light, signaling the start of day and the making of breakfast. Further down the shore and inland, the flat, snow-covered roof of Tillie's glistened in morning sunshine. Would the sign on the front door be changed to read: "Closed for good?"

Below the pines, parked in the distance under Tillie's jingling poem, stood my Jeep that had been rescued by

Beanie's husband the previous night. Looking back to the sweep of the lake, the brilliance of day melded the shores from every direction into one. Thief Lake was all the world.

I calmed my breathing. Was it Granny's voice I heard soothing me? Removing my mitts once more, I loosened the tie that fastened the furry earflaps of my hat over my temples. I lifted the flaps and listened.

I heard the sound of the air sweeping around the papered birch trunks that marched down to the lake in file. I attended to the scurry of cold-hardened snow over the crust from which particles were loosened and over which they tumbled. I heard the misery sung through sheaves of white pine needles, one to another as together they hung low with ice and snow. I waited for a long time for that nothing to come. Would it be there?

From the direction of the lake, coming along the birch corridor, I heard the sound of black boots crunching on the crusted snow. A dark figure rose from below, walking stiffly, measured and direct, dressed in funeral clothes—black pants fitted over the boots, a formal tie binding his white collar, a tight-fitting black coat, a white carnation pinned to its lapel. Hatless, he stopped, centered in the aisle of birches, the lake below steaming behind him, his hair stirred by wind. He stood, silent.

I had expected my father those nights on the train to Tattamagouche. I had cried ice at his death, had turned away from his people and from him, from the north, from the cold, from remembrance. I turned from the sight of death, but it had followed me, nevertheless, breathing down my neck all that time. Like a shard of icy glass driven as deep as understanding must go, his death had wounded me. I felt dangerously bare. Each of us stared, wordless, frozen together. I waited. Cold bit my bare ears. My fingers lost feeling. My face frosted. I listened.

I stood still to hear the drunken, raucous Mi'kmaq chanting, the chilling accusations reaching out from darkness, to hear the yellow flashing words echo in a midnight kitchen, but nothing broke the air. The wind died.

My black-clad father stood as a stark silhouette against the lake. Above the frozen surface of the hill we had both climbed, over the rilled drifts and flooded steaming plain of Thief Lake, I cast a scorching groan, released moaning waves of pent-up grief piled high over more than three decades. My wail rebounded from Granny's hill, from the Canadian rise to the north, from the granite outcrops above Tillie's. I heard my own cry lift and swirl and carom around the lake. "Father, forgive me."

As I gazed at my father's face, I saw that he was no longer looking at me. He was looking through me at what stood behind. Nothing could be there, but I knew at the same time what it was. I thought I heard a snort.

Just as my vision of Roscoe had passed through my own dream-state body, the image of my father passed through me. I felt a warming, an expanding thaw radiate, then withdraw at my back straight to what I knew would be there before turning to see it for the last time: the white, shining, full-antlered deer. What it had snorted, I knew very well.

I turned and stood fast. I cupped my numbed hands to mold the apparition of my father together with the vision of the buck, swirling and spiraling tightly and majestically in union at my fingertips, into something resembling an ancient birch, straight and lofty, black and white, which, to save my sight, I could not watch.

Then one clap from hands I could no longer feel made everything disappear.

Tiny swallows the last of his coffee and rises. He tends the lines suspended over each hole, carefully reels in, removes the bait, and hooks the barbs to the cork handles.

I gaze out though the burlap curtain to the afternoon sun. I'm spent.

"Some say the People discovered spirits in the woods," Tiny says. He leans over the table to rack the fishing rods on staves above the window. The bells tinkle faintly.

Rehooking one of the barbs, he says, "Others say it was the Indians themselves who loosed the spirits into the land."

I'm watching him stow the rods.

"Still others say they never existed at all, that it is just wind."

He covers the two holes with wood slabs fitted with handles and returns to the table. "I don't bother. I fish. I make my syrup. I harvest *manomin*."

He is bringing me back. "I've held each of those opinions, and for a long time I didn't bother either."

Tiny sits. "But now you have a story to tell."

"If anyone has the patience to hear it."

"It needs more telling," Tiny says.

I get up. "It'll be dark before you know it."

I move to the bunk where I left my jacket. I slip on the parka. I start the zipper.

Tiny hands me the newspaper parcel. "Take your fish," he says.

"Thanks."

We move to the door.

Outside, the sparkle of sun on snow lined with the long shadows of birches and pines slaps our vision. We stand at the icehouse door, blinking out across the lake.

I pocket the fish. I move off. I have nothing left to say.

The sun sets behind the granite outcrops of the hills to the south.

Walking steadily, I sense Tiny and his cabin behind me growing smaller in the last light of day.

Like a timber wolf stirring from a storm-burrow he has dug, my thought rises from the lake past the golden light to that which lives beyond. I check the fish pack deep in my parka pocket. I beat my hands across my sides to force blood to flow and gently rub my ears and cheeks to flush the warmth. I finish zipping my coat, and with bared hands, tie my earflaps against the cold. I beat my hands another time and pull on the mitts. I know Tiny, still in his shirtsleeves and long johns, is watching me. I go on down the trail from the fish-house village. It's two miles to shore.

CPSIA information can be obtained at www.ICGtesting.com
Printed in the USA
LVOW07s1049300815

452056LV00001B/1/P

9 780991 476305